The Suicide Murders
J.M. Sutter

PublishAmerica
Baltimore

© 2007 by J.M. Sutter.
All rights reserved. No part of this book may be reproduced, stored in a retrieval system or transmitted in any form or by any means without the prior written permission of the publishers, except by a reviewer who may quote brief passages in a review to be printed in a newspaper, magazine or journal.

First printing

All characters in this book are fictitious, and any resemblance to real persons, living or dead, is coincidental.

ISBN: 1-4241-9388-5
PUBLISHED BY PUBLISHAMERICA, LLLP
www.publishamerica.com
Baltimore

Printed in the United States of America

To my beautiful daughter, Elizabeth, without whom this book would have never been possible…because without you I would have never lasted this long. I love you.

Prologue

It was his thirty-second birthday and he was celebrating it alone in a dive bar called the Hi-Ho. Not only was he celebrating his birthday, he was celebrating a new start to a life that had been filled with turmoil. Today, however, was a new beginning. Today was the turning point in his life.

Danny Taylor ordered another beer from the bartender. It was his third beer so far, but that was okay, because even on a bad night Danny could drink a twelve-pack. On a good night? Well, that was another story. That was the old Danny. From now on the new and redirected Danny was going to control his drinking. He was going to control his temper.

As Danny looked through the want-ads for the Riverside, San Diego areas, he remembered how hot it was outside. It was just after two p.m. One more beer went hot.

On August 15, 1998, outside it was 95 degrees. Danny woke just after midnight in his horrible one bedroom nightmare of an apartment in Sacramento. Why he ever chose to live there he will never know. The only thing he knew at that moment was if he ever wanted to amount to anything, he had to get away, now! That is exactly what Danny did. He packed his clothes, left a note for the landlord, and said goodbye to his old life.

As the bartender brought over another Coors, Danny thought about the three other times he had made this exact getaway—every time looking for sanity and every time finding exactly the opposite. What did he really expect before? In the past he would change his address, but he would never change himself; his behavior; his attitude. Today was completely different because today was his thirty-second birthday. Today, Danny Taylor felt alive.

Closing the paper, he laid it on the bar and went to the men's room. A quick pit-stop and he would be on his way. As he was washing his hands, he looked in the mirror. He was six-feet-two inches and just over two hundred pounds. The lines around his eyes showed the countless nights of his drinking. This, however, added to his rugged good looks. When he was tanned, just as he was now, his baby blue eyes became almost transparent. Women loved him for his eyes. Women were fooled by his eyes. He reached for a paper towel, but the dispenser was empty. Not uncommon for a bar of this caliber. Danny wiped his hands on his jeans and went to pay his tab. As he approached his spot at the bar, he noticed the bartender had replaced his old beer with a new one—also not uncommon in a place of this caliber. Most people would throw a twenty on the bar and get round after round until the money was gone, then they usually threw another twenty out after that. People paid a lot to escape their dull, miserable lives, to escape loneliness. Every one of these bars had a regular crowd that came in every day and, even though it was a sad life, it gave them a sense of belonging. Danny had always been one of these people.

The day was still plenty hot, so Danny welcomed his new beer. At two-twenty-five apiece you couldn't beat it. As he took a gigantic swallow of beer, he tried to think of the defining moment he realized he was an alcoholic. Oh well, no matter now—that was a thing of the past for him. From now on he would be more responsible in his drinking. Feeling proud of himself for this, he figured he better get some food in him, something the old Danny would never have done. He motioned the bartender over, pointed to his beer for another and asked for two bags of peanuts. He remembered how his first wife used to tell him that peanuts didn't constitute a meal.

Danny swiveled around on his bar stool and surveyed the place for the first time. Funny how the immediate proximity of the bar itself drew his attention for so long. As he tore a corner from the peanuts, he dumped some into his mouth. Planters, Extra Hot—the best! This place was like all the other dive bars Danny loved so much. In the corner was a jukebox that played outdated CD's of artists such as Patsy Cline (who, by the way, kicks ass), Elvis Presley and Garth Brooks, as well as a meager selection of contemporary tunes.

The center of the bar had a pool table, long in need of being replaced, and the walls had NASCAR banners, as well as other sports related items. One wall was completely covered with humor items. Danny chuckled at one with a guy picking himself and his barstool off the floor. He was looking at the bartender and the caption read: *I'm not as think as you drunk I am.*

Another had a guy sitting on the hood of his Rolls Royce drinking champagne. The caption read: *Poverty Sucks*.

His favorite one was a girl in a miniskirt who was bending over to pick up something she dropped. She had no underwear on. Everyone behind her had turned toward her, eyes big, mouths open. The next picture she was standing up and everyone was looking the other way. No caption.

Danny opened his other bag of peanuts, got another beer and noticed the day crowd had mostly left and the place was filling up with a crowd who presumably had just gotten off work. The crowd was a little younger and a little more fashionably dressed, but not much. God he loved this atmosphere. God he loved to drink. Whoa, how easily it was to forget about changing. This place was definitely fun, but he remembered he didn't even have a place to stay. He drank down half his beer and stepped outside to familiarize himself with his new surroundings.

The Hi-Ho was located on Van Buren Boulevard in Riverside, California, about one mile north of the 91 Freeway. Danny checked his pockets and found only forty dollars left. Forty plus the ten bucks inside would get him a motel room. Tomorrow he could cash his last paycheck, get the motel for a reduced weekly rate and see where he was at that point. Something fortunate would happen. It always does. Danny took a deep breath, preparing himself for the smoke-filled air in the bar, turned and re-entered.

Damn, it's dark inside these places when you first enter from daylight. Danny slowly walked to his stool, let his eyes adjust and looked at the clock—4:45 p.m. He felt his drink, which was half-empty. It was warm.

The bartender brought a fresh one over, took the old one and said, "Welcome back. This one is on the house."

Ice Cold. God, he loved these places.

Danny made another men's room stop, and upon his return to his stool, he was pleased to see a blond sitting on the stool next to him. *Not bad*, he thought. She ordered a "7&7" (Seagram's 7 and 7-Up).

As Danny sat down, she said, "My, my."

Instantly he thought back to a thought he had outside. *Something fortunately will happen. It always does.*

She looked to be in her early forties with the recognizable wear on her face that came from years of drinking. Danny saw it in the mirror every day. Still, she was very attractive, especially with his beer goggles on.

Danny took a drink of his beer and nodded. This was what he loved. He tilted the bottle back and easily finished it. They went down so easy after a while.

As if being challenged, she just as quickly dispelled of her drink.

It was Danny's turn to say, "My, my."

In a sultry voice, she softly said, "Well, now that I have your attention, can I buy you a drink?"

True love.

"Another Coors Light?" she asked.

He couldn't remember exactly when he learned it, maybe in college, but Rule #1 to taking a woman home from a bar is to never let her drink anything stronger than you. Danny swears women are impressed by how much a man can drink—at least the women in these places.

"It just so happens that 7&7 is my favorite drink," he explained.

"I do believe the gods have blessed me," she said. "A 7&7 it is."

They picked up their newly acquired drinks in a toast. "To new friends," she said.

"And to new beginnings," he added.

Her name was Margaret. Her friends called her Margi. She was thirty-nine, younger than Danny previously thought.

They were on their third drink when Margi said, "You actually drove all the way from Sacramento today? You don't even look tired. You want a pick-me-up?"

Hallelujah!

"What do you have in mind?"

"Do you do speed?"

"Of course," Danny replied. He really shouldn't. This was no way to make a new start. Still, he was spending his motel money on drinks for them, and if he wanted to go home with her he knew what he had to do. Rule #2 to taking a woman home from a bar is to indulge in whatever it is that she is indulging in. A little "spirit" lifter wouldn't hurt anyway. This way he could drink more.

"Here," she handed him a small round item under the bar, "you first." It was the size of a large marble and twisted in the corner of a small plastic bag.

"Holy shit," Danny whispered. "I can smell it from here." He had in his hand, roughly an eightball of real, real good shit. Not only was he going to get laid, he was going to get laid well. She was trusting somebody she just met with a package that cost $250, easy. He motioned toward the men's room. "I shall return."

It never fails, he thought as he was locking the restroom stall. To this day, the mere sight or smell of speed or cocaine sent his bowels through an immediate hell. *Oh well*, he was thinking as he sat on the toilet, *I'll kill two birds with one stone.*

As he untied the knot on the baggie, he saw that this was crystal meth and it was still wet. Margi probably knows someone who manufacturers it themselves. No wonder she so easily gave him the package. This stuff was cheap to make, but was highly profitable to sell. If she knows the cook, it probably only cost her a blow-job. Danny couldn't help but think how much money he could make selling this stiff if he hooked up with Margi for a while.

He dipped a corner of a credit card into the bag. This stiff was "glass." The best. Normally he could chop this up, but it was so hard that it scatters everywhere when you break it up. You need at least a twelve by twelve flat surface. Fuck it. It would hurt his nose more if he snorted it straight, but he had no choice.

Danny snorted the meth into his left nostril and quickly dipped the credit card back in for another little pile. He snorted it up his right nostril just as the pain in the left side was registering. He immediately tilted his head back before his sinuses could react and try to drain the poison out. His eyes were tearing into his ears. "Glass" is the most painful of the drugs to snort—especially when it's un-chopped. The only thing Danny could compare to this burn in his nose was salt.

Once, as a boy, he and his best friend had imitated a grownup they had seen snorting a white substance into his nose. They went straight to Danny's house, shook some salt out of the shaker, made a little line and snorted. He and his friend must have poured a gallon of water up their noses before the burning stopped.

Instantly, Danny opened his eyes wide. How could he have forgotten? He vowed he would never do speed again; not after what happened last time. But this was different, wasn't it? Yes! Today was a new start. Today he was in Riverside and not Sacramento. Today, Margi, a woman who was looking better by the drink, was waiting for him. He took one long sniff and returned his head back to its normal position, wiped the tears from his eyes, tied the baggie and cleaned himself up. He already felt more awake. More everything. He washed his hands and checked his nose in the mirror to make sure there wasn't anything dripping. He must remember to check again in about five minutes. How many times before had he done a quick snort of something, only to look in the mirror later and see a white residue around his nostril? What a bust. The drug user term for that residue was called a "Felony Ring."

"All better?" Margi asked.

"I'm a new man." He handed her the baggie under the bar. "Your turn."

She leaned over, gave Danny a tender kiss on the mouth and explained she'd be right back. Just before she entered the ladies' room, she called to Danny, "Oh, Danny Boy, be a dear and order me another drink. The ice cubes seemed to have soaked up my last one." She smiled.

Danny smiled back. He looked around the bar and tried to guess who she would be with tonight if he wasn't here. It made him sad. Funny though, how she had called him Danny Boy. Whenever he got to drinking with someone in a bar, he always somehow became Danny Boy. Nowhere else, however. He turned around to grab his glass and he saw that his drink, once full before his trip to the restroom, was now empty. His ice cubes must have soaked up his drink, too. This girl was truly a drinker. Today has been fun so far. He couldn't wait until later.

Two more drinks were brought over as Danny wiped sweat from his forehead. *Man, speed makes you sweat.* No worries though; he felt great. A man on top of his game. He downed his drink, ordered another one and two shots of Jagermeister. Risky? Yes. The last time Danny drank Jagermeister a guy bumped into him and he...no! That was before. Nothing can possibly ruin tonight. Tonight was Danny's thirty-second birthday. His new start in life.

Margi came back to the bar with fresh makeup on. She smiled as she saw the shots. She smelled it and made a face. "Jagermeister," she said.

"Is that alright?" Danny asked.

"Of course, as long as tomorrow we don't want to remember what we did today." She smiled again. "Jagermeister always makes me black out."

"Me too," he said. This lady and he had a lot in common. Danny heard somewhere that Jagermeister was banned in some states because they wouldn't list the ingredients. It was rumored to have deer blood in it. "One shot won't hurt us though."

Margi picked up her shot glass. "Another toast. To the man with the sexiest eyes I have ever seen. May I still feel this way even after we've had sex." She laughed.

They clicked glasses and instantly the black liquid that tasted like original NyQuil was gone; swallowed with the ease of two veteran drinkers.

"You know," Danny said with a smirk, "there's only one way to find out about my eyes."

Two minutes later their drinks were gone and they were walking out the door.

"I just live five minutes away," Margi said. "We'll just take my car and in the morning we can come back for a Bloody Mary."

"If you keep that up I might fall in love with you."

"Promises, promises."

Margi handed Danny the keys to her car. She owned a 1995 Honda Civic. Danny made a right on Van Buren Boulevard, drove about a mile and pulled into Parkwood Apartments. He pushed a remote control on her visor and an automatic gate opened. Margi's stall was the fourth one on the left.

As they walked to the apartment, Danny took her hand in his. They walked past the pool and down a path to the left. She lived in apartment 45, on the bottom floor. As he went inside, he saw a small, well-kept room that had just enough room for a small kitchen table and couch. They went straight to the bedroom.

He pulled the curtains together as she opened the closet and pulled out a mirror. She put it on the dresser, reached into her purse, took out the speed and set it on the mirror. She grabbed a book and pressed it down hard onto the baggie, rotating it left and right. She then dumped it out onto the mirror. Danny admired her skill. Crushing the hard drug in the baggie prevented it from scattering everywhere. She pulled a playing card from the frame around the mirror and separated two huge lines from the pile. She rolled up two one-dollar bills and they snorted at the same time. Her head automatically tilted back and she did a little high-step dance that reminded Danny of the dance Snoopy did when he's happy.

"It burns so good!" she was saying. "It burns so fucking good!"

Danny's nose started to run, so he laid on his back on the bed. Margi joined him.

"Is all the shit you get this good?" Danny asked.

"It took awhile, but I got rid of all the connections and now I get it straight from the source."

Just as Danny thought. Just then she rolled on top of him and put one leg on each side, straddling him.

"What's your favorite position, lover?" she asked.

"You're doing good so far," he said.

"So far, so good, huh? Well, lover, get ready for a night you'll never forget."

Margi left Danny on the bed as she went into the bathroom to freshen up. She had a nice oak bed with extended bed posts, firm mattress and big fluffy pillows that smelled of both perfume and cologne.

Margi came out of the restroom wearing only a smile, which turned to a frown when she saw Danny was still dressed. Twenty seconds later he was buck-ass naked. She reached under the bed and pulled out a bag. "Take your pick," she said.

Danny looked in the bag and saw sex novelty central: dildos, vibrators, handcuffs, leather whip, lubricant, colored condoms, feathers, blindfold, porno tape, porno magazine, candles, and a Kama Sutra book. He took out the candles, a feather, the blindfold and fumbled around the bottom and found four silk scarves.

"Don't forget the condoms," she said.

"Of course. Thank you," he replied. *Smart woman*, he thought.

Tying a woman to the bed had always been a fantasy of Danny's, but he had never done it until tonight. As he stood looking at her, he felt himself becoming larger. He had tied her up, but at her request he tied her face-down. As she lay waiting for him, he turned off all the lights and lit the candles. She had the blindfold on and was calling for him to hurry. He asked her, "How bad do you want me?"

"I want you fucking bad—and I want you to fuck me good!"

"All in time," he said. "All in time." He slowly ran the feather from her right calf to the inside of her thigh. She twitched as he ran it softly up her leg, gently brushing her hot skin. She was grinding herself against the bed in slow, steady strokes. Danny twirled the feather in small circles up and down her wet center. She pushed her hips in a circular motion, pressing against the bed as hard as she could. She was moaning.

"I'm so hot, baby! Fuck me, baby!" she exclaimed. "Fuck me, Danny!"

Danny slipped a finger inside her, running it up and down, in and out. He grabbed one of the candles and dripped wax onto her firm ass. She gasped. "More Danny, more!"

Danny did. He put the candle back and lightly spanked her. A little harder and a little harder. Still, she wanted it harder. He took the whip from the bag. She begged for it, so he obliged. He whipped her until he almost drew blood. Between his excitement and the speed, he was sweating wildly, and his head felt like it was going to explode. He lay on top of her and asked, "Now?"

She just nodded her head. Her legs were spread far apart and tied, and she was waiting. He put the tip of his penis in her and asked if she wanted more. She tried to push herself down the bed to take all of him, and as she did, he thrust forward. In and out, over and over, harder and harder. She called out his name as she came instantly, pulling her arms and jerking her body. She came with such intensity that she almost passed out.

He then slowed his rhythm and they were as one. Gently they flowed with each others body, him thrusting, her lifting to meet him. Two bodies sweaty and hot. Two bodies fulfilling their lust, their passion. He was getting close to orgasm when she came again, and as she called out his name, it pushed him over the edge and they climaxed together.

"How long until you can do it again?" she asked.

"Not long if you stay in that position."

"Then don't you dare untie me."

"Do you want to get in the shower with me?" Danny asked.

"I'll wait here, but you only have five minutes."

The thought of her waiting for him tied up started to make him hard again, but he absolutely had to take a shower. He could smell the speed coming out of his pores, so he kissed her on her shoulder, slapped her on the ass and went into the bathroom.

He turned the water on, waited for the temperature to adjust, and stepped in. He grabbed the shampoo. It was Herbal Essences. He laughed and thought, *For a totally organic experience—if they only knew.* Danny always liked shampoos that lathered up well, and that is exactly what this shampoo did. As he rinsed it out, he stood for a long while, letting the warm water wash down his body. He reached for the soap, but stopped. It was Caress. Chick soap, what did he expect? He grabbed the shampoo again, squeezed a large amount into his hand and lathered his body.

What a rip-off those commercials are, he thought as he rinsed himself off, once again letting the water run over his body, feeling the old Danny wash away. He had no idea what his future held, with or without Margi, but right now he liked the way it was heading.

Danny came out of the bathroom with a towel wrapped around his waist. He walked over to the dresser and asked Margi if she wanted him to bring her a line. No answer.

I put the girl to sleep with my magic wand, he thought. He took the playing card and pulled away two lines from the crushed pile, re-rolled one of the dollar bills and quickly snorted one of the lines. There was no reason for him to have done another line, of course. His heart was beating out of control, and he'd be lucky if he saw sleep within the next three days. What he really needed was a drink. He called to Margi, "Do you have any alcohol in the house? Hey, baby. Margi!" he called. "Margi!"

He was at the head of the bed now. There was something not quite right about her neck. He nudged her. "Margi?" It came out a whisper. Danny rolled her head so he could see her face. He pulled the blindfold down and jumped back as huge unseeing eyes stared at him. He saw bruises on her neck. *What in the hell was going on?* He stumbled backward and fell. His face was a mixture of horror and disbelief. His heart was beating so fast and so hard that he seemed to be bouncing off the floor. The room, the whole world was spinning out of control. He tried to get to his feet, but his legs denied him. He closed his eyes and started crying. "What the hell is going on?" he wailed. His heart was beating too rapid and he clutched his chest. He couldn't breathe. The room was fading in and out as his head throbbed. He realized he was passing out.

The last thought that went through Danny Taylor's mind before darkness overtook him was, *This is my thirty-second birthday. Today is a new beginning, a new start. This wasn't supposed to happen."*

Chapter 1

"Well," Dr. Richards was saying, "it took us two years, but I think we finally have your medication right."

Danny Taylor was sitting across from the Chino State Prison psychiatrist.

"That, of course, is not uncommon," he continued. "What we are dealing with here is not an exact science. It is basically hit-and-miss, if you will, until we find the right combination for the specific individual."

No shit, Danny thought. *Doesn't this asshole know we've had this talk about twenty times?* Danny had stopped taking his medication a long time ago. After countless talks with this idiot, and countless variations of psychological drugs, he realized he was getting worse, not better. At one point he was so fucked up that they had him on suicide watch. So, now he told the doctor what they wanted to hear and sold his medication to the other inmates.

Dr. Richards wasn't employed to pass judgment on the inmates. He was merely here to try the best he could to figure out why the inmates committed the crimes they did. When Danny first met him, he tried to have Danny admit to himself that he, in fact, killed the woman he called Margi. He informed Danny that once he admitted it, he would begin healing. After repeated talks and denials, Dr. Richards finally came to the conclusion that Danny did not believe he had killed Margi. He diagnosed him as a multi-personality schizophrenic.

During his trial, Danny remained insistent that he was innocent. It was a two day trial with a thirty minute deliberation. The jury found him guilty. The papers called him a drug-addicted, spaced-out murdering rapist. Because of the way

Margi was found, a lot of publicity surrounded the case for about a week—until a hotter story came along. Thank God when it did.

Danny would gladly give his life to find out what happened that night. Hell, sometimes he thought maybe he was crazy and that maybe he did kill Margi. He even admitted to himself it was the only thing that made sense. Even though he thought Dr. Richards was a quack, he met with him every other week to see what the doctor had to say.

"So," Dr. Richards said, "unless you have something else you would like to discuss, I'll see you again in two weeks."

"No," Danny said. "I'll see you next time."

Chapter 2

Chino State Prison in Chino, California separated its inmates by classification. The prisoners were put in three main levels: maximum, medium and minimum. The inmates in the minimum security housing unit were made up mainly of drug offenders, low-level drug dealers, or people with multiple drug possession charges.

Medium security housed drug dealers of a little higher caliber—people with weapons charges and those who had minor violence on their record.

Maximum security had murders, rapists, major violence offenders, major drug dealers and anyone with ten or more years to serve on their sentence. Until Dr. Richards' schizophrenic diagnosis, maximum security is where Danny was housed. Now he was in with the truly scary people—psych med users. He and the other inmates ordered on mandatory medication by Dr. Richards lived in a separate wing called the Annex. They all take some form of psychological drug. Dr. Richards deemed these prisoners in need of extra supervision for their own well being.

The combined housing units of maximum, medium and minimum security make up the general population. Prisoners in general population were housed in two-man cells. This was the same for the inmates in PC (protective custody). The people in PC were hated by everyone in prison. These were the people who did a crime, got caught, and told on people they knew in order to get a reduced sentence—snitches. PC is also made up of anybody afraid to be put in general population. The Annex, however, is dorm-style living. Inmates in the Annex were generally referred to as the "psychos" by the people in general population. The inmates in PC were just glad somebody else took shit besides themselves. They didn't say anything about anyone.

There were sixty bunks in the Annex in an area that was ninety by forty feet. The Annex was one big cage surrounded completely by bars. There was an eight by three foot section in one cover with a sliding gate. This opened only twice daily. Once to let you out for breakfast at 4:00 a.m., and once to let you back to your bunks to sleep at 9:00 p.m. From 4:00 a.m. to 9:00 p.m. you stayed in an adjoining ninety by forty foot room, also surrounded completely by bars. It was in this room that you ate, watched TV, made phone calls, played cards, took showers, used the bathroom and so forth. There was twenty-four hour video surveillance and a guard that walked the perimeter every fifteen minutes. When it was mealtime, everyone lined up in order of their bunk number and handed a tray through a one foot by six inch hole in the bars. When everyone was finished, you handed the tray back through in the same order. At 5:00 a.m. and 5:00 p.m. you were given your medication through the same slot, in the same order.

Outside recreation is mandatory and on weekends only. Saturday recreation is from 12:00 p.m. to 2:00 p.m.; Sunday is from 6:00 a.m. to 9:00 a.m. The Annex also has their own yard, separate from PC and general population. It is the size of a football field, with half of it concrete and the other half grass. The grass is worn out around the edges where people jog. On all four sides of the concrete there are four basketball hoops with no nets. Inmates have access to three basketballs, two soccer balls and one football. Saturday is the only day you see everybody participating in activities. Since medication is taken at 5:00 a.m., most people find a spot on the grass and sleep on Sundays. Everyone must go to Rec., rain or shine.

It was during recreation one day when Danny heard through the grapevine that another inmate was planning to kill him.

Chapter 3

Meeting people that you wanted to be friends with was a hard thing to do in the Annex. Either people came and went too fast to get to know them, or they were just too crazy to associate with. Danny did manage to find a few people who he would classify as friends. The person he hung around with most was a guy named Tom Prescott.

Tom was a peculiar one. Everywhere he went he carried a bag of Fritos. He couldn't get enough of them. Whether he was on the phone, on the toilet, watching TV, playing cards or playing basketball, Tom would have his bag of Fritos with him. Naturally, Danny nicknamed him Frito.

Frito was only five-foot three inches tall and weighed one hundred twenty-five pounds. How he stayed so skinny no one will ever know. Frito looked just like Horshack on the TV show *Welcome Back Kotter*. Danny took him under his wing the day he was diagnosed schizophrenic and transferred to the Annex. Danny felt sorry for Frito. It was instantly obvious that he had an inferiority complex. Frito had no self-esteem and always sought recognition and assurance. He never stood up for himself and people were always taking advantage of him. Danny protected him.

Just as Danny did, Frito had ended up in prison on a raw deal. Frito was twenty-four years old and was working as a bag-boy at Sunny Foods Supermarket in Redlands, California. He was a good worker who never called in sick and never showed up late. For a little over a year he had been bagging groceries for a very beautiful woman. Frito fell in love with her the first time he saw her. During the last few months it seemed she was paying more attention to him. Was it his imagination, or was she standing in the line he was bagging groceries in, even if other lines were shorter? One time he handed her a bag of groceries and she touched his hand. That was the final sign Frito needed. He wrote her a poem that night and carried it in his pocket until the next time he bagged her groceries. His heart was beating wildly as he slipped the letter into her bag.

She returned to the store thirty minutes later and went straight to the Manager's office. Five minutes later, Mr. Stewart, the manager, came out of his office with a scowl on his face. Frito's heart fell as Mr. Stewart approached him.

"Tom," the manager said, "will you please come with me to my office?"

"Tom," Mr. Stewart stated, "this is Ms. Thompson. She just left here not too long ago with a bag of groceries that she claims you bagged. As she was taking her groceries from this bag, she noticed a piece of paper at the bottom. This piece of paper, Tom." Mr. Stewart held it out to him.

He's handing my broken heart to me, Frito thought as he grabbed the paper.

Mr. Stewart says, "Please read it."

"I don't th…" Frito began, but was cut off.

"If you want any chance of keeping your job here at Sunny Foods Supermarket, Mr. Prescott, I suggest you read what is on that piece of paper."

Frito glanced quickly at Ms. Thompson, then shamefully away. He knew he had done the wrong thing by giving her the letter. He read:

> *God made you pretty like the flowers.*
> *You smell like you always take showers.*
> *Writing this is hard for me to do,*
> *Do you love me, because I love you.*
>
> *Tom From Sunny Foods*
> *XOXOXOXO*

Frito handed the note out in front of him, never taking his eyes off the floor. He was so embarrassed his face felt as hot as the sun.

Mr. Stewart took the note, and said, "Tom, look at me. Did you write this poem and place it in Ms. Thompson's bag?"

He knew there was no way out. "Yes, but—"

Mr. Stewart cut him off again.

"Tom, I have no choice but to let you go," Mr. Stewart said. "As of this moment you are no longer employed at Sunny Foods Supermarket. You may come in tomorrow for your final paycheck."

Tom quickly left the office and went straight to his car. He had to apologize to Ms. Thompson. He saw her come out five minutes later. *How could such a beautiful woman do something so mean to me?*, he said to himself.

When she pulled out of the parking lot, he started his '82 Celica and carefully followed her, far enough behind to not be seen and close enough to not lose her. He felt just like Jim Rockford, his favorite TV private investigator.

As she pulled into her driveway, he slowed and stopped two houses down. There was a man waiting for her at her front door. When she approached him, he tried to hug her, but she pulled away. She walked past him, and while she was unlocking the door she turned around and pointed to the street as if telling him to leave. When she opened the door, he pushed his way in and slammed it behind them. Frito didn't know what to do. He sat in his car for at least thirty minutes, playing out heroic rescues in his head. Finally the front door opened and the man came out with a torn shirt. He was almost running to his car, looking both ways before he got in and drove away. Like a good P.I., Frito looked at his license plate: *STUD4U*.

Why can't I think of a cool license plate like that? Frito thought. He started his car and was beginning to pull away. "This obviously isn't a good time to talk to her," he whispered. *She probably just got done having sex with STUD4U.* He stopped when he saw flames through her living room window. Frito jumped out of his car and ran to her house. He looked inside and saw the entire bottom floor on fire. He stood on her lawn not knowing what to do when a neighbor came out of her house and yelled to him.

Scared, Frito ran to his car and drove away. An hour later the police found him at his apartment. While questioning him, Frito told them about what happened at Sunny Foods and that he had followed her to her house to apologize. He said he left when the lady called to him because he didn't want to get in trouble. He never told them about STUD4U. Frito was arrested and later convicted of first degree murder. Ms. Thompson was found burned to death in her home. This is how Tom "Frito" Prescott ended up in Chino State Prison and became Danny Taylor's friend.

Chapter 4

It was 9:00 p.m. on Friday night and everyone had just been let back into the room with the bunks. Whenever they were in the bunk area, the main lights were off and the only lights on were in the walkway around the cage. At night, the surveillance camera had a hard time seeing the inmate's activity, so this is when all the "shady" behavior started.

As soon as the guard passed by on his perimeter check, Danny pulled the bag of Pruno from underneath his bed. Every week he made two gallons of jailhouse alcohol. He and Frito saved their fruit from the week, squeezed the juice and threw the pieces into a garbage bag, added lots of sugar and poured in cups of hot water periodically. At the end of the week they strained it through a towel into two one-gallon containers Danny had gotten from a friend on the kitchen crew. He then threw the pulp back into the bag and had a "kicker" for next week's batch.

Friday at 10:00 p.m. new arrivals come in and anybody scheduled to leave within the week are taken out and held in single-man cells until their release date. This helped to open up beds for newcomers and prevented any last minute jealousy killings of an inmate going home by somebody with a lot of time left. The new arrivals were either newly diagnosed patients of Dr. Richards who were now required to take psych meds, or people that have had previous psychological problems, just sent to prison and were waiting to talk with the doctor.

Danny used to only make one gallon of Pruno, but quickly learned to make two. Every week at least one newcomer would keister drugs in, and alcohol was a great trading item. It used to make him feel weird snorting coke or speed that used to be up someone's ass, but, like everything else in prison, you got used to it.

Just as Danny finished preparing and pouring next weeks Pruno, the guards called out the names of the people leaving. Nobody he cared about was on the roll-up list. They had five minutes to roll up their shit, say goodbye and line up at the gate. Five minutes after that, the new people would be brought in.

He and Frito started drinking from their container. Danny always liked to get a good buzz before he did drugs, otherwise he was too jittery. The batches of Pruno always varied in alcohol content, but, for the most part, twenty-four ounces would get him shit-faced.

Danny was taking another drink when a buzzer went off—new arrivals. He and Frito stood as they filed in. Danny remembered how bad it sucked going into a new environment, not knowing anybody. He and Frito slept in the furthest corner from the gate; Frito on the top bunk, him on the bottom bunk. There were seven bunks open, and four people were coming in. Two bunks over was an open spot, and that is exactly where a huge, ugly, mean looking guy was heading.

In prison, just as in life, you can't tell a book by its cover. Danny had seen guys the size of trees that had a sweet old lady's disposition. He had also seen midgets who would try to bite your balls off if you weren't looking. The man appeared to be forty years old, six-foot-three and roughly two-hundred fifty pounds. He was white, just like he and Frito.

Frito looked at Danny, and said, "He's taller and bigger than you." He sounded worried.

"Don't worry. Has anybody been able to take me yet?"

"No."

"And nobody will. Besides, look at his eyes. He's scared of us."

Frito laughed nervously.

They walked over to him as he was making his bed. "How's it going?" Danny asked. "My name is Danny and this is Frito."

Frito gave a half wave.

The man stopped, looked at them both briefly, went back to making his bed, and said, "They call me Mad Dog."

"Did you just come in, or did they transfer you from general population?" Danny asked.

"I got picked up last week on a violation. They gave me a year. Fucking bastards. I got out of this same fucking place three and a half years ago. I haven't been caught doing nothing for three and a half years and they bust me with a half gram of speed. I was gonna be off probation in six months. Fucking cocksucker cops."

"We were hoping you brought some drugs in with you. We have an extra gallon of Pruno to trade," Danny whispered.

"Oh, I got drugs," Mad Dog replied. "I said they busted me with a half gram, I never said I didn't have more on me. Some motherfucker must have tipped the cops off that I was selling because I was sitting at home watching TV when the cops started banging on my door. I had the half gram out on a mirror in front of me. I also had four eight balls under the seat cushion. Thank God I was in my underwear because as soon as I heard the banging, I knew it was the pigs. I can usually smell them coming.

"I reached under the cushion, dropped my drawers, and shoved them up my ass one by one. I was just grabbing the mirror to dump the rest in the toilet when they busted down the door. I was standing there with my boxers around my ankles and a half gram on the mirror I was holding. I stuck my nose in the center of the pile and snorted.

"The looks on this fuckers' faces—they almost shit! Three of them took me down and knocked the mirror on the floor. I almost shot those bags straight out of my ass like a bullet.

"Thank God I shoved them up there dry. Anyway, they scraped the powder off the carpet and got enough to nail me. I saved myself at least a year by hoping that half ounce. Instead of a sales charge, I only got a possession."

Danny and Frito looked at each other and started laughing. Mad Dog finally joined in. They made a trade. A gallon of Pruno for a half gram of speed.

Chapter 5

Six months had passed by since the arrival of Mad Dog. Danny, Frito, Mad Dog and Fruit Loop (the resident 'bitch') were sitting in the middle of the grass on a Saturday afternoon.

"I still can't believe you're getting out in six months," Frito was saying. "What am I going to do when you leave?"

"You're gonna be just fine. Besides, maybe I'll pick up another charge like Mad Dog and have to stay longer."

"I hope so." He munched on his chips.

"Fuck you both sideways!" Mad Dog exclaimed. "I still can't believe they gave me another six months for a shank. How do they expect us to protect ourselves?"

Fruit Loop spoke up. "Like you need protecting. You're as big as this building." Fruit Loop was exactly the same size and weight as Frito.

"Big deal. You're safer than me. Nobody in their right mind would kill you. Where else would we get our blow jobs?"

"Is that what I was doing to you? I thought you were flossing my teeth." Everyone was laughing. "Big body, small weenie—what a shame."

"Hey, Danny," Frito said, changing the subject. "Do you think I did the right thing by telling my lawyer the truth and filing an appeal?"

"Come on Frito, are you serious?" Danny asked. "I spend four months convincing you to do it, and now you don't know? Do you like the fact that you're in here while the cocksucker who actually set that fire is on the street? Trust me, you did the right thing. You have nothing to worry about from that guy. Fuck, if there was any way I could catch the motherfucker who set me up…"

"Uh, oh! Here he goes again, claiming his innocence," Mad Dog said. "Didn't you know that everyone is innocent in this place?"

"I am innocent!"

"Then why don't you tell us what happened? Why don't you ever tell us about your case?"

Danny had learned a long time ago not to talk about his case. He had told a few people when he first got in, but they didn't believe him. Reliving the nightmare only made him want to cry anyway. He could remember telling Dr. Richards about that night. He swore that pervert got off when he explained about the sex he and Margi had. Fuck Dr. Richards. How could he say Danny had strangled her in the middle of their love making? How could he say Danny had imagined talking to her before taking a shower? Fuck that and fuck everybody!

"No need. Frito knows the truth, and that's enough. By the way, you know what will happen if you tell anybody, right?"

"I'm taking it to my grave, Danny."

"One way or the other," Danny explained.

"Holy shit!" Fruit Loop exclaimed. "I'm sorry, Danny. I can't believe I didn't tell you this earlier, especially with talking about shanks and such!"

Danny got a sinking feeling in his stomach. "You can't believe you didn't tell me what?"

"I heard through the grapevine that someone is coming over from general population that has it out for you."

"He's being transferred to the Annex?" Danny asked.

"Yes. I hear he's faking his problems to Dr. Richards just so he can get to you."

"When is he being transferred?"

"Next Friday," Fruit Loop said sadly.

"Who?" Danny questioned.

"I don't know him. Some guy named Timmy."

"Tiny Tim? I haven't seen him since my first month here, before I got transferred from general pop."

"Did you fuck with him when you were there?" Mad Dog asked.

"Yeah," Danny said, "but everyone did. He's a weasel. I caught him stealing some chips from me one day."

"Were they Fritos?" Frito asked.

"No, they were Doritos."

"Yuck!"

"Who cares, Frito!" Danny shouted. "This could be serious."

"What did you do when you caught him stealing?" asked Fruit Loop.

"I had some guys hold him down while I shaved his head and eyebrows. That was over two years ago though. Why come after me now?"

"Wait a second," Mad Dog said. "Tiny Tim…Tiny Tim." Mad Dog had his eyes closed, and he was rubbing his head, obviously thinking. He opened his eyes and said, "Tiny Timmy needs to be shaved, 'cause Tiny Timmy just won't behave."

"He's gone crazy," Fruit Loop joked. "I must have sucked his brain right out of him."

"Fuck you," Mad Dog snapped. "I remember hearing that being chanted when I first got in. I was in the holding cell and it was right down the hallway from general population. It sounded like a fucking lynching. The guy probably snapped. It looks like the shaving you gave him has become a weekly tradition."

"Great," Danny said, disheartened. "Tiny Tim is in here for splitting his wife's head with an ax while she slept. I'll have to stay awake the next six months. Fruit Loop, find out for sure if he's being transferred. If he is, find out if he is absolutely, positively coming just to get me. I only have six more months and I don't need any problems."

Chapter 6

"Alright, everybody," Danny was whispering to his friends, "tomorrow is Friday. We have verification Timmy is coming after me right away. This is my problem, not yours. I have no other choice but to take him out first. We all know how it works on the inside. I don't want to kill the guy, but if I don't, I'm as good as dead as soon as I close my eyes. I have to be careful though, 'cause I'm getting out of here in six months no matter what! I'm going to have to make it look like an accident and no witnesses! I am going to do this alone, but I need your help with how I'm going to do it. This needs to be the perfect crime."

The four of them were huddled around Danny and Frito's bunk. It was 10:00 p.m. Thursday night.

"It's going to be hard to commit the perfect crime when there's fifty potential witnesses," Mad Dog pointed out.

"Maybe the best way to do it is when everybody is sleeping," Fruit Loop added.

"That sounds good," said Mad Dog.

"I agree," Danny remarked, "but I don't think I'm going to have that long."

"The best thing to do is to hit him right away then. As soon as he comes in." Mad Dog thought for a second, then continued. "When he gets to his bunk with his belongings, I'll create a distraction so everyone will look in my direction. That will be your time to do whatever it is you're going to do."

"Not much of a perfect crime," Danny said, "but it will have to work.

On Friday, at 4:45 p.m. Frito grabbed a handful of corn chips and munched away absentmindedly. "I'm so nervous," he muttered.

"Calm down, you idiot," Mad Dog snapped. "You want to draw attention and get us busted? If you look as guilty afterward as you do now, we're all finished."

"He's right, Frito," Danny whispered. "Everything is going to be alright. With any luck we got the information wrong and Timmy won't even be coming in."

The guard called the roll-up list; everyone said goodbye to those who were leaving. They lined up at the gate and two minutes later they were gone. Five minutes later the buzzer sounded.

"Showtime," Mad Dog declared.

Mad Dog, Fruit Loop and Frito walked to the gate area where the new people were coming in. Danny waited by his bunk and watched the people appear. The second to last was Tiny Tim. Danny's heart sank. He didn't realize until just that moment how badly he wanted to have heard wrong information about Timmy. Now there was no turning back. He nodded to Mad Dog that Timmy was there. The next nod meant "action."

Danny still didn't know what Mad Dog was going to do. He imagined Mad Dog didn't know either.

Tiny Tim was walking to an open bunk straight across the room from Danny. This was perfect. His bunk was just on the other side of the two-foot dividing wall. As he approached his bunk, he spotted Danny and gave him the most wicked look Danny had ever seen. Timmy then gave a devilish grin and mouthed the words, "You're dead."

Danny looked Timmy straight in the eye and nodded. The signal was sent.

Mad Dog yelled as loud as he could, "I'm sick of your retarded, Frito loving ass." He grabbed the bag of chips from Frito and dumped them on the floor. Frito dropped to the floor and was shoving chips in his mouth. Everyone turned to watch, including Timmy.

As soon as Mad Dog started yelling, Danny was already moving toward Timmy. When Frito fell to the floor in his idiotic attempt to retrieve his precious corn chips, Danny was over the dividing wall grabbing Timmy. Danny kicked his legs out from under him while pulling back with all his force on Timmy's shirt. Danny kept pulling until Timmy's head hit the edge of the wall. Thank God for all the cheering and yelling going on because Timmy's head sounded like a watermelon hitting the ground after being dropped from a ten-story window. Danny quickly hopped back over the wall and ran to Frito's rescue. Mad Dog and Danny had some words, Mad Dog scuffed Frito's hair and said he was joking, and everybody went back to their bunks.

Tiny Tim was first seen by the person in the bunk over from him. The guards were called in, everybody was questioned, and no one had seen a thing. The warden ruled Timmy Wagner's death an accident. It was concluded he tripped, then, unfortunately, hit his head on the concrete divider wall. The following week the wall was taken out.

Chapter 7

"I see this will be our last meeting with each other, Mr. Taylor." Dr. Richards was looking at Danny's file.

"Yes, sir. I get released next week."

"Please realize, Danny, that the adventure is just about to begin for you. We have made terrific progress, but it is paramount that you continue to take your medication. Without it, the world that makes sense to you today will become distorted and confusing. You will be more apt to get angry, then violent. Your other personalities will resurface, and if that happens, it is almost a guarantee I will see you in here again. It is a vicious cycle, Mr. Taylor."

"I know, sir. Thank you for all you've done." Danny wondered what this moron would say if he told him he hadn't taken his medication for the last two years.

Dr. Richards stood and extended his arm. Danny did the same. As they shook hands, the doctor wished Danny luck.

"I just had my pre-release interview with Dr. Richards," Danny was saying to his friends. "I've been cleared to leave and tonight I'll be going to the single man cells for my last week."

Frito was lying on his bed eating his corn chips and moping. Mad Dog was sitting on Danny's bed next to Danny. Fruit Loop was five bunks down making money.

"It's hard to believe it was almost six months ago that Tiny Tim situation happened," Mad Dog said.

Frito finally spoke up. "Yeah, asshole! I'm still pissed off at you. Did you have to dump my Fritos on the ground?"

"If you call me asshole again, I'll throw *that* bag on the floor."

Danny laughed. "Hard to believe, but I'm actually going to miss this place a little."

"Then don't go!" Frito yelled.

"You'll be just fine. Besides, you go back to court on your appeal in two months. Just give them all the information and you'll be a free man. You have the name of the halfway house I'm going to be at. Look me up."

"As long as I don't fuck up again, I'll be out of here in half a year. Poor Fruit Loop has three more years." Mad Dog laughed, and continued. "Hell, he probably makes more money in here than on the street. That kid has a gift."

At 9:50 p.m. they called Danny's name to roll-up. He said his goodbyes and gave a final wave to his friends as he walked through the gate. When Danny was gone, Frito cried.

Chapter 8

Danny was sitting in the waiting room of the San Diego probation office in downtown San Diego. This wasn't the first time he'd been on probation. As a matter of fact, he had just gotten off of probation before the Margi situation. Danny had been drinking Jagermeister at some nightclub and a guy bumped into him while he was walking to the restroom. The two exchanged words and punches were thrown. Danny broke the man's nose, shattered one of his kneecaps, then emptied his bladder on the man as he rolled on the grown in agony. Danny did a year county time for that.

The probation, however, was worse than the jail time. For two years Danny lived under a microscope. He only had to report to his PO once a month, but he had to go in for a drug test at the PO's request. That was roughly once every two weeks. In addition, his PO would make unannounced visits to his apartment and work. It was both embarrassing and humiliating. Now Danny was starting the nightmare all over again, and this time for four years.

A door opened next to the reception window and a balding head stuck out. "Danny Taylor," the head said as a statement.

Danny stood and walked to the door. He saw the body that belonged to the head.

"Danny, my name is Bill Wakefield. I'll be your probation officer. Follow me, please."

Danny did. The man was roughly fifty years old, five-foot-eight, brown hair and brown eyes. Average. Boring. They walked down a long hallway with offices on the left and cubicles on the right. His was the last office on the left. Panic raced through Danny's body. The offices were occupied by senior probation officers—the worst. POs have been around the block. They have heard every lie, every story, seen everything, been there and done that. They trusted nobody, and thought everyone was trying to get something over on them.

They entered the office and sat down. Bill Wakefield and Danny sat silent for a full minute. His PO was obviously studying him, or trying to intimidate him.

He took a breath and spoke. "I'm a busy man, Mr. Taylor, so I'm going to cut right to the chase. Coming from prison and starting life again is no easy task. There are many pressures no one but the person in that situation can understand. The last thing you need is for me to breathe down your neck. I've read your file, Danny, and it is not hard to figure out you're an alcoholic. Also, I see you're taking "Haldol" for a form of schizophrenia."

Danny thought about telling him he wasn't taking the medication prescribed to him, but thought better of it.

"I see from the prison psychiatrist that you have made tremendous progress. On his recommendation, you were released after three years on a six year sentence. As long as you continue to take your medication, visit AA at least once a week, and stay in the halfway house you're assigned to, I will give you the trust and freedom I feel is necessary in making a new start. You will, of course, be required to make your monthly appointments with me, as well as submit to a monthly drug and alcohol test." He paused and observed Danny for another full minute, then asked, "Is this a fair chance I'm giving you, Mr. Taylor?"

Danny had a hard time concealing his excitement. Finally he smiled and said, "It is a blessing, sir. I won't let you down."

"See to it that you don't because, if you do, I assure you I will slam your ass."

"Yes, sir," Danny said. He had no doubt he meant it.

"You'll need these." Mr. Wakefield handed Danny a handful of AA attendance slips. "Give one of these to the person running the meeting you attend. Have them sign it, then bring at least four of these back to me every month, without fail."

"Yes, sir."

"Don't try signing them yourself either. I do check up on them."

"Yes, sir."

Mr. Wakefield stood and Danny did the same.

"Alright, Mr. Taylor. I'll see you next month."

"Thank you, sir."

Chapter 9

The halfway house Danny was staying at was nothing special, but it was better than prison. The house was called New Beginnings, located in downtown San Diego, on 6th Street near the South Freeway. It was an old eight-bedroom decaying eyesore. It reminded Danny of a haunted house.

During the six months Danny was staying at New Beginnings he followed all the rules. He went to his AA meetings—which he hated—kept all his appointments with his PO, and saved money for an apartment when his six month agreement with New Beginnings was over.

He was doing so well it almost scared him. Was this the quiet before the storm? He hadn't drank, or, more importantly—hadn't wanted to drink since he was released from prison. Now he was truly on his own. He had just finished moving into his studio apartment in Chula Vista. The locals called it Chulajuana. It wasn't much by a long shot, but it was in San Diego County and within the perimeters set by his PO. It also wasn't very far from his work.

Danny had gotten a job as a courier for a company called On Time Couriers. It wasn't a bad job for him, since he loved to drive. Danny picked up packages he needed to deliver for the day, checked locations and delivery times, put together a route and was free from a boss all day. He reported to work in Old Town at 7:00 a.m. and generally got off at 3:30 p.m. before the traffic started. All his deliveries were in the San Diego County limits.

As Danny pulled up to his apartment with a large pepperoni and jalapeno pizza from the Pizza King, he thought about his buddy Frito. Frito never contacted him at the halfway house. His appeal must not have gone through after all. Either that or he wimped out and decided not to give the information about STUD4U to the judge. Mad Dog was supposed to keep after him about that. Danny sure missed that guy. The whole time he was at New Beginnings, he kept a super-size bag of Fritos just in case his friend showed up.

Danny stepped out of his 1994 Toyota 4x2 pickup and looked around. He wondered if he was the only white person in this city. He locked his door and rechecked to make sure it was locked. Danny didn't like leaving his car on the street, but there was a waiting list for a carport, so he had no choice. He told his truck to behave and started walking toward his apartment. As he was inserting his key into the lock in the six-foot security gate, he noticed somebody had jammed the lock so it stayed open. Typical.

Danny climbed the steps to the second floor, made a left at the top and went halfway down the hall. His apartment was number 21, the legal age to gamble. *Funny*, he thought, *because staying here is definitely a gamble.* He unlocked his door and bolted it behind him.

The place was small and pretty much a dump. Luckily, Danny's mother lived not very far away in Poway and had helped him out with a couch, TV, VCR and refrigerator. She had also put the down payment on the truck. His mother had stuck by him the whole time he was in prison, believing in his innocence. Moms are great.

Danny pulled a video from the Blockbuster Video bag that was sitting on the VCR. Earlier he had rented four classic movies: *Grease, Boogie Nights, The Buddy Holly Story,* and the greatest movie ever made, *Halloween*. He put *Halloween* into the VCR and pressed play. If he was going to be scared staying here, he might as well be scared shitless.

He sat on the couch, grabbed a slice of pizza and was pleased it was Friday night. Two more days until he had to work again. As he listened to the spine-tingling music from the John Carpenter masterpiece, he was proud of himself for being sober, especially on a Friday night.

Chapter 10

Danny woke Saturday morning at 10:30 a.m. and got up to turn the TV off. It had a blue screen, reminding him to pop the tape out. He lifted the lid of the box of pizza and saw four pieces left. Danny loved pizza any time of the day. He grabbed a piece and ate happily. He would take a shower, then get his truck washed, since there was no place around the apartment to wash it.

As Danny locked the door of is apartment on the way out, he heard birds chirping in the distance. It reminded him of when he was a kid, not having a care in the world. Oddly enough, he didn't have a care in the world today. He didn't have to work, or see his PO for another three weeks, and he had gotten his weekly AA meeting out of the way Thursday night.

He walked through the broken gate and was happy to see his truck was still there. As he got closer, he noticed someone had left him a message under the driver side windshield wiper. *Great*, he thought, *I probably took someone's regular parking spot.* Then he jokingly thought, *Maybe some hot chick saw me park here and left me a note with her address.*

It was a large envelope. Danny removed the envelope from under the wiper and got in his truck. He started it and turned on the air conditioner.

Danny opened the envelope and pulled out the contents. There was a piece of paper and a Polaroid enclosed. He turned the Polaroid around and instantly dropped it as if it were on fire. He sat a quick moment registering what it was that his eyes had seen. He left the picture where it was and opened the note. He quickly looked up and looked around from his left to his right. He looked in his mirror, but saw nothing suspicious. He looked down at the note again. The message looked like a ransom note, with letters cut out from a magazine. Danny read:

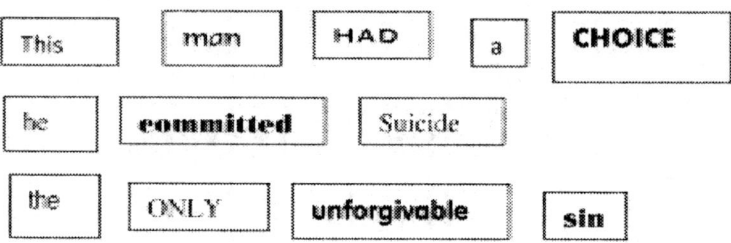

Danny put the note down; a shiver went through his body. He quickly looked around again, then slowly picked up the picture. He felt dizzy and sick to his stomach. He forced himself to look at it without turning away.

The picture was of a man lying on the floor, his head blown off. His brains were splattered all over the wall. Danny drove straight to the police station.

Chapter 11

Danny drove to the police station in downtown San Diego because it was the only one he knew of. He went to the front counter, explained his situation, and showed the officer the note and Polaroid. The desk clerk looked at Danny suspiciously and picked up the receiver on his phone, punched in three numbers and waited.

The cop spoke into the phone. "Detective, this is Thompson. I have a Mr.—sir, what did you say your name was again?"

"Danny Taylor."

Officer Thompson continued, "I have a Mr. Taylor at the front desk. I think it wise that you speak with him. May I bring him to your office? Thank you, sir." He hung up the phone. "Follow me, Mr. Taylor."

As Danny walked through the room, he was thinking that this place was nothing like the movies. There was no commotion. There were no "bad guys" being interviewed. Nobody was handcuffed to the desk. In fact, it was nice and quiet, a pleasant working environment.

Officer Thompson knocked lightly on a door marked with the words "Detective Miller,"

Just like the TV show Barney Miller, Danny thought. He heard the words, "Come in!"

They entered a small office. This looked just like the movies. Detective Miller was seated behind a small, cluttered desk. There was a coat rack next to the door with one coat on it. A small fan was oscillating on top of one of two file cabinets.

"Detective, this is Mr. Danny Taylor."

"Come in. Have a seat."

"Thank you," Danny said. He sat in one of two metal chairs that had padded seats. Officer Thompson remained standing. Danny felt suddenly uncomfortable. Detective Miller was sitting down, but he appeared tall. He was definitely husky. Danny guessed he was over six feet and easily two hundred fifty pounds. He was a very confident looking man, slightly graying at the temples. The rest of his hair was jet black, and he wore it slicked back. He had brown eyes and a two-day growth on his face—very rugged looking. Not a person you would want to fuck with.

"What's this about, Thompson?" the detective asked.

"I think it would be better explained by him." The officer motioned toward Danny. All eyes were now on him.

Danny cleared his throat, "When I went out to my truck today, I saw something under my wiper. I took it off and got inside my truck. It was hot outside, so I wanted to turn the air on."

"Get to the point please."

"I opened the envelope, took out the contents, and found that." He pointed to the letter and picture Officer Thompson was holding.

"Let me see those," Miller said. Officer Thompson handed it to him. The detective looked first at the picture, his stone expression never wavering. Next he read the letter. He looked at Danny and asked, "Why do you suppose this was left on your truck? Do you think you might know the person in this photo?"

"I doubt it. I don't even think the envelope was intended specifically for me. Last night was my first night in my apartment. Nobody knew I was there besides my mom."

"When did you find this?"

"Not even an hour ago."

"And you came right here?"

"Yes."

"Where do you live?"

"Chula Vista."

"Why did you come all the way over here? There are other facilities closer than this."

"Like I said, I'm new to that area. This is the only police station in San Diego I know by heart."

Detective Miller looked back down at the picture, then the note. He handed them to the officer. "Take these to Sharon and have her check for fingerprints. I can finish with Mr. Taylor. You may go back to the desk. Thank you."

Officer Thompson nodded and left the office. Danny shifted in his seat. The detective took out a notepad and pen. He wrote down Danny's name, address and mother's phone number, since his wasn't hooked up yet. He gave Danny his card.

"I don't know why your truck was chosen as the destination for this material. All I know is there are a lot of sick people who would consider this a practical joke. I wouldn't worry about this. We'll run some tests on the letter and picture. Most likely we'll be able to pull some prints other than yours and ours and find out who they came from. Thank you for cooperating and bringing that in. You would be surprised at how many people would have just thrown it away, not wanting to be bothered."

He stood and walked Danny to the door. "We will be in touch if we have any further questions. You know your way out?"

"Yes. Thank you."

Detective Miller nodded and shut his door.

On his way out, Danny said goodbye to Officer Thompson.

When he got into his truck, he closed his eyes and rested for a moment. He looked at himself in his rearview mirror, shook his head and reflected; I *don't need this aggravation in my life.*

Chapter 12

Danny drove to a coin-operated car wash. As he was washing his truck, he started sweating uncontrollably. He slowed his scrubbing down and added more quarters to the machine so he could take his time. *It must be close to a hundred degrees out here*, he said to himself, and for the first time since being out of jail he very badly wanted a beer.

Summer was always Danny's drinking season. Summer and winter, that is. Hell, who was he kidding—summer, winter, spring, fall, Lakers games, Angel games, Super Bowl, playoffs, sunshine, rain, good times, bad times, morning and night. All were reasons to drink for Danny. The problem was, one drink leads to three, three to ten, ten to twenty, and so on. He'd fooled himself into thinking he could handle alcohol way too many times. Deep down, however, he knew he wouldn't be able to stop. Not when his philosophy was—*Why drink unless you are going to get drunk?*

The machine started beeping, letting him know he had thirty seconds left. He dropped another quarter in the machine and flipped the control knob to rinse. He rinsed all the soap off, making sure to get the rims good, and finished just as his time ran out. He had forgotten to bring towels to dry his vehicle, so he drove around until his truck was dry—somewhat spotted, but dry. He headed toward his apartment, but remembered he had nothing to eat or drink at home.

He would go shopping later. Right now he would get a Dr. Pepper and some chips at the Quick Mart.

He pulled into the spot directly in front of the store. As Danny stepped out of his truck, he was blasted by the outside heat. Once inside the store he felt better. Before Danny knew what was happening, he was opening the beer cooler and was reaching for an eighteen pack of Coors Light. He stopped abruptly and just stood there letting the cold air surround him. He slowly closed the refrigerator door and moved to the soda section. Danny grabbed a liter of Dr. Pepper and a bag of Doritos. He stopped, smiled, put them back and grabbed a bag of Fritos. He paid for his purchase, got in his truck and drove home.

When he got out of the truck, he left his windows cracked so the heat wouldn't be trapped. He would roll them all the way up for the night after he went shopping.

Danny woke up at 5:00 a.m. Sunday morning with the blue screen on the TV again. He must have fallen asleep while watching *The Buddy Holly Story*. Having no bedroom or bed, he saw falling asleep in front of the TV becoming a regular thing.

Suddenly he remembered he had never made it shopping, which meant he hadn't rolled up his truck windows. He quickly went outside to make sure it was still there. It wasn't much worth stealing, but it is all he had.

A wave of relief passed over him as he saw his truck where he had left it. Since he was awake, he decided to go to the twenty-four-hour supermarket down the street. The windows were fogged up so he couldn't see inside, but as soon as he opened the driver's side door, he panicked at what he saw. Someone had slipped another large envelope through the slit in the window.

This time Danny wasn't going to give anybody watching him the satisfaction of seeing him scared. Even though his heart was pumping wildly, he calmly picked up the envelope and shut his door. He stuck his key in and locked it.

While walking back to his apartment, he casually let his eyes roam ahead of him for anything suspicious—someone peeking out of their curtains maybe? He saw nothing. He climbed the steps and entered his apartment, locking the door behind him without delay. He opened the envelope carefully as he sat on the couch.

Suddenly he wondered if he should have opened it. The smart thing to have done would have been to take it to Detective Miller. *Too late now. It's already open*, he thought. He pulled out two pieces of paper. No picture this time—thank God!

The two pieces of paper were folded individually. There was one word on the back side of each. The letters were once again cut from a magazine. On one were the letters: "FIRST." On the second were the letters: "NEXT." Danny opened the one that said "First."

The letters on the note itself weren't cut out from a magazine. The words were in individual strips from an old-fashioned labeler; the kind kids used where you would hold it in one hand and turn the circular top with the other until you reached your desired letter, at which point you would squeeze the grip and the letter would be imprinted on a piece of tape. You kept doing this until you spelled your word, then you turned the circular top to the picture of a pair of scissors, squeezed the handle and the word would be cut from a large roll of tape. This was how the entire note was—one word cut from the other.

Danny opened the other note. It was the same style. He went back to the letter stated "First." He read:

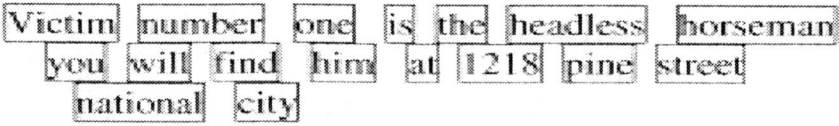

Danny sat in stunned silence. Not knowing what else to do, he picked up the letter stated "Next." He sat on his couch contemplating whether or not to read it..

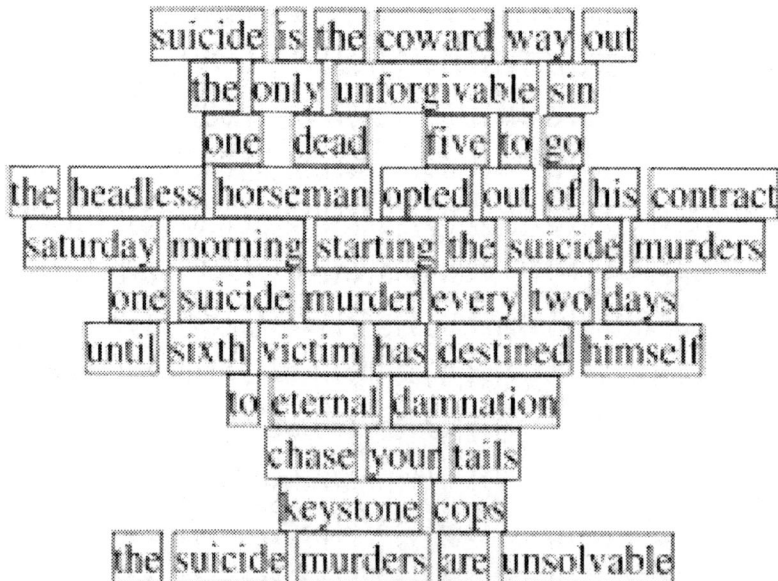

THE SUICIDE MURDERS

Fear was seizing him, but curiosity was overwhelming him. Wouldn't it be better not to know what was in the letter? He needed to know what it said. After giving this to the police, he was bound to be questioned.

"Great!" Danny whispered. "Mine are probably going to be the only prints found on this." He picked it up and read:

Wonderful, Danny thought. *Not only is this guy a psycho, he's a cocky psycho.* Maybe if he just threw these letters away he could save himself an incredible headache. He could foresee the cops questioning him already. Why shouldn't they? So far Danny was their only link to this nutcase, besides the notes. Once again Danny pondered; *I don't need this aggravation in my life.* What was his PO going to say? Any contact with law enforcement meant notifying him. Either that, or run the risk of going back to jail on a violation. Right now a ninety day or six month vacation didn't sound too bad.

Danny put the letters in the envelope and drove to a payphone. He took Detective Miller's business card out of his wallet and called the station. Of course, he wasn't in. It was 6:00 a.m. Sunday morning, but Danny knew he better try there before calling him at home. Danny took a deep breath, put a quarter in the slot and dialed Detective Miller's home number.

Chapter 13

The phone range three times and was picked up by a groggy sounding female. "Hello?"

"May I speak with Detect...Mr. Miller please?"

"Honey, I think it's someone from work," the woman said out of the receiver.

Danny heard grumbling, then the detective's voice in the phone. "This is my only day off, so unless someone's dead, you're gonna be!"

Danny almost hung up the phone on an intimidated impulse, but quickly thought better of it. "Sir, uh, Detective Miller, this is Danny Taylor, the one who brought you that note I found on my truck yesterday."

"I know who you are. Look, when I talked with your mother I told her that I had some more questions for you. I didn't mean for you to call me at—what time is it?"

"A little after 6:00 a.m., sir," Danny said hesitantly.

"Are you out of your mind!" he exclaimed.

"Detective Miller, I don't know anything about you calling my mom. I'm calling you because I got another envelope this morning. I found it in my truck when I was going shopping."

"It was in your truck?"

"Yes. I accidentally left my windows cracked last night and the person must have slipped it through the opening."

"Is the envelope sealed?"

"I opened it."

"I suppose your fingerprints are all over what's inside."

Danny knew he shouldn't have touched the damn letters. How stupid could he be? "I did read the letters, sir, and that's why I'm calling."

"You read the letters." He sounded exasperated. "You're tired of prison, so now you want to be a cop, huh?"

Danny stood holding the phone dumbfounded.

"That's right," the detective was saying. "I know all about you and your criminal record. Your prints were the only set besides Officer Thompson and mine that were on the note and envelope. I ran a check on you and came up with your whole life history. That's when I called your mother's house."

This is exactly why people throw things like this away when they find them, Danny thought. *It never pays to get involved.*

"Do you want the letters or not?" Danny was fed up.

"Meet me at the station in an hour, and don't give them to anybody but me."

Danny drove straight to the station and waited for Detective Miller on the stairs out front.

Chapter 14

"The letter gives the address of the guy in the picture," Danny said as the detective was walking toward him.

"Come inside," Miller said back. "Try not to smother the envelope with your prints."

They walked back to Detective Miller's office. Danny sat in the same chair as yesterday and felt a slight wave of déjà vu.

Miller sat in his chair behind the desk. He held out his hand, "May I see that, please?"

Danny tossed it to him, receiving a dirty look in return. Miller took the two letters out of the envelope, only after he reached into his desk and plopped a box of latex gloves on his desk. He slowly put them on while never taking his eyes off Danny.

What a prick, Danny thought.

The detective opened the letter labeled "First." He read it and set it aside. He then opened the letter labeled "Next." When he was finished, he looked at Danny and asked, "Why?"

"Why what?" Danny asked.

"Why has this person chosen you as the messenger?"

"I don't know. Didn't we go through this yesterday?"

"Yesterday you told me you didn't think you were specifically targeted. Today appears to be an entirely different situation, wouldn't you agree?"

"I guess so. Maybe the person saw me open the envelope yesterday and then followed me here. You yourself said most people would have thrown it away—not wanting to get involved. The person probably figured if I brought the first envelope to you, then I'd most likely bring this one to you too."

They sat looking at each other. Danny spoke again, "If you want to know the truth, I wish I would have just thrown the damn thing away. I don't need this aggravation in my life!"

"Neither do I, Mr. Taylor."

Detective Miller pressed a couple buttons on his phone and a voice said, "Yeah?"

"Would you come in here, please?" Miller asked.

Twenty seconds later a uniformed officer knocked twice and opened the door. Miller copied the address from the letter and handed it to the cop. "Take another officer with you to this address. We're looking for a possible homicide or suicide. Break the door down if you have to, and use caution."

"Yes sir," the cop answered. He closed the door behind him.

The detective punched some more numbers on his phone and waited. A female voice asked, "What can I do for you, Detective?"

"Sharon, would you come in here please? I have two more letters for you to take a look at."

"Be right there."

She wasn't lying. In a matter of seconds a fairly attractive brunette with permed hair walked in the room. She looked to be about five-foot-five, one hundred thirty pounds, maybe thirty-five years old. Danny couldn't help but admire her breasts, and just as if she had read his mind, she said, "Nice tits, huh?"

Danny's face grew red. She then patted her ass. "It ain't nothin' compared to my 'pooper' though."

Miller laughed. "Thank you again for working today."

"Hey, as long as the OT keeps coming in, I can afford the finer things in life—like these tits." She smiled at Danny.

He smiled back, his face going back to its normal color. He liked her.

"Have you found out anything else from the letter?" Miller asked.

"Besides the fingerprints of that convict? Not really."

Miller laughed loudly and held his hand out in a sweeping gesture toward Danny. "Meet the convict behind the fingerprints."

Danny's face got redder than before. This time from both embarrassment and anger. He must have been crazy to try to help the cops. Fucking ingrates.

"Too bad," Sharon said. "He's cute."

"Here are two more letters we've just come into possession of. Mr. Convict,

I mean, Mr. Taylor's prints will once again be on them." He gave Danny an amused glance and pulled out two pairs of gloves from the box on his desk. He started to hand them to her and stopped. "Oh, I see you planned ahead." She already had gloves on.

She looked at her hands and said, "Oh, these? I was just giving one of the new recruits a hand job. A little bonus for having to work on a Sunday." She winked at Danny.

Danny felt as if he could fall in love with this woman. Too bad he was deemed a loser, and a convict loser at that.

"I'll let you know what I come up with." She looked at Miller this time. "With the letters I mean—not the rookie." She left the room, leaving behind a lighter mood and a hint of cheap perfume.

"I'm sure you can appreciate the job I have to do, Mr. Taylor," Miller was saying. "I need to keep all avenues and possibilities open until I can safely eliminate them. Do I think you have something to do with these letters, other than being in the wrong place at the wrong time? No. Otherwise, I would have had you watched last night at your apartment. I chose not do that, even after I saw your criminal record.

"I will probably have a car follow you now, to see if this person contacts you again, but it will be strictly for your protection. Would that be alright?"

What other choice did he have? They were going to tail him anyway, so he might as well take some heat off himself and volunteer to be followed. "Of course," Danny said, "I have nothing to hide."

"Thank you for your cooperation."

"I'm sorry about the fingerprints—especially on the letters today. When I saw the envelope in my truck I didn't know what to do. I had it opened before I even thought about leaving prints. At that point it was too late. I was overcome with curiosity as to what the letters said. Now I wish I had never opened either envelope."

"I can understand, Mr. Taylor," Miller said. "I'm not saying what you did was right, but I can understand. Do me a favor, though. If you're contacted again without my boys seeing it, don't touch anything. Signal them and let them handle the situation accordingly."

"I will. Am I free to go?"

Detective Miller smiled and said, "You always have been."

As Danny got up, he asked, "Are you going to let somebody know to follow me?"

Detective Miller smiled again. "It's already been taken care of."

THE SUICIDE MURDERS

After Danny left, Miller sat at his desk thinking. The person behind the notes was most likely certifiable, maybe even an extreme religious fanatic. He thought about some excerpts from the letter: *One suicide murder every two days, The headless horseman opted out of his contract Saturday morning.*

Today was Sunday. Tomorrow would be another victim. He thought about the last part of the letter: *Chase your tails, Keystone Cops. The suicide murders are unsolvable.*

That part is what really pissed Miller off. "Nobody is going to get away with this shit," Miller whispered angrily. "This Keystone Cop is going to shove his Keystone cock right down your fucking throat!" Just then his phone rang. He pushed the intercom button. "Detective Miller here."

"Detective, this is Duncan. I think you better get over here. We have verification of a body, and there's a cassette tape on a table with your name on it."

"I'll be right there—and don't touch anything!" Miller shouted into the speaker. As he hit the button to hang up, he wondered how the killer knew his name.

Chapter 15

Miller pulled to the curb in front of 1218 Pine Street in his 2000, 4-Runner.

Duncan met Miller at his vehicle. "Homicide is already here, but everyone is waiting for you to hear what's on the tape."

"Is there a cassette player inside?"

"Yeah. The victim's name is Ross Tyler. This is his house. There's a tape player on his stereo system."

The two of them were now walking across the lawn to the house. Duncan was five-foot-eight and skinny. Walking next to Miller he looked tiny.

"You know," Duncan continued, "when you told me to check this place out, I didn't think I was going to find much—and I almost didn't."

"What do you mean?" Miller asked.

They stopped at the door.

Duncan said, "I searched the whole house, top and bottom and found nothing. I almost left when I realized I hadn't checked the closets downstairs."

They walked through the front door. Duncan led him toward the kitchen, pointed at an open door in the side of the wall, and said, "I opened this and found stairs leading to the basement."

As they descended the stairs, a smell grew more powerful with each step.

Duncan said, "Once we reach the bottom, you might want to breathe through your mouth."

Miller did exactly that.

At the bottom of the stairs they faced a wall. There was a hallway of about fifteen feet that led to the right. When they emerged from the hallway, Miller saw the bloody scene.

"Detective Miller," a voice called, "over here."

It was Ron Turner from homicide. The two men shook hands.

"Pretty messy, huh? Fucking shotguns really know how to blow a head apart," Turner stated.

"How did you ID him?"

"Fingerprints. We have our laptop here with the print pad."

Miller took a minute and studied the scene, taking everything in. It was worse than he expected. The man lay naked, with the front of his head completely blown away. His neck and remaining back part of his skull were only inches away from the wall. It appeared as if he were sitting against the wall when he pulled the trigger and was propelled straight down. The wall and surrounding area, as well as the ceiling, were splattered with blood, skull and chunks of brain.

The bizarre part was that the man's penis was missing. His mid-section was completely covered with blood. That was when Miller noticed the trail of blood from between his legs. It led to a table in a corner of the basement about ten feet away.

Turner saw where he was looking and said, "There's a cassette tape over on that table with your name on it. We've been waiting for you to get here until we played it."

The three of them walked over to the table. Miller reached for the tape, then stopped. He looked back at the body and asked, "Where's his penis? I assumed since the blood led over to this table it would be here."

"Forensics has it," Duncan said.

"The thing is," Turner added, "our killer appears to be a little unbalanced."

"What does that mean?" Miller asked.

"The shotgun was found upstairs in the den. The victim has a rifle rack on the wall there. The shotgun was found on the rack, with the victim's penis shoved into the end of the barrel." Turner cleared his throat and asked, "Do you want to listen to the tape now?"

Chapter 16

As Miller put the tape in the cassette deck, he looked around the room. It was full curious officers—too many officers. He wasn't sure yet how much he was going to tell the press. In a situation where a serial killer is loose, you have to be extremely careful. Certain clues are kept secret in case a copycat killer joined the fun. That was the only way to be sure you had two nuts to catch instead of one. Take the notes for example. Only he, Sharon and Officer Thompson knew about them. Only he and Sharon knew the killer coined the slayings to be the "Suicide Murders." If someone tried to imitate, there was no way to know a victim needed to be claimed every two days.

He pulled the cassette out of the stereo and asked Turner if he had a tape player in his car. He said yes. Miller announced to everyone that the cassette was confidential. He and the homicide detective walked to his car.

When in the car, Miller explained about the notes and how he had come into possession of them.

Turner listened carefully and asked, "So, this Danny Taylor is clean?"

"He's not spotless."

"What does that mean?"

"He's an ex-con on probation for murder."

"You're kidding me! You don't have him in custody?"

"This guy isn't the killer, Ron. He would have to be crazy to give me the notes himself. Think about it."

"You mean crazy enough to cut off a man's dick and shove it into the end of the murder weapon?"

"I hear what you're saying, but hear what I'm saying. I have nothing to hold him on. If I find evidence here that links him, then I'll arrest him. For right now I have to settle for tailing him."

"Alright, alright…let's have a listen to the tape."

Miller pushed the tape in and the two of them listened. It was silent at first as the reels spun the leader tape through. Suddenly the car was filled with the sound of empty recording.

Turner turned the sound down a little. A man's voice came on. It was shaky and scared. Turner turned the radio back up.

The voice said, "My name is Ross Tyler and this man is making me talk to you."

Miller pressed the power button. "How old is this man?" he asked.

"Sixty-five," Turner answered. "Computer check showed no record."

"I've got a bad feeling about this," Miller said. He pressed the power button again.

The voice continued, "He's holding a gun on me. Says he wants me to blow my head off with my own shotgun." He started to whimper. "Man says he knows where my grandchildren live. He's fucking crazy is what he is!"

Miller and Turner listened to what sounded like the man being slapped repeatedly. When the slapping stopped, all you heard was his sobbing. The tape recorder was shut off, then started again. There was the sound of footsteps, then what sounded like a chair being scooted around wildly. This went on for about twenty seconds, then the man's voice spoke frantically.

"Oh, God! This can't be happening! Dear God, No! I don't know who'll hear this tape, but this guy is crazy! He just went to get a knife! He says he's gonna cut my pecker off! He says he's gonna cut my pecker off if I don't kill myself. He's crazy! He's crazy! He's got me tied naked to a chair and he's goi…"

The footsteps sounded again.

"I never done nothing to you, mister!" The voice was hysterical. "I never done nothing to nobody!" The man was screaming, "Nooooooo!"

The two men sat in the car, horrified. The screaming went on and on. Terrible, horrifying, pain-filled screams echoed in their ears. After what seemed an eternity, the screaming subsided. They heard the man sobbing. Through the sobs they heard him say, "I'll do it. God forgive me, I'll do it. Please, just leave my grandchildren alone." The tape shut off.

Miller popped the tape out and put it in his pocket. "Do you mind if I take this to my analyst?" Miller asked. "It's just that she already knows about the notes and the less people that know about the details, the less chance we have of information being leaked to the press."

"I don't mind at all. Sharon's the best in the business. Tell me, has she come up with anything from the letters?"

"That's what I'm going to find out. I just gave her the second and third letters today—right before I came over here. The first letter only had Mr. Taylor's prints on them from when he opened it. I suspect his will be the only ones on the other two also."

"Naturally," Turner said sarcastically. "The man sounds clean to me."

"I got a tail on him now, so it would be impossible for him to do anything. Let me go see if Sharon has come up with something. If she hasn't, I'll start an investigation on Taylor. The next victim is supposed to be killed tomorrow. If that happens while we have Danny in our sights, we'll know it's not him."

Turner looked Miller straight in the eye, and asked, "Have you ever heard of an accomplice?"

Chapter 17

As Miller drove back to headquarters he had his mind on Danny Taylor. Not putting a tail on him last night suddenly seemed like a very foolish thing. It would make sense if he was the killer. How else could the tape have had his name on it? The man was killed on Saturday morning (the picture verified that) and Danny had come to see him Saturday afternoon. The killer wouldn't have known he was going to go to the downtown office; not when he lives in Chula Vista.

Miller slowed his thoughts down. Being a veteran detective, he had investigated countless crimes. Everything wasn't always as it appeared. He had seen murder investigations go together simply, every piece of the puzzle fitting together nicely. He had also seen them appear simple, only to go spinning out of control, going in directions he never would have dreamed of. Right now he had to collect the facts and the facts only. No speculations. Right now he had to trust his greatest ally—his instincts. His instincts almost always steered him right, and right now they were telling him Danny Taylor was innocent.

When Miller arrived at the station, he went straight into the lab where Sharon was working. She was looking under a huge magnifying lens.

"Tell me some good news," he said.

"I just got my period. You're not a father."

"That is good news. Tell me better news."

"I wish I could, Jim, but this guy is good. The only prints are from our convict. I've got the crew trying to track down the specifics; what type or types of magazines the letters were cut from, what stores still sell those kid labelers, how old the paper and envelopes were. You know—the exciting stuff."

"I always thought you were the exciting stuff," Miller said, smiling.

She gave him a chuckle. "I'm rubbing off on you. You're becoming a degenerate."

They laughed. Miller then changed the mood. "Sharon, we need to pull something from these letters. I just came from the murder scene and it was pretty messy. I have a feeling this guy is going to try to outdo himself with every victim, making each killing as gruesome and bizarre as possible."

"I've notified everybody on my crew they are on mandatory overtime until we catch this guy."

"Good. I told Turner from homicide that I wanted you to head the analysis of the letters and any other clues that need to be investigated by forensics. He agreed. In fact, he said you were the best in the business."

"I've always perceived Turner to be an intelligent man, but now I know he borders on genius."

Miller reached into his pocket and pulled out the cassette tape. He handed it to Sharon and said, "This was left at the crime scene with my name on it. See if you can find anything from it, and keep this and the letters as quiet as possible. I don't want a leak to the press."

"No problem," Sharon said. "My people hate the press."

"Who doesn't?" Miller replied. He started to leave, then turned around at the door. "Prepare yourself before you listen to that, Sharon. It's pretty gruesome—even for you."

She walked to her portable cassette player with a look on her face that could have been perceived as excitement.

Chapter 18

Detective Jim Miller sat at his desk. He was leaning back in his chair with his eyes closed. He was thinking about the letters. He had buzzed through to Sharon about five minutes ago and was waiting for her to bring him copies of the letters and tape. As he was reaching for the phone, she walked in.

She handed him the copies and said, "That tape is something else. I'm going out on a limb, but I agree with the victim—the killer is crazy. You think he might be related to me?"

Miller shook his head no. "He's not that far gone yet."

Sharon was about to leave, when she said, "I forgot to tell you something strange. All three letters we have from this guy have cut-out words. While I didn't expect to find his prints, I did expect to find some prints. Every time we've received notes like this, there are usually at least partial prints on the cut-out letters themselves. You know, from people thumbing through them in the liquor store or supermarket. This is the only time I've never been able to get anything."

"Interesting. What do you think it means?"

"Either he subscribes to the magazine, or it's one of those porno-mags that come individually wrapped. I need to first see if I can identify which specific magazine or magazines the letters come from, and if I can do that, then the tracking process begins."

"I have faith in you. Keep in mind religious magazines or publications. We may have a Jesus freak on our hands. Two of his letters make a reference to suicide as being the only unforgivable sin."

"Yeah, I was thinking of that," Sharon said. "He also made a reference to eternal damnation."

"Exactly. I'm going to pull all our records of any previous offenders who are eccentric in their religious beliefs."

"Looks like we both got our work cut out for us. Oh, by the way, are you going to bring that ex-con in for more questioning since his are the only prints we got?"

"No. I got a tail on him right now, but I fucked up and told him about it," Miller said, embarrassed.

Sharon laughed. "I never have understood all your methods."

"Me neither," Miller admitted.

Sharon left the room and he rubbed his temples.

It was 12:10 a.m. Monday morning and Miller had just put the last of the files away from the religious offenders.

Unfortunately, nobody fit the profile. Not yet at least. He would keep them within reaching distance though, because the upcoming murders, or suicides, or whatever the hell they were classified, would present new clues. New clues represented patterns. Patterns represented carelessness. Carelessness represented arrests.

Miller looked at the clock and wondered if the sick fucker had already made his killing for the day. He then opened Danny's file, which he had downloaded from the main computer earlier. He opened up his top drawer on his desk, took out a bottle of aspirin, dumped four out into his hand and washed them down with cold coffee.

"Why you, Danny Taylor?" he asked. "Why were you given the notes? It just doesn't make sense."

Miller laid his head straight down so his forehead was resting on the desk. His arms were hanging down. "I swear to God," he said, "if you are the killer, Mr. Taylor, I'm going to cut your dick off and shove it into the barrel of my gun and shoot you with it."

He picked his head up, drank some more coffee and read aloud from Danny's file. "Three drunk drivings, one at twice the legal limit, and two at three times the legal limit. All three in different states. Two bar fights, with one of those ending in the draining of the bladder onto the victim. One drunk in public and, of course, one homicide." Miller closed the file.

He finished the cold coffee, grunted from the taste and stood up. *That's it for tonight—I mean this morning*, he thought. *I better get some sleep before I can't think straight.*

Miller picked up the phone, dialed the number of the officers who had pulled night duty on Danny. The cell phone was picked up on the second ring. "Hello?"

"This is Detective Miller. What's the word on our boy?"

"He's been inside his apartment since we took over at ten."

"Okay, you have my home number if anything happens."

"Are you still at headquarters, sir?"

"Not anymore," Miller answered. "You guys stay alert." He hung up the phone, gave a big yawn and headed for home.

Chapter 19

The alarm clock Danny had bought the day before was beeping. He hit the off button and got up from the couch to stretch his back. Unless he wanted to be a permanent patient of a chiropractor, a bed was going to need to be bought soon. There was no room for one, however, not until he at least moved into a one bedroom apartment.

Danny walked over to the window and looked out. He had a full view of the courtyard. No one was watching his door. A couple of times last night he walked around the complex to see if he could spot the cops watching him. They were easy to spot. Two white guys smoking cigarettes in an obvious undercover cop car wasn't very typical in Chula Vista. He knew they would be there, so they weren't trying very hard to be inconspicuous. What if the killer was going to leave him another letter? They were blowing their chances of catching him in the act, that's for sure. Shit, they were only three cars down from Danny's truck. That's another thing—they were only watching his truck. He could have slipped away last night through the back of the complex, killed some poor sap and returned with the perfect alibi. The notes appeared to be right it seems. These were Keystone Cops.

After a shower and breakfast, which was again cold pizza, he locked his apartment and walked toward his truck. Danny laughed to himself as he walked past the gate. *These guys are going to have a fun time following me,* he was thinking. *I drive at least a hundred miles a day.* He was still laughing as he got into his truck.

THE SUICIDE MURDERS

Even though Danny's truck was watched all night, he was still relieved to see no note today. He wondered how long it would be before he wouldn't think about the notes anymore.

He started his truck and was suddenly second guessing his decision to not tell his PO about what had been happening. It isn't worth it though. All this will blow over as soon as the killer is caught. Hell, today is Monday. There's supposed to be another killing today. All this will probably blow over when he isn't contacted. Why wouldn't it? He's been watched since yesterday. He will receive no note, the victim will be found some other way, and he will be free of this nightmare. The killer will start giving his messages to some other unlucky soul. Yes. That is exactly what will happen. No way was he going to volunteer himself to an unwanted headache with his PO. No way.

Danny pulled into the parking structure at work and the electronic gate closed behind him before the cops could follow him in. He was stepping into the elevator that was located by the gate just as they were following another car in.

It's nice to know I can lose these guys if I have to, Danny thought. He got off on the second floor and walked into On-Time Couriers, right on time. It was 7:00 a.m. on the dot.

As he was getting a cup of coffee from the automatic machine, his boss approached him. His name was Trey Reynolds. *A soap-opera name*, Danny thought the first time he heard it.

"How's my best driver?" he asked. He said this to everybody.

"I'm doing well, thank you."

"You're not tired from getting your new place in order?"

"I don't have much stuff. It didn't even take an hour to get everything I own in the apartment."

"Well, I scheduled you an easy day, just in case."

"That was nice. Thank you."

"Think nothing of it," he said. He turned and left as quickly as he came.

Danny walked over to the box that had his deliveries for the day. Mr. Reynolds wasn't kidding—he only had six drops. That was good. After what happened this weekend, he was dreading a long day.

He sat down, sipped his coffee and put together his route. With any luck, his day would be over at 12:30 p.m.

Chapter 20

Detective Miller woke at 8:30 a.m. and called the cell phone of the officers following Taylor. The phone was picked up on the second ring, just like last night.

"Yeah?" the voice asked.

"Yeah! This is Detective Miller."

"Oh, sorry sir. This is Peterson."

"How's everything look?"

"Good. Right now we're in Rancho Bernardo. It seems this guy has a delivery job or something."

"Are you having any problem keeping up with him?" Miller asked. He was walking over to look at himself in the mirror.

"No, but we're hungry. When do we eat?"

"When he eats. God, I look like shit." He was running his hand over his facial hair and turning his head side-to-side.

"What?" Peterson asked.

"Nothing. Just keep a close eye on him and keep me updated. I'll be in the office by nine-thirty."

"Yes, sir."

Miller hung up and set his phone on the toilet. He opened his medicine cabinet, took out a razor and shaving cream, then closed it. He stared at his reflection for a good ten seconds, then asked himself, "What adventure does the day hold?"

THE SUICIDE MURDERS

Officer Peterson sat in the unmarked squad car with his partner. It was 12:15 p.m. and they were waiting for Danny to come out of a business complex in the city of Escondido.

"Man, I hope this prick stops and gets something to eat soon," Peterson was saying, "I'm starving!"

His partner was wiping his forehead with his hand. "They need to fix this fucking air-conditioner. How do they expect us to follow this guy in the middle of summer with no fucking air?"

"Nice working conditions, huh? No air, no food, and no sympathy."

"We won't be rookies forever—thank God!" Hudson exclaimed. He was getting frustrated. In his opinion, there was nothing worse than hot weather. He didn't agree with it, but he could see how people lose their minds in the heat and end up killing someone. Right now he was wishing Danny would do something that would warrant him kicking the living shit out of him.

Peterson noticed his partner's rapid breathing. "Cool off," he said. As soon as he heard his own words, he wished he could take them back. He turned his head and grimaced.

"Cool off!" Hudson screamed and laughed at the same time. "Cool fucking off?" He then spoke calmly. "I can't cool off, Peterson, old buddy, old pal, because we don't have a FUK-KING AIR CON-FUK-KING DISH-N-ER!" He blared the horn every syllable when the shouting began.

Danny came out just as the honking started. He looked over at the car, and when the honking stopped, he waved.

Hudson saw him waving, looked over at his partner and said calmly, "I'm going to kill that motherfucker." He then exploded like lighting for his door handle. He was halfway out of the car when Peterson grabbed him by the back of his pants. Hudson fell down face first, pulling Peterson over the driver's seat.

"What the fuck?" Hudson screamed.

Peterson let go and hurried back up to a sitting position. Hudson jumped up, turned around, and bent down into a crouching position. Peterson, who was looking straight ahead, slowly turned his head to the left until he was looking right into the eyes of his partner.

Hudson gave him a finger wiggle wave and said, "Hi, I'm Hudson." He stopped wiggling his fingers. "I'm your partner—remember me? We work as a team."

Peterson started laughing and said, "That's why I stopped you from killing him. Now get in the car before he loses us." He made a hand gesture out the front window. Danny was pulling out of the parking lot.

"Shit! Miller will have my ass if he gets away." He scrambled in the car and screeched the tires onto the street.

Danny turned into the very next complex. Hudson said, "He did that on purpose. Please, let me kill him—just a little."

Peterson laughed. "How the hell did they ever let you on the force?" he asked joking, then said, "Wait, I don't think I want to know."

"Alright, he's pulling into Carl's Jr. He's going in too." Hudson quickly parked the car and said, "You watch the outside, I'll get the food." In a flash he was out of the car and walking toward Danny. Peterson jumped out and joined him.

"What are you doing? One of us has to stay out here," Hudson explained.

"I'm not letting you go in there alone with him."

"We won't be alone. The place is packed."

"You know what I mean."

"Yeah, I know what you mean. You don't trust me."

"Not with him I don't."

They were standing in the middle of the parking lot. "Fine," Hudson said. "You get the food. I'm just going to use the bathroom and I'll meet you back out here."

They walked toward the restaurant, and Peterson asked, "What do you want? It's my treat."

"I'll have the number four with a Coke."

As they walked in the door, they saw Danny. Peterson pushed Hudson toward the restroom and said, "Splash some cold water on your face. It will help you cool off."

Hudson shot him a look. "I mean," Peterson corrected himself, "it will make you feel better."

The two men had finished their lunches and were sitting in the car waiting for Danny to come out.

Hudson said, "This fucker sure is taking his sweet-ass time. He knows we're out here baking like a toasted cheeser."

"A toasted what?"

"You know, a toasted cheeser...a grilled cheese sandwich."

"Whatever," Peterson said, joking. He then saw Danny walking out the front door. "Here comes our boy."

"Look at him," Hudson said. "Look how refreshed he looks. How nice for him."

Danny was walking across the parking lot, sipping his soda when he stopped abruptly.

"What's he doing?" Peterson asked.

Danny was staring at his truck. He then looked over to the cops, then back to his truck. Slowly he started walking again. When he was about fifteen feet away from his parking spot, he stopped again. He turned to the cops again and waved his arm for them to come over.

Peterson and Hudson got out of their car and walked side by side over to Danny, wondering what it was that was wrong.

The two of them looked like twins. They were both five-foot-ten with black hair, and both were roughly one hundred-eighty pounds. Hudson was twenty-four and Peterson was twenty-three. Coincidentally, had they entered the academy on the same day. Now they were walking together toward Danny Taylor in their blue Hagar slacks, white Oxford shirts with ties loosened at the neck and tan Florsheim shoes.

Hudson spoke to Peterson. "If this guy is yanking our chains I'm going to shoot him."

"No, you're not," Peterson replied. "I am."

"What is it?" Hudson asked.

"It's not possible," Danny said, bewildered. "How is it possible?"

"How is what possible?" asked Hudson.

Danny pointed to his truck. "There's an envelope on my windshield."

Chapter 21

Miller was sitting at his desk. He had just come back from talking with Sharon. The cassette tape was a standard sixty minute TDK. Tests run on it showed it to be five years old. There was no way to track it because sales of that particular tape were way too common. The handwriting of Miller's name on the cassette didn't match the victim's, and no prints were found. Sharon had asked for a writing sample from Danny.

As Miller was reaching for his phone to call Peterson, it rang. After a slight flinch from the surprise, he picked it up and said, "Detective Miller here."

"Detective, this is Peterson. I have…"

"It's about time you called." He looked at his watch. "I asked to be kept updated—that was almost five hours ago."

"I know, sir. I'm sorry." Peterson swallowed hard and wiped the sweat from his brow. He wanted very badly to win the coin-toss between himself and Duncan, but he lost. So now he was on the phone with his superior about to tell him they fucked up. "Sir, we have a problem."

Miller opened up his drawer and reached for his aspirin. "What is it Peterson? Don't tell me you lost Taylor!"

"No sir. The thing is, sir—"

"Out with it!"

"Taylor was contacted again without Duncan or me seeing it. There is an envelope under his windshield wiper. Do you want me to open it?"

"No!" Miller exclaimed. "Do you guys have any gloves?"

"Of course, it's standard. There's a box of latex gloves in the trunk."

Miller thought for a second, resting the phone between his shoulder and ear while he dumped some aspirin into his hand. "Put the gloves on and bring the envelope to me. Also, tell Taylor he's not under arrest, but we need for him to come to the station now. Something isn't right. When he gets here if he needs to have me call his boss, I will. If he refuses to come voluntarily, read him his rights and bring him in for interfering with an investigation. Do you understand me?"

"Yes sir," Peterson said, relieved someone else was going to be taking the heat off him and his partner—at least he hoped so. "We're in Escondido, so we should be there in half an hour."

"Come straight to my office." Miller hung up and took the aspirin.

After he hung up with Peterson, Miller called Ron Turner. The homicide detective said he would be there in twenty minutes. He then buzzed Sharon and told her they had another letter coming in.

The three of them were in Miller's office when Officers Hudson and Peterson entered with Danny. Miller saw no handcuffs on Danny, and said, "I see he came willingly."

Hudson answered, "It just so happens he was done for the day. He finished his route right before he went to Carls, Jr. for lunch."

"That's where the envelope was put on his truck," Peterson added.

Miller was putting on gloves while the officers talked. He held out his hand toward Peterson. "Could I have that please?" He was referring to the envelope.

"Of course. Sorry, sir." He handed it to Miller.

"Before the three of us take a look at this," he made a motion of his hand toward Sharon and Turner, "I would like to know how it ended up on Mr. Taylor's windshield without either of you seeing it placed there."

The two officers looked at each other, both wanting the other to explain. Peterson finally answered the question. "What happened is, when Taylor went to lunch, I went in to get some food and Duncan needed to use the restroom."

"Are you telling me you went into the restaurant at the same time?" Miller asked incredulously.

"It was only for two or three minutes, tops."

"Well, it appears to have been more than enough time for the killer to place the note, doesn't it?"

"Yes, sir," the officers said simultaneously.

"Mr. Taylor, we would like for you to volunteer to give us a handwriting sample." Miller continued. "Would that be alright with you?"

"I don't see why not."

"Good. Peterson, you and Hudson take him to the interrogation room. There is a standard three page form to be copied, and make sure he signs his name at the end three times. Put the papers in the lab so Sharon can do what it is she does."

"Am I in trouble?" Danny asked.

"Not at all, Mr. Taylor. Just follow the directions on the form in a normal, relaxed manner and everything will be fine. When you're done, you may go home. Peterson and Hudson will continue to follow you for your protection, of course." Miller then looked at the officers. "You two will come back here and wait for me to talk with you further when your backup arrives. Understood?"

"Yes, sir," they again answered at the same time.

When the three of them left the room, Miller picked up the envelope and looked back and forth between Sharon and Ron. He opened the envelope and pulled out a single sheet of paper and unfolded it. He put it on the desk for everyone to see, and they both stood up to get a better look. It was once again cut-out pieces of tape from a kid's labeler. Miller read the letter out loud as they all looked at it.

> such a beautiful girl doing such
> bad things for money
> no wonder she did drugs
> i guess she did not know drugs kill
> go to 343 second avenue apartment
> number four san ysidro
> you will find rapunzel

They sat silent for a moment.

Sharon spoke first. "Let me see what I can do with this." She put on a latex glove and grabbed the letter. Two seconds later she was gone.

Turner picked up Miller's phone and sent a crew to the address. "You want to ride over with me?" he asked.

"No," Miller replied, "I'll follow you."

Chapter 22

When Miller and Turner arrived at 343 Second Avenue, the front of the apartment complex was blocked off with yellow crime scene tape. If they hadn't known the girl was dead before, they certainly would have now.

They walked in together, showing their identification to the officer at the door of the apartment. He directed them to the bedroom. As they were walking in the bedroom, the crime photographer was walking out.

"That is one of the most interesting set of pictures I have ever taken," he said as he past them without slowing down.

"Holy shit! That is interesting!" Miller agreed. The two of them stood at the door looking at what was in front of them.

The victim was lying naked on her back. Her legs were hanging off the bottom of the bed, and her arms were spread out over her head. She had syringes hanging out of the middle of her arms, right at the part that bends. There were syringes stuck between every finger and every toe, held in place by a long strip of duct tape that ran over the plungers. Her mouth was overflowing with pills and there were some scattered around her head. Two metal sniffing straws were rammed up her nose and dried blood lead from them down her cheeks to just under her ears.

Miller and Turner walked to the bed and examined her closely. Even in death they saw she was very pretty. She had blond hair of about three feet in length and it was laid out directly above her head. She appeared to be in her mid-twenties. Her eyes were wide open, but there were little squares of green paper stuck to her irises. On her belly were her areolas and nipples. They were cut out whole. Mounds of white power was heaped where they used to be. Dry blood ran down her stomach and sides. Another piece of duct tape led from just below her navel and went between her legs to the small of her back. The duct tape was holding in two dildos, one in her vagina and another in her rectum.

"We need to catch this sick fucker," Miller said.

"Repunzel, huh? Isn't this guy original?" Turner remarked. "What do you think the paper over the eyes is?"

"It would have to be drops of acid."

"Makes sense," agreed Turner.

Miller started looking around the room as Turner investigated the body more thoroughly. There wasn't much to look at though, besides the dead girl. There wasn't much for furniture or decorations. The walls were completely bare and the curtain over her window consisted of a blanket nailed to the wall. Pretty typical of a drug user actually. They were always paranoid someone was watching them. She had only the bed, a dresser, a small combo VCR/TV set and a hand-held camcorder. The camcorder was the type that had a screen you could watch while you were recording. Miller popped open the tape deck on the boom box, but it was empty. He pressed eject on the VCR and a tape noisily came out. He read the title: "Robo-Cock." He then pressed eject on the camcorder. The deck popped open and revealed a tape. Miller pulled it out and said, "Bingo! The bastard left us another present with my name on it."

Turner posted an officer outside the bedroom door and instructed him to keep everyone out. The camcorder was 8mm so they couldn't play the tape in the VCR without a compatible cartridge for it to fit into. They also didn't have the proper accessories to play it through the camcorder to the TV. Luckily however, they could view the tape on the camcorder screen itself. Miller pressed the power button, then hit rewind. They could hear the gears spin the reels.

"What do you think the chances are of his face being on this?" Turner asked.

Miller made a head gesture toward the girl. "About as much a chance of that girl coming back to life."

The gears slowed down and they heard a click as the reels stopped. Miller pressed the play button and they huddled together to view the screen.

The image came on and they were looking at the girl. She was on her knees in the middle of the bed. She was topless, but her hair hung down over her shoulders covering her breasts and continued between her legs. She was beautiful.

"Are we rolling?" she asked. The camera nodded up and down.

THE SUICIDE MURDERS

"I thought it was too much to hope for, but I was guessing this guy might be cocky enough to let us hear his voice."

"Give him time," Turner said.

She had a half-empty bottle of Jack Daniels in her hand and took a drink. She started giggling. "My name is Tiffany Adams. Oh shit! I said my last name." She started laughing and shrugged her shoulders. "Oh well. Fuck it is what I say. Joke 'em if they can't take a fuck, right?"

She was obviously drunk. She took another drink and leaned forward on her left hand and handed the bottle straight ahead and out of the picture. The camera tilted and turned slightly, then the sound of the bottle being set on the dresser followed. The camera re-centered on her. She was on all fours and the picture zoomed to her face. "I got me a guy who likes to watch, isn't that right, hon?" The camera again went up and down.

Tiffany started crawling backward to the headboard. The camera panned back to get a full view as she did. When her feet touched the tope of the bed, she stopped, stood on her knees again and flipped the right side of her hair over her shoulder. Her right breast was exposed. She was looking directly into the camera. "Do you like what you see?" she asked. The camera nodded. She flipped the left side of her hair over her shoulder. Her breasts were tan and big. Not huge, but probably a size "D."

She stuck her chest out and shook back and forth. Her breasts were very firm, but very real. Her body had no idea what gravity was yet. She stopped shaking and squeezed them together, then let them go, then squeezed them together, then let them go. She looked down and pinched her right nipple, giving an exaggerated moan. She then picked up her breast and lowered her mouth to it while looking seductively into the camera. She stuck her tongue out and ran it around the nipple, then flicked it back and forth on the hardened point. Her tongue then went back in her mouth and she lowered her breast.

She placed her hands on her belly and slowly moved them into her underwear. She let out a gasp as they past under her. Still on her knees, she rubbed up and down between her legs. She had her eyes closed and her heard was turned to he left. Her hips started rotating as she moaned. The camera zoomed on her pelvis as she gyrated and stroked. Her left hand moved to her breast and the camera panned out to view her whole body.

She was rotating her right hand in fast circles between her legs while squeezing her breast with her left hand. Her hips started moving up and back as her right hand circled even faster. As her body jerked wildly in the height of ecstasy, Tiffany screamed, "Number six! Number six! Oh God, number six!" and, as her body slowed its convulsing, and as her hand slowed its rubbing, Tiffany said something in the final pulsing of pleasure that stopped the hearts of both Miller and Turner. "Danny Taylor is number six."

Tiffany Adams then asked the man holding the camera, "Was that the right thing to say, baby? Did that get you off?" The camera moved up and down.

She then asked the man holding the camera another question. She asked him with the words that most likely formed the last sentence she would ever speak. "Can I have that shot of heroin now?" The camera moved up and down, and as she smiled her beautiful smile, the camera shut off.

Chapter 23

Turner and Miller were outside at their cars talking at the crime scene with a San Ysidro policeman.

"We identified the woman as Tiffany Adams. She is twenty-five years old and a known prostitute. We're interviewing the neighbors right now, but so far no one has seen anything. So many people come and went from her apartment that no one paid any attention. It wasn't unusual for screams and banging either," the officer reported.

"Thank you," Turner said. "Let me know if you come up with anything else."

"I will, sir." The officer walked away.

"An autopsy will be done for an official cause of death, even though we all know what it is," Turner said.

"Of course," Miller replied. "Let's get men on the streets today in every fucking city in San Diego County. I want to know if a drug buy went down consisting of a mixture of drugs. Spread the word that helpful information will represent a 'get out of jail free card.' I want this motherfucker bad. Nobody leaves me messages on crime scenes and gets away with it."

"This guy has been error-proof so far. He most likely bought each drug separately from a different dealer," Turner added.

"I know, but spread the word anyway. Ask if anybody new has been buying. If we can get the same description in different cities, we may be on to something."

"Will do. Get that tape over to Sharon and let's see what info she can get from it. We have today and tomorrow to catch this guy before he strikes again," Turner continued.

"Are you going to bring Taylor in for interrogation?"

"Right now I have Sharon analyzing his handwriting to see if on the outside chance it matches the writing of my name on the cassette tape. I'll also have her check it to this." Miller held up the videotape. "If that comes up cold, which I foresee it will, I'm going to investigate him more thoroughly. I'll talk with his PO, and maybe even head to Chino and talk with the warden at the prison he was at—see if he did anything there that will raise a red flag."

"Call me tomorrow morning and let me know what's going on and I'll let you know if I come up with anything from the streets."

The men got in their cars and drove off. Miller couldn't stop thinking about the video tape. What a shame such a pretty girl ended up being a prostitute. He saw it all the time though. Either a girl tries drugs and gets addicted and has to start hooking to pay for her habit, or a girl is so pretty she finds guys lining up to pay her for sex. Easy money. If they only knew how often they ended up dead.

Miller had just gotten to the lab and was talking with Sharon.

"Remember, Jim, I'm not a handwriting expert, but I can clearly say Taylor's handwriting is not the same on the cassette tape, or this video tape."

Miller was sitting in a chair in the corner of the lab. It always made him nervous to be in this room, as if he was going to disrupt evidence or fuck something up somehow. "Well, is it possible he could have faked his writing?"

"You know the form is set up to find changes in writing patterns and styles. Even if he was trying to change his writing style, it would be impossible to keep it consistent all the way through. His writing was smooth and natural. He has definitely written that way his entire life."

"What if he changed his style on the cassette and videotape?"

"Like I said, I'm not a handwriting expert, but in my opinion, I say it still isn't him. The videotape and cassette have the same writing pattern. Your name is exactly the same on both of them. The person who wrote your name has been writing like that for a very long time."

"Alright. Did you get anything from the last letter?"

"Nothing. He obviously wears gloves because the letters are as clean as clean. Also, the envelopes and paper are standard. Every store in America sells them."

Miller let out an exaggerated sigh and asked, "Any news about the labeler he's been using?"

"Funny enough, they aren't very uncommon. We found four main toy stores that sell them. The tests we ran on the tape showed it was over twenty years old. Either the killer has had the thing since he was a kid, or he picked it up at a garage sale, swap meet or something. Either way, it's going to be a bitch to track. We have people going to neighborhoods asking about recent garage sales and we've also got a list of all the people who rented spaces at the swap meets in S.D. County. The department on top of shit duty is calling them as we speak. If anybody sold one of those things within the past three months we'll know."

"You are the best, aren't you?"

"You want to do a quickie and find out?"

"Maybe later. Right now I've got my sights set on Mr. Taylor's PO."

As Miller walked out the door, Sharon asked him if there was anything good on the tape. "I have a feeling you're going to love it," he answered.

Am I doing the right thing by not telling Danny his name was given as the sixth victim? Miller was thinking to himself. He and Turner had discussed what they thought while in Tiffany's room, after viewing the end of the tape again. Their first inclination was to get Danny protection. They then discussed the possibility of something Turner suggested yesterday. Maybe Danny was working with an accomplice. If he were, then putting himself as the sixth victim would stop the police from suspecting him. If that were the case, wouldn't he expect police protection? Something wasn't making sense about this case and they both knew it. They had decided to tell Danny they were pulling the surveillance they had on him and see how he reacted. Of course, they were still going to tail him, but they were going to be a tad more secretive.

While in the bedroom, they discussed bringing Danny in and interrogating him, then telling him they thought he was clean, thus pulling the surveillance team. When Miller was talking with Turner outside by the cars, he inwardly decided to handle things his own way. Since his handwriting didn't match either the cassette or the videotape, and there were already two people dead with no clues, he decided he was going to talk with Danny's PO and see if he could give him any useful information. He was driving there now.

"Thank you for seeing me. I know you must be busy," Miller said.

"Think nothing of it. So, you are here in regard to Danny Taylor? Has he done something wrong? Something I should know about?" Bill Wakefield asked.

"I'm here confidentially, Mr. Wakefield."

"Call me Bill."

"Thank you, and please call me Jim. As I was saying, I'm here confidentially, Bill. This conversation must only be between us. Would that be possible?"

"Of course. You don't want me to mention this to Danny."

"Or anyone else for that matter."

Miller was sitting in Danny's probation officer's office.

"The thing is," Miller continued, "I'm heading a murder investigation and Danny is a potential suspect."

"You know, of course, Danny is on probation from a murder change. One in which he claimed, and still claims, his innocence."

"I didn't know he claimed he was innocent," Miller stated.

"Yes, and did you know he was diagnosed a multi-personality schizophrenic by the prison psychiatrist?"

Miller's mouth about hit the floor. "No, I didn't. Interesting."

"Interesting indeed. He did so well in therapy sessions that his doctor recommended he get out early.

It was as if pieces of a puzzle were being put together in Miller's head. "That's why he only did three years on a murder-one charge. Tell me, has Danny been a headache for you?"

"Not at all. He reports every month with his required AA meetings, holds a steady job and gives me a clean drug test."

Miller instantly became suspicious. What an amazing coincidence it is that he claimed his innocence in a previous murder investigation, and now he is supposedly innocent again. Not only that, but he's now targeted to be the sixth victim. There was more to Danny Taylor than meets the eyes. Miller decided that tomorrow morning he was going to make a trip to Chino State Prison and have a little talk with the psychiatrist.

Miller stood and shook the PO's hand. "Thank you for your time, Bill, and please, let's keep this conversation between us."

"You have my word, Jim."

Miller was in his office and had just spoken with Peterson and Hudson. He informed them that the surveillance on Danny was now to be covert. He assigned them a new car (with air-conditioning) and told them if they fucked this up they would be giving parking tickets until they retired. He then called the team that was presently watching Danny and explained the same thing. He had them go to Danny's apartment and inform him he was no longer being followed because of lack of manpower. When asked if that was okay, Danny said it was.

It was now time to see what Danny Taylor's next move would be.

Chapter 24

Danny was on his couch watching *Halloween II*. After the police informed him they weren't going to follow him anymore, he went to Blockbuster, returned his old videos and picked this one up. He also picked up another pepperoni and jalapeno pizza, which made four pizzas in four days. Tonight, however, he craved beer with his pizza. After all, it should be illegal to eat pizza without beer. He'd been thinking about how it would be to feel that delicious liquid cascade over his taste buds. He'd been thinking about nothing else for the last two hours. Hell, why shouldn't he drink? After what he's been through the last couple of days, he deserved a drink. He looked at the clock. It was 11:45 p.m.—two more hours until the bars closed.

He left the TV on and went for a walk. Fresh air would do him good, except the air wasn't that fresh. The night was muggy and uncomfortable. Suddenly he realized how dangerous it is for somebody to be walking in this neighborhood this time of night, especially a white guy. *Too bad I don't have my police escort anymore*, he thought.

Danny had been walking for about ten minutes when he decided he better turn around and go back. The walk was only making him sweat, which was making him thirstier. At the end of the block he would turn around and go home.

When he got to the end, he noticed a bar on the corner he didn't remember seeing before. He could have sworn there was a mini-mart on this corner, but the neon sign in the window read, The Watering Hole.

"Who am I to run away from my destiny?" he said out loud as he pulled the door open and entered. He wasn't a smoker, but the unmistakable and overpowering cigarette smell that hit him when he walked through the door brought back to him hundreds of memories instilled in his brain by places like this.

He walked up to the bar and sat at the only stool that was available. There was a female bartender, and Danny said, "Nurse, my medication please."

The woman behind the bar was weathered, but attractive. She looked to be about forty with brown hair and brown eyes, and was slightly skinny. "What has the doctor prescribed for you, handsome?" she asked.

"Plenty of Coors Light and plenty of sex."

"Well then, you came to the right place, sweetheart, because I have the coldest beer and the hottest pussy in town."

Danny gave a wicked grin. How lucky was it for him to find this place? She reached under the counter into the open ice bin, pulled out a bottle of beer that was dripping with ice shavings, and set it on the counter. "I get off at two. There's the coldest been in town, just like I promised. If you want to find out about the other thing, I suggest you stay right there in that seat until my shift's over."

"I'm not going anywhere." Danny raised his eyebrows and slightly tilted his head forward, luring her name from her.

"Melissa," she said.

"Isn't that a coincidence? That just so happens to be my new all-time favorite name."

She laughed. "I'm sure it is, honey, I'm sure it is." She started to turn and tend to another customer when Danny asked, "Melissa, before you leave, would you mind getting me another Coors Light?"

She looked at the beer in front of him—it was full. She laughed again as she pulled another beer from the ice.

"I have a feeling I found the man of my dreams." Melissa raised her eyebrows and slightly tilted her head forward in a mock imitation of before.

"Danny," he said with a smile.

"Well, Danny," she said as she set the beer next to the other one, "that just so happens to be my new all-time favorite name also." She left him with a smile.

At 1:50 a.m. Danny was walking back to his spot at the bar from a visit to the restroom. Melissa had just announced "Last call," and, as he sat down, he saw two fresh beers in front of him. He looked over at her and gave what he hoped was a sexy smile. She gave him a seductive wink in return.

Besides himself and Melissa, there were only two other people still there. Melissa had already cleaned the place up as much as she was going to, and was finishing up icing the beer down in the coolers for the night. She had started drinking shots of Southern Comfort at 1:00 a.m., and now was pleasantly buzzed. Danny was pleasantly buzzed until his trip to the restroom. Standing up and walking had him feeling downright drunk, and why wouldn't it? Since arriving at a little before 12:00 p.m., he had drunk ten beers, and he had two more in front of him. Normally that amount would be no problem, but he hasn't drunk since his latch batch of Pruno.

It was 2:15 a.m. and Melissa had just let the last customers out. She locked the door and walked over to Danny. He finished the last of his beer and stood up to meet her. As they met, they embraced and kissed wildly. Danny pushed the empty bottles out of the way and picked her up and laid her on the bar. Her head hit the bottles and they tipped over, one of them falling on the floor, the top breaking off. Danny was pulling her jeans and panties off as she was kicking off her tennis shoes and unbuttoning her top. He then kicked his shoes off and quickly discarded his shirt and pants. Melissa slipped out of her bra as Danny climbed up on the bar. They both kept their socks on. As Danny lay on top of her, he was already hard.

"Put it in me, Danny," she whispered.

Danny did. He expected a little bit of effort at least, since there was no foreplay, but he slid inside her with ease. She was far from being a virgin, but she was hot and wet, and as Danny slid in and out of her, her hips instantly matched his rhythm.

"You feel so fucking good."

"Faster Danny. Harder, baby!" she shouted on the verge of orgasm already.

Danny put his arms on the sides of the bar and raised himself up. He thrust into her with such force that they moved further up the bar with each push of his hips. She grabbed his butt and pulled him into her harder with each stroke. "Oh, baby! Yes, baby! Yes, Danny!" she screamed as she came. She was screaming so loud that he looked toward the door to make sure no one outside heard and came to the window for a free show.

She stopped screaming and let go of his ass, but her hips were still moving with his. He looked down and watched her little tits jiggling and immediately became aroused to the point of ejaculation. He continued his thrusting as he lowered himself onto her. He grabbed her arms and held them above her head, and then transferred them to his left hand, holding them together by the fingers. She heard his grunt as he came, and felt his body tighten.

Danny stayed motionless on top of her, and in her, for about ten seconds. Melissa then wiggled her hips and asked, "Did you empty it all out?"

Danny then laughed a horrifying, evil laugh. He squeezed his fingers together like a vice, grabbed the beer bottle that lay by her head and smashed it against the bar ledge. Melissa struggled, but he held her tight. Danny looked into her eyes and spoke to her in a voice that reminded her of the devil. It reminded her of her worst childhood fears.

It sounded like a madman's laughter echoing through the halls of an asylum. "Suicide is the only unforgivable sin, Melissa!" Danny shouted, his face contorted into a mask of range and terror. He raised the broken bottle and spoke calmly, his face now peaceful and sympathetic, "May God forgive you."

He brought the bottle down between her wrists with such a force, it tore a gaping hole in both arms. Blood spurted all over the bar. Melissa was thrashing wildly and Danny held her tight, but he couldn't control her and they fell to the floor. He had dropped the broken bottle, but had already picked up the one that had fallen on the floor. Melissa was screaming and blood was gushing from her wrists. She tried to crawl away, but Danny flipped her over and had the bottom of the beer bottle in his palm. He raised his arm and rammed the mouth of the bottle into her windpipe. She looked up at his with horrified eyes, gave a death-ridden gargle, and died with her face frozen in terror.

Danny went to the bar and got a beer. He drank half of it down and walked over to the window to look out and see if it was clear to leave. The streets were empty. He looked down at his clothes, which had blood splattered on them and wondered if he would be able to make it home without being seen. "Fuck it," he said, and he downed the rest of the beer. He threw the bottle at Melissa and it crashed on her head. "Fucking slut!" Danny shouted to the corpse and unlocked the bar door.

When he opened it, Detective Miller was standing with a gun pointed at his face. He was smiling. "I caught you, you sick fucker," Miller said calmly. "The problem is, you're a day early. You're not supposed to kill until tomorrow." Detective Miller fired his gun into Danny's face.

Danny bolted straight up on his couch. He awoke from his nightmare soaked with sweat. His heart was pounding like a jackhammer, and he sat there thinking about what was going on. It took awhile to realize what had just happened was a dream. He stood up to go splash water on his face and felt wet between his legs. *Unbelievable. I had a wet dream of killing someone.*

Chapter 25

Detective Miller was driving to Chino State Prison. He looked at his watch and saw it was 9:00 a.m. It was also Tuesday, which meant the killer was going to strike tomorrow.

He had called Turner when he first woke up and was told some interesting news. A couple of dealers in Imperial Beach said they had a new face come around on the weekend, maybe Friday night, and make a buy. The guy was at least six feet tall and bought both speed and coke from one dealer and heroin and acid from the other. The dealer who sold the heroin and acid is the one who remembered the height of the buyer. It was such an unusual combination he said, and hardly no one buys acid anymore, he added.

Miller said to Turner, "Danny is over six feet, isn't he?"

"Yes, he is."

"He also didn't contact me until Saturday afternoon. He could have made the drug buy on Friday night in anticipation of us putting a tail on him."

"I've been thinking this Taylor guy is pretty clever," Turner stated.

"I've been thinking the same thing. Anyone who can claim innocence on a murder one charge and be found guilty, but get released after only three years because of outstanding progress reports by the prison psychiatrist must be smart. Smart and manipulative."

"Are you going to the prison today?"

"I'm calling the warden as soon as we hang up."

That was almost two hours ago. Miller still didn't know what he was going to do with the information he had gotten from the warden. No matter what he was told negatively about Danny, if anything, he couldn't use it to arrest him. Deep down he figured he was trying to find reasons to believe Danny was innocent.

Miller pulled up to the outside gate at Chino State Prison and pressed the button on the speaker.

"Can I help you?" a rough voice asked.

"Yes. My name is Detective Jim Miller of the San Diego Police Department. I'm here to see the warden, Jerry Simmons."

"Do you have an appointment?"

"Yes. He knows I'm coming."

"Just a moment please," the voice said.

Miller waited for about fifteen seconds. The man was presumably checking his log sheet or appointment schedule for Miller's name.

The gate started to open and the voice said, "Follow the yellow line on the ground to the visitor's parking. Walk to the main building and ring the bell."

"Thank you," Miller said, and pulled through the gate. When he got to the building, he rang the bell and waited five minutes. He rang the bell again. The voice came over the box, "Can I help you?"

"Yes. I'm waiting outside the building," Miller said.

"Who are you?" the same rough voice as before asked.

"I'm Detective Jim Miller from the San Diego Police Department."

"State your business," the voice said rudely.

Miller rolled his eyes. Was this guy serious? It must have been a time frame of seven minutes since he had talked to him at the gate, and five of that was spent standing at the door waiting like an idiot. "I'm here to see Warden Jerry Simmons." Miller beat him to the next question, "I have an appointment."

"Just a moment please." Another fifteen seconds went by and the voice said, "Thank you for waiting. When the door buzzes, pull it open and follow the yellow line on the ground to the next door. When you get there, ring the bell on the wall."

I'm in the fucking "Twilight Zone," Miller thought to himself. When the door buzzed, he opened it quickly. He didn't want to miss it. He then ran along the yellow line to the next door. He wanted to be sure he was fresh in this moron's mind.

It took ten seconds to get from outside to the next door. Miller rang the bell.

"Can I help you?" the rough voice asked.

It took every ounce of his willpower to not yell into the box that this guy was

THE SUICIDE MURDERS

a fucking idiot. Miller took a deep breath, then another, then spoke as calmly as he could. "My name is Detective Jim Miller. I'm with the San Diego Po—" Miller was cut off by the voice on the box.

"I know that already. When the door buzzes, pull it open and follow the yellow line on the ground to the end of the hall. Go into the visitor's room—it's the last room on the right. The warden will be with you shortly." The door buzzed and Miller almost pulled it right off its hinges.

The hallway was about thirty yards long and had a camera mounted on the ceiling every ten feet. Miller couldn't help but think he must be on Candid Camera. He reached the room and went to the vending machine in the corner that sold cold drinks. He put in three quarters and pressed the Cactus Cooler button. His drink fell to the bottom. He grabbed it, took a seat and checked his watch. It was 11:25 a.m. *Not bad*, he thought, considering he stopped for gas and a quick hamburger.

At 12:15 p.m. the warden walked into the visitor's room. He was an average man at five-foot six inches, one hundred sixty pounds with reddish-black hair and brown eyes. Miller stood and the warden spoke as they shook hands. "Detective Miller, I presume."

"You presume correct. Obviously you are Warden Simmons."

"Please, call me Jerry," the warden said.

"And please, call me Jim," the detective returned.

"Well, now that's out of the way, I would guess that you want to talk about Danny Taylor. That is what you said on the phone, correct?"

The men sat down in two chairs that faced each other. Miller wondered how he should start.

"That is correct, Jerry. Before I start, I need to ask that this conversation be confidential."

"Of course," Jerry replied.

"I'm heading a murder investigation and Mr. Taylor is a suspect."

The warden was nodding his head as if not at all surprised by what Miller was saying.

"The return ratio in prisons is eighty-five percent," Simmons said. "Did you know that, Jim?"

He shook his head no. "I knew it was high, but not that high." Miller changed the subject. "What I need to know is if Danny had any problems while here. Are there any 'red flags' in his behavior that I should know about?"

"Actually, Mr. Taylor was a good inmate. He was on medication, you know. He was housed in the Annex."

"The Annex?" Miller asked.

"Yes. The Annex is a special section of the prison our psychiatrist Dr. Richards set up for anyone on mandatory medication." Jerry put a finger to his temple as if contemplating something. "You knew he became suicidal after Dr. Richards transferred Mr. Taylor out of general population to the Annex?"

Miller's eyes perked up. "He was suicidal?" he asked.

"Yes. The doctor put him on suicide watch for almost a month. Mr. Taylor claimed it was because of the medication he was on. Dr. Richards changed him around to a different type of drug and Danny was taken off suicide watch."

"Is there any way I can talk to Dr. Richards?" Miller asked.

"Does that mean you have no more questions for me?"

Miller took a business card out of his wallet and handed it to the warden. "I don't have any more questions at this moment, but when I leave I may think of some more. Would it be alright to just call next time?"

"Of course," the warden answered.

"If you can think of anything later that may help me, please call me. My home number is on there also." Miller pointed to the business card.

The warden got up and shook Miller's hand. "Good luck to you, Jim. I'll send in Dr. Richards."

"Thank you," Miller said. "You have helped me more than you know."

Warden Simmons smiled and left the room.

Miller looked at his watch, then went to the vending machine and got another drink. The time was 1:00 p.m. Coming out here was going to end up costing him a day, but it looked like the information he was getting would be worth it. Aside from the lead they got from the drug dealers, he didn't have much to work with. He drank the soda and threw the cup into the trash can. When he turned around, Dr. Richards was standing in the doorway.

"Warden Simmons informed me you would like to discuss a former patient of mine, Danny Taylor. Is that correct?" He stood straight and spoke with confidence.

"That's correct, Dr. Richards. I was wondering if you could tell me a little about him. Mr. Simmons told me at one point he was suicidal."

"I don't make it a practice to discuss the very personal and very private conversations between my patients and myself." He came from the doorway and sat in the first seat closest to the door. He made no attempt to shake Miller's hand. Miller remained standing.

Dr. Richards continued. "I definitely don't agree with Warden Simmons doing it. He has asked me to answer your questions in regard to Danny Taylor;

however, and unfortunately, I have no choice. He is my boss, and since Mr. Taylor paid no money to me for my services, I cannot keep information from members of law enforcement if they inquire. What exactly would you like to know, sir?"

Miller was going to tell Dr. Richards to call him Jim, but thought better of it. The cocksucker probably wouldn't anyway. "As I was saying, Jerry told me that Taylor was on suicide watch for a month. Is that true?" He called the warden by his first name in hopes it might piss the doctor off somehow. In fact, he would call the doctor by his first name if he knew it.

"It took two years for the correct medication in the correct amounts to finally be achieved in finding a stable, sane and happy person in Danny Taylor. There were some ups and downs in his emotions until this puzzle, if you will, was solved."

Miller sat looking at Dr. Richards. Dr. Richards continued. "In answer to your question, yes, Mr. Taylor had talked about committing suicide for a short period of time. I had him transferred to solitary confinement and put on suicide watch. His medication was then changed, and after a brief monitoring period, Mr. Taylor was put back in the Annex and we never had a problem again. Mr. Taylor made excellent progress in our one-on-one sessions, and upon my recommendation was released from custody early." Dr. Richards smiled in satisfaction as to the power he had.

Miller sat thinking for a moment, and asked, "Why did Danny come talk to you about killing himself. Why didn't he just do it?"

Dr. Richards looked at Miller as if that was the most absurd question he'd ever been asked. "Really, Detective! I guess if a man lives long enough, he is bound to hear everything. The reason he didn't kill himself is presumably he did not want to die. He simply wanted to feel normal; a thing most of my patients have a hard time feeling." Dr. Richards squinted his eyes as if he was studying Miller. "Are you a religious man, Detective?"

"Why?"

"I was just wondering if you knew suicide was the only unforgivable sin."

Miller was astonished at what he had just heard. The words were echoing in his head. The room had suddenly elongated like that of a hallway in a scary movie, and Dr. Richards appeared to be a hundred feet away.

Dr. Richards saw Miller turn pale and asked, "Are you feeling alright, Detective?"

"What did you just say?" Miller asked.

"I asked if you were feeling alright."

Miller had control of himself now. "No, what did you say about suicide?"

"I asked if you knew it was the only unforgivable sin."

Miller collected his thoughts for a second. "Do you tell that to all your patients in the Annex?"

"No. Well, I've told that to a handful of people in the Annex for one reason or another over the years, but I mainly save that for the patients that come to me with thoughts of suicide. It works, too. I haven't had one person commit suicide while I've been here."

"Did you say that to Danny?"

"Of course," Dr. Richards said. "He, however, told me he already knew that."

Miller had his wallet out and was handing Dr. Richards his business card before the psychiatrist knew what was happening.

"If you think of anything that might be helpful, give me a call." Miller was out the door.

Dr. Richards got up and threw the card in the trash.

Chapter 26

Miller pulled over at the first gas station and used their payphone. As he was dialing Turner's cell phone number, he thought to himself that he must be the last person alive without one of his own. He hated them. He had one when they first came out, but the damn thing kept hanging up on him, and when it wasn't cutting him off, he couldn't hear what the person talking to him was saying. He realized he needed one though, especially at times like this. Maybe he'd try the digital phones. He'd heard…Miller's thoughts were cut short by Turner's voice.

"This is Turner."

"Ron, it's Jim."

"Jim, I didn't recognize the area code on my caller ID. Are you still in Chino? It's almost 2:00 p.m."

"I know. They move pretty slow at the prison."

"What did you find out?"

"Remember when I showed you the first letters we got, how they made a reference to suicide being the only unforgivable sin?"

"Of course."

"Well, get this. I was talking with the prison psychiatrist about Danny, and out of nowhere he asked me if I knew that."

"What? He asked you if you knew suicide was the only unforgivable sin?"

"Yes, and get this—he said he tells that to all his patients who talk about committing suicide." Miller listened for Turner's reaction.

"You're not telling me Taylor was, or is suicidal?" Turner asked. He was amazed at what he was hearing.

"It appears as if he's alright now, but the prison psychiatrist had him on suicide watch for a month."

"How long will it take you to get back? I'll meet you at your office and we'll discuss everything you found out."

"I'll meet you there at 4:00 p.m.," Miller answered.

Turner was sitting in Miller's office. Miller had just run down everything that was told to him by both the warden and Dr. Richards.

"Is Taylor supposed to be taking his medication, or was that just while he was under the psychiatrist's care?" Turner asked.

"That's an excellent question. I thought of that while I was driving back from Chino. I called Dr. Richards when I got back, but he was gone for the day. When I called Danny's PO, he said it wasn't a form of his probation."

"So, it sounds as if he needs to take it, but it's not mandatory by the courts," Turner noted.

"Exactly," Miller said. "But Danny may be taking it. His PO hasn't asked him if he has because he feels his clients do better rebuilding their lives if they aren't suffocated with authority. Danny hasn't given him any reason to believe he hasn't been taking it."

"Except maybe mutilating two people," Turner noted.

"Nobody's perfect," Miller joked.

"I don't know," Turner said smiling. "I think Sharon's pretty damn close."

"That's funny that you say that. She was asking about you yesterday."

"Really?"

"No," Miller replied.

The two men started laughing and Turner said jokingly, "You're an asshole."

"Have you been talking to my ex-wife?" Miller asked with a big smile on his face.

The laughter died down, and Turner asked, "So, what's your next move?"

Miller started laughing again, leaned back in his chair and put his hands behind his head. "My next move is to break the law."

"In what way?"

"I'm going to bring Taylor in for questioning and see if he'll submit to a drug test. I'll make up some reason why, but I won't tell him it's to test for psychological drugs. While he's here, I'm going to have a team go in his apartment, tap the phone and bug the place."

"If you come up with anything that leads to an arrest, you won't be able to use it in court," Turner explained.

"That's only if we divulge how we got our information, which we won't," Miller said. "Our information will have come from an anonymous tip."

"It's not the most ethical approach to law enforcement, but if it saves victim number three's life, I'm all for it."

"Exactly. The fucker's lucky I don't install hidden cameras."

"Alright," Turner was saying. "I need to go check in with my team. Let me know right away if something happens."

"You'll be the first person I notify."

When Turner left, Miller got a team together, called the surveillance team to make sure Danny was home and headed to his apartment.

Miller was briefing his three-man team outside of Danny's apartment. The surveillance team was watching the door in case he came out.

"This is simple. I'm going to take Taylor downtown for questioning, so we'll be gone for a good two hours. I expect you guys to be in and out in no more than thirty minutes. That will be more than enough time to plant the bugs and search his place. His phone was supposed to be hooked up today, but if it wasn't, leave it alone. Plant bugs where you would expect him to put it—his bed stand, in the kitchen, etc. I won't bring him back until I see you back at the station. Are there any questions?"

The men shook their heads no. "Good," Miller said, "I'm going to go get our boy."

"You know, Detective Miller, the only reason I agreed to go with you downtown is because I have nothing to hide." Danny and Miller were driving to the station. "What I don't understand is, yesterday you pulled the surveillance team and now you're bringing me in for questioning."

"You were never being followed as a suspect, Danny," Miller was saying. "We were only following you in case the killer contacted you. Unfortunately, we are short in men and the department feels we can better utilize the team that was following you before in other areas of the investigation."

"I understand," Danny said. "This won't take long I hope. I have to work tomorrow." Danny was nervous. Something was going on that the detective wasn't telling him. He understood that they would want to question him further when he saw the note on his car at Carl's, Jr. He was, after all, contacted successfully while being tailed by the cops. The drug test was what puzzled him. Did he look high or something?

"I can't imagine us being at the station more than thirty minutes," Miller said.

Miller and Danny were in his office, and he was stalling until he saw his team return. He was embarrassed at some of the questions he was coming up with. Finally his team walked by his window and gave him a thumbs up.

"That will be enough questions. You've been very helpful in clearing up some loose ends."

Why it matters where I got my pizza from over the weekend I will never know, Danny thought to himself. In fact, most of the questions Miller asked didn't make a whole lot of sense to him. If it was going to please Miller though, Danny would have answered the stupid questions all night. He most certainly didn't need any more problems than he was having. "No problem, sir," Danny said.

"Now, we'll just go do a quick drug test, and I'll drive you home." Just as Miller said that, in walked Sharon.

"Oh, I see our convict's here."

"Yes, Mr. Taylor was good enough to answer a few of my questions. I'm going to give him a drug test right now—you know, standard procedures." Miller held his eyes on Sharon's, hoping she would catch on.

"Oh, yeah—standard procedures," she said. "I'll tell you what, why don't you let me give him the test."

"Are you sure?" Miller asked.

Sharon's smiled instantly vanished. "Blood? You mean I'm not monitoring a urine sample?"

Miller laughed and Danny blushed. "Sorry, Miller, you're on your own." Sharon turned and left the room.

"I guess it's just you and me, Danny," Miller said.

As Miller was driving Danny home, neither said a word the whole way. Miller couldn't stop thinking that he could possible have the killer in the car with him. Maybe even the mastermind of a murdering duo. He also couldn't help but hope Danny was innocent. He had been very cooperative and even submitted to the drug test when there was no justifiable reason for one. Miller sighed and thought to himself, *Are you the killer I'm after, Danny Taylor, or are you just a person with a shitload of problems trying to put his life back together?"*

Chapter 27

It was Wednesday morning and Danny had just left for work. Peterson and Hudson were following him for the day, and after a night of sitting in a van listening to Danny snoring, Miller's team when home to do some snoring of their own. Danny's phone had been hooked up, but he had made no calls and received no calls. He also had no visitors, and the only voices Miller's team (that is what they like to call themselves) heard at all were those of the people getting slashed by Michael Myers.

Miller was already in his office and on his second cup of coffee. Since his team had come up with no information last night, he talked with Peterson and Hudson this morning and told them to call him if anything seemed remotely strange about Danny's day; calling from a pay phone, talking with someone on the street, waving to someone from his car, etc.

The phone on Miller's desk rang. He picked it up in the middle of the first ring. "Miller here."

"Jim, it's Ron Turner," the voice said.

"How you doing, Ron? Are you going to make my day and tell me you have groundbreaking information about the case?" Miller asked hopefully.

"Sorry, not yet. We do know officially that our hooker died of an overdose of heroin."

"What other drugs were found?"

"The pills were a combination of downers. The white powder on her breasts was a mixture of cocaine, speed, and PCP. The syringes in her arms were heroin.

The syringes in her hands all contained cocaine. The syringes in her feet contained a combo of speed and bleach. Last, but not least, her eyes were covered with paper saturated in acid."

Miller had his eyes closed and was shaking his head. "Her feet had a combo of speed and bleach?"

"Yeah, I guess he wanted to make sure she had no chance of living."

"Any new leads from the streets? Did anyone sell any pills recently to anybody new?" Miller asked.

"That's a negative. We can't rule out that he didn't go to Mexico and buy them though. He could have bought all the drugs there for that matter. It's easy to carry drugs across if you're an American."

"I know."

"Did you come up with anything from Taylor's apartment?" Turner asked.

"That's a negative also. There was nothing incriminating or suspicious, and the guy didn't speak a word all night. He had no visitors and made no phone calls."

"It seems like we're chasing our tails, doesn't it?"

"You can say that again. I feel like there's nothing to do but sit back and wait for the next victim," Miller said angrily.

"I know what you mean. This guy will fuck up somehow though. They always do. Call me if anything happens."

"You too." Miller hung up the phone and reached for his bottle of aspirin.

Chapter 28

Peterson and Hudson had been tailing Danny since he left for work at 6:30 a.m. It was now 2:00 p.m. They were waiting for him to come out of a law office in San Marcos.

"I'm glad we thought ahead and packed lunches today," Hudson was saying. "This guy still hasn't stopped to eat."

"I know. He's been going so fast today that I wouldn't be surprised if his drug test comes up positive for speed."

Peterson was eating a sandwich and some Cheetos. Hudson was eating leftover chicken he had for dinner last night. Both were comfortable and cool in their new air-conditioned car. "He's been in that place an awfully long time, don't you think?" Hudson asked.

"I guess so," Peterson answered. "We'll give him five more minutes, then we'll check it out." He took the last bite of his sandwich and turned on the radio. After flipping through the stations, he turned it off. Hudson was staring at him with his mouth open, showing his partner a mouth full of chicken and a look of surprise. "What?" Peterson asked.

Hudson spit the chicken into the bucket he was holding on his lap and returned his surprised look to his partner. "What do you mean, what? You know what?" Hudson said, his voice rising with each word.

"No, I don't know what. What?" Peterson asked again.

Hudson turned the radio on and pushed button Number 2. "Kashmir" by Led Zeppelin was on. He sat there looking at Peterson. Hudson raised his eyebrows as if reminding his partner of something, then made a head gesture toward the radio. Peterson couldn't help but let out a chuckle because he didn't know what the hell his partner was getting at. He finally asked, "Do you like this song?"

Hudson stuck his face in the bucket of chicken and laughed a crazy laugh. He then slowly lowered the bucket to his lap, while slowly raising his head. He was looking straight ahead, then he spoke to the radio in a damn good impersonation of Howard Cosell, "Can you believe it, Robert? Without a doubt, this is the saddest display of friendship the world has ever seen."

Peterson laughed. "You've got some problems, don't you?"

"No, they're not problems. My mom says they're what make me special."

The two men laughed until they cried. Hudson then asked, "Why did you turn off my song?"

"How am I supposed to know that's your song?"

Hudson thought about it, then laughed. "Oh, yeah. I guess you wouldn't."

I think you were born with one too many chromosomes," Peterson joked.

"Maybe, but now you know. If you turn off the radio again when that song is on, I'll shoot you."

"Speaking of shooting someone, I think it's about time to go hunt Taylor down."

"That's my job," Hudson said. He opened the driver's side door and was getting out when he stopped and looked at his partner. "If I'm not back in five minutes, call the police."

They were parked straight across the street from Danny's truck in a business complex. There was a four-foot tall hedge that blocked them from view. The hedge was thin enough where they parked so they could see across the street. It was thick enough that you couldn't see them from across the street. Hudson walked around it and come back to the spot in front of the car. It was about fifteen feet from where they were parked to the edge. He wanted to be in view of his partner in case something happened. He was halfway across the street when Danny came out of the building. Hudson froze.

Only twenty yards separated the two of them. If he was spotted, you might as well stick a fork in him, because he was done. Peterson was watching in a stunned silence. Danny was still walking forward, but was looking at his paperwork. Hudson spun around and sprinted straight for the bush. There was no time to go around. He knew the spot on his side of the car had no one parked in it. Peterson started laughing, knowing what was about to happen. Hudson was running full speed, and three feet before he crashed into it, he dove head first over the bush. Only he didn't nearly make it all the way.

Peterson saw him jump, then saw him appear like magic on his side of the hedge, eyes wide, mouth open, and tongue hanging out, his body stopped halfway over. He reached down and pulled on the leaves and his legs went flying over, sending him crashing on his back. Peterson was laughing so hard his sides hurt. Hudson crawled to the car.

"Did he see me?" he asked as he got in.

Peterson couldn't stop laughing to answer.

"Did he see me?" Hudson asked louder.

"No. Nice recovery." Peterson continued his laughter.

"Fuck you!" Hudson said, then laughed with him.

Hudson pulled out of the business complex and followed Danny down the street. Danny pulled into a Jack-in-the-Box and Hudson pulled into a McDonald's across the street. Danny went inside the restaurant.

"I'm going inside to clean up. I'll be right back," Hudson said.

Peterson stayed in the car and kept watch. He started laughing again, thinking about what his partner had just done when Danny came walking out of the restaurant.

"Oh, shit!" Peterson said. He looked back at McDonald's and there was no sign of Hudson. Danny got in his truck and pulled away. Peterson was giggling like a little kid as he moved over to the driver's seat and followed him, leaving his partner behind. "Hudson," he said, "this just isn't your day."

Danny drove two blocks down the street and pulled into Burger King. Peterson pulled into an Arco Station next door. Danny went into the restaurant and Peterson could see that he was ordering. He pulled over to the far corner of the Burger King parking lot, reclined his seat and waited. A minute later the cell phone rang. "Please be Hudson and not Miller," Peterson said to himself. He picked up the phone on the second ring. "Hello?"

"Where the fuck are you?" Hudson growled.

"I'm out catching bad guys. Where are you?" Peterson asked, holding back his laughter.

"I'm up shit creek without a paddle."

"It's not that bad, partner," Peterson said smiling. "Do you feel like doing some more running?"

"What do you mean?"

"I'm two blocks down, at Burger King."

"Is he inside eating?" Hudson asked.

"Yes, and no, I am not going to pick you up. There's no fucking way I'm going to make a bad situation worse."

"Fuck!" Hudson said, then there was silence. "Fuck!" he said again, then silence. "Shit, you're right. The Burger King is north of McDonalds, right?"

"Yes, and you'd better hurry."

"I'm on my way."

Hudson got to the car so fast that Peterson didn't even see him until he opened the passenger door.

"Honey, I'm home," Hudson joked as he got in the car.

When Danny took the 78 Freeway to the S South, Hudson made a call to Miller and informed him he thought Danny was heading home. Miller had his team stationed in front of Danny's apartment in their '95 Econoline van within twenty minutes. When Peterson and Hudson got to Danny's place, the night surveillance team was already there. They ran down the day's events to them, leaving out the fuck-ups, called Miller again and did the same and went to get a cold beer.

Chapter 29

Miller was in the lab talking with Sharon. He had just gotten off the phone with Hudson. They had successfully delivered Danny to the night surveillance team without any contact from the killer. He looked at his watch. "It's 4:30 p.m., and all is well," he informed her.

"If all was well, Mel Gibson would be in here stretching my sausage pocket."

Miller was drinking his coffee and spit it out, almost choking. He looked at her with a surprised look and started laughing. "Damn, Sharon. Are you trying to kill me?"

Sharon smiled, pleased with herself. Never before had she got a reaction like that from Miller. Other people, of course, but never him.

Miller continued, "Isn't he a little past his prime, anyway?"

She threw her head back and laughed. "I'm quite sure his weapon is still plenty lethal. Besides, saying he's past his prime is like saying you're past your prime. I still got my heart set on going a couple rounds with you one day."

"I don't think I could handle you, Sharon."

"No, you probably couldn't," she said playfully, "but I guarantee you would die a very happy man."

Miller was nodding his head in agreement, and it almost looked to Sharon as if he was considering giving her a try. There was something in the way he was looking at her.

He regained himself and took a drink of coffee. "What have you come up with since the last time we talked?" he asked.

Shit, Sharon thought. *He changed the subject.* She wondered what would happen if she told him that she wanted him; that she wasn't joking about the things she said to him. She couldn't though, because she didn't want to ruin their friendship.

"Sharon?"

Miller's voice brought her out of her thoughts. "What? Oh! Ummm, no. Sorry, no." Sharon shook her head and smiled. "Sorry. Sometimes I swear I'm a blond. My crew is striking out on the garage sales and swap meets. Nobody has sold anything, or has anything matching the description. Oh, by the way, the tape of the hooker; it was clean of prints, and again the tape was too common to trace. We ran Taylor's name by every place that sells that kind of stuff, but it came up clean. He would have used cash anyway. Hell, it most likely was the girl's tape anyhow."

"Okay," Miller said. "Just keep at it." He left the lab.

"Hey, Miller!" Sharon shouted. He stuck his head back in the door. "I have a video of myself that blows the one of the hooker away. Why don't you come over for a private screening?"

Miller smiled. "Because, if I go into your house, I don't think I'll ever get out." He winked at her and went to his office. He was just sitting at his desk when his phone rang.

"Miller here."

"Jim, it's Ron. The shit has hit the fan. I'm on my way to victim number three."

Miller stood up. "What! How do we know it's one of ours?"

"The woman was found at the bottom of her pool by her husband. There's another video with you name on it and another note. We're in trouble with this one. The victim is Allison Hayword."

Miller sat down like a bag of rocks. "You're not serious!"

"I'm afraid I am. You got a pen and paper for the address?"

Miller fumbled on his desk. "Yeah, go ahead."

"...3821 Oceanfront Court, Cardiff by the Sea. You got that?"

"Yeah. I'm leaving right now." Miller hung up the phone and sat in stunned silence, thinking of the implications this was going to have. They had done such a good job at keeping this out of the media until now. Now a media frenzy was about to take place. Allison Hayword was the number one news anchor in San Diego.

Chapter 30

When Miller pulled up to the Hayword residence, the media was already swarming. He saw vans from every major network. He parked in the middle of the street. The road was blocked off for a hundred yards each way, and the only people able to cross were police and emergency crew. Allison's house was a large, ocean-front estate. Miller showed his ID and was let into the house.

Turner spotted him and took him to the backyard. The body was already out of the pool and bagged. The backyard consisted of a ninety by forty foot immaculate lawn, a huge rock formation waterfall that poured into a fifty by twenty foot swimming pool, a connecting fifteen by ten foot Jacuzzi, a gazebo, and a horseshoe pit. Between the far end of the backyard and the beach was a five-foot privacy wall. In the middle of the privacy wall was an iron gate that led to the sand. The water was about one hundred fifty feet from the privacy wall. The whole section of beach in this area was private property.

Miller made a head motion toward the body bag, which was on the grass. "Any reason for me to take a look?"

"Not unless you're curious to see what she looks like dead," Turner answered.

"No thanks. Where's the note and video?"

Turner led him back inside the house and into the master bedroom. The place was crazy. Cops were everywhere. The tape and the letter were on a dresser already in evidence bags. Miller picked up the bag with the letter. Once again the message were single words cut out from a kid's labeler. Miller read:

> the rich and famous are notorious for being unhappy
> so many beautiful people committing suicide
> pills and alcohol and water equal death
> juliet left romeo all alone while she swims in the river of
> fire for eternity

Miller looked at Turner and asked, "Do you have any objections to getting out of this circus and viewing the tape at the downtown lab?"

"Not at all. What are we going to say to the vultures outside?"

"As little as possible."

When Miller and Turner crossed the crime scene tape, they were swarmed by reporters. Cameras were flashing, questions were being screamed, microphones were shoved in their faces and TV cameras were everywhere. Voices were coming from all around. Miller heard:

"Is it true there is a serial killer on the loose?"

"Was Mrs. Hayword found in the nude?"

"Why haven't we been told about this series of deaths?"

"Are there any suspects?"

"Why was your name found on evidence, Detective Miller?"

"We hear you might know who the killer is."

"It's our right to know the truth—how come you're not answering our questions?"

Miller stopped in his tracks and Turner bumped into him. He held his hand up to the crowd. "Please, everyone!" he shouted. "Please, listen to what I have to say!"

The crowd became quiet.

"Thank you." Miller could see the red lights on in the front of the TV cameras, some of them most likely doing live feeds to the networks. There was no way to get around telling these people that Hayword was dead. Hell, how they came up with the information they already knew was a mystery to him. That was their job though, and they were good at it.

"As you probably already know, Mrs. Allison Hayword is dead." Cameras started clicking and murmurs went through the crowd. "As of this moment, we do not know the cause of death. We do know, however, that she was murdered." More cameras were clicking. "Obviously, for security reasons, we cannot tell you any specifics about this case. I will tell you we have some leads we're following up on. We will release more information when we have it. Thank you." Miller and Turner started walking and the questions were flying at them again.

"I'll meet you there," Turner shouted to Miller as they separated for their cars. The camera crews split and followed both men to their cars, shouting questions at them that went unanswered. The cameras continued filming the cars until they were out of sight. The cameramen then swung around to their respective reporters as they eloquently delivered the story.

Miller, Turner and Sharon were in the lab at the downtown station. The video was shot from the Hayward's personal video camera. Sharon put the tape in the special 8mm adaptor attached to her system. She hit rewind and asked Miller, "Has anyone seen this yet?"

Miller looked at Turner.

"No," Turner said, "we're the first to see it."

"I wish we had popcorn," Sharon joked. The tape finished rewinding and she pressed play. She looked at the two men, and said, "I hope it's like the last tape."

Miller and Turner were sitting down and Sharon remained standing. There was a brief period of static, then Allison's face appeared. She was crying and her makeup was running down her face. The camera panned back and showed her tied to a chair in her house. She was in her bathing suit.

"Please don't make me say that." She was trying to get herself under control, trying to regain composure. Presumably because the camera was on and she knew the city she loved, if not the whole country, would see this. Miller could see in her eyes that she knew she was going to die.

"Please don't make me read that."

The camera shut off, then came back on. Allison's nose had blood trailing from it, over her mouth and down her chin. It had dripped onto her chest, but was dry now. Her makeup was even more smeared, but she wasn't crying. The camera zoomed on her face and she spoke as if on cue.

"Hello, San Diego." Her voice was extremely shaky and scared. "I am on location at my home. I am a very sad person and about to—no! I won't read it!" Allison was shouting at the camera with a sudden look of defiance on her face. "You'll have to kill me!" The camera was shut off, then came back on.

Miller, Turner and Sharon looked at each other when the camera shut off, knowing some sort of pain was going to be inflicted upon her.

Allison was now in a different location. There was no longer a wall behind her. She was now tied to the chair in front of the sliding glass window that led to the backyard. You could see the pool in the distance. The camera was now stationary and at about head-level. The camera panned out so you could see her face and breasts, nothing more.

Allison was consumed with fear, her eyes filled with horror. She was whimpering, "Oh, God. Please, I'll read it."

You could hear what sounded like cowboy boots slowly cross the linoleum floor.

"Please! I'll read it! I'll read it!" Allison was struggling with the ropes, trying to free herself, but she and the chair remained in place. She was looking up and to her left. She was now motionless, except for the heaving of her chest. A huge kitchen knife came into view and slid between her breasts. The killer had gloves on and a long sleeve shirt that was duct-taped at the wrists, holding the two together. Allison had closed her eyes and was crying. The blade of the knife was facing the camera, in between her breasts and under her bathing suit top. She was trying her best to keep still, her bosom rising and falling around the cold steel.

With a snap of his wrist, the killer cut the center piece of her top off. Allison flinched. The suit flung open and hung at her sides, leaving her breasts exposed. The knife was laid flat on her left nipple, her hard point being covered midway on the twelve-inch blade. Slowly the blade slid along her until the sharp tip of the knife was pressing directly on her nipple. He kept the point pressed firmly as he moved the handle away from her body toward the camera. He twisted the knife and blood started flowing down her breast.

Allison screamed, but was afraid to move. He then moved the blade back flat and ran it to the base of her nipple.

With one quick downward swipe, her nipple was gone. A spurt of blood shot from the opening, then flowed down her body like a small river. The knife disappeared from the view of the camera.

Allison was screaming and struggling wildly in the chair. The hands of the killer appeared with a roll of duct tape. He stuck a piece on one side of her breast and unrolled the roll to the other side, covering her nipple. He then did that two more times, making an X over the first piece of tape. His hands disappeared from view again and the camera was left to film Allison.

Five minutes went by in her transition from screaming, to crying, to the beginnings of shock. Slowly, during that time her bleeding stopped. Allison sat in the chair, makeup smeared like an oil painting in the hot sun, breasts exposed— one mutilated and duct taped, tied up with her head hanging down. The sound of the cowboy boots on the linoleum started again. Allison lifted her head and looked to her right.

She was visibly haggard, her willpower gone. She nodded her head up and down. A hand appeared, showing a handful of pills. Two were put in her mouth and the killer's other hand held a glass with brown liquid to her mouth. Allison tilted her head back and took a drink. She swallowed, then coughed as if trying to catch her breath. When she regained control of herself, she opened her mouth again and two more pills went in, followed by another drink, which produced no coughing this time. Three more times she opened her mouth for pills, and three more times she drank from the glass until it was empty. A hand patted her head, signifying what a good girl she was. The sound of walking again led to the camera being picked up. The camera zoomed on Allison's face and again. As if on cue, she straightened up, shook her hair back and spoke into the camera.

"Look how brave she's trying to be," Sharon said with a tear in her eye.

Miller about fell on the floor. Sharon was the toughest woman he knew. Ice ran through her veins. He had never seen her show emotion over a victim before.

She then looked at him. "Catch this guy, Jim. Catch this guy and bring him to me." She then looked back at the VCR.

Allison Hayword began the last broadcast of her life. "Hello, San Diego. I am on location at my home. I am a very sad person and am about to...I mean, I just took some sleeping pills with a glass of whiskey." Her eyes kept shifting to the left, then back at the camera. The camera tilted a little and there was a sound of cardboard rubbing together, the killer flipping to another cue-card. Allison began speaking again.

"I know what you're thinking, and you're right—suicide is the only unforgivable sin, but I'm taking the coward's way out. Now, if you'll excuse me, I'm going to go take a little swim to an afterlife of eternal damnation." The last sentence was spoken through tears. The camera shut off.

Sharon turned the monitor off. "Well, what are your guys going to do to catch this sick fucker?"

"This guy isn't leaving us any clues we can use," Turner was saying. "He's leaving us pictures, letters and home movies, but we can't get anything from them. We're on our hands and knees trying to find some DNA at the crime scenes. Hell, we can't even find a hair from this guy."

"Did you see how careful he was?" Miller asked. "He duct-taped his long sleeve shirt to his gloves. I wouldn't doubt if his head was shaved, and the rest of his body, for that matter."

"What about witnesses?" Sharon asked.

"Nobody saw anything from the first two murders," Turner answered. "My guys are interviewing neighbors right now, but the murder appears to have happened a little before noon. Everyone in her neighborhood works, and the houses are about a hundred yards apart anyway," Turner replied.

"So, is Taylor off the hook now?" Sharon questioned Miller.

"Definitely not. Right now the only thing we've got going for us is our theory that Danny is working with an accomplice."

"Exactly," Turner agreed. "I was thinking that tomorrow I would question Taylor's boss and his family to see if I can come up with anything useful."

"Good idea," Miller said. "See if there is anybody he hangs around with. Get their names and run checks on them—you know—the usual."

"Of course. Look, I hate to spoil the party, but I need to be getting back to the crime scene and wrap things up." Turner got up and shook both their hands. "Don't worry, we'll nail this bastard. Call me in the morning, Jim." Turner walked out of the room, leaving Miller and Sharon alone.

"I need to check in with my team and see if anything is happening. Do me a favor and watch the tape a couple more times to see if you can get anything from it. I'll be in my office." Miller left the lab.

Sharon pressed rewind and sat down. She didn't want to watch the tape again—especially alone. For some reason, what the killer did to Allison Hayword affected her. Never before had she felt sympathy in her work. This time was different—perhaps because she felt like she knew Mrs. Hayword. After all, she had watched her report the news five nights a week for twelve years. Now Mrs. Allison Hayword was the news.

Chapter 31

It was 9:30 p.m. and Miller had just gone over the files of the religious offenders again. He came across a couple that raised suspicion. He called Turner and gave him the names. Turner's guys would check on them tomorrow. Miller also informed him he was going back to the prison first thing in the morning. He was going to find out about anybody Danny hung around with in the Annex and see if any of them were out now, possibly helping him. At first he was only going to call, but more information was given when you were face-to-face. That was something he had learned long ago.

Nothing was happening at Taylor's house his team reported when he called. He got up, stretched, and decided to go home for the night. On his way out he stopped by the lab. Sharon was viewing the tape and he stood and watched the end of it with her. When it was over, she turned the monitor off.

"I feel real bad for her, Jim. I just keep thinking how scared she must have been. At first she probably had some hope her husband would come home and save her, or maybe a neighbor would hear her screams and call the police. People rely on us, Jim. People rely on us to catch the guys like this sick fucker, and here we are dumbfounded." She shook her head and turned away from him, trying to hide the tears forming in her eyes.

"We'll get this guy, Sharon." He walked over to her and put his arm around her. She stood up and put her arms around him, placing her head on his chest. He held her close. They stayed that way for a full minute. Miller kissed her on the head. "How much sleep have you gotten since Friday?" he asked.

She let out a tired sigh. "About ten hours."

He held her out in front of him, his arms on her shoulders. "Come on. I'm taking you home." He had grown close to Sharon over the years. They had worked together a long time and he had never seen her like this. His heart went out to his friend.

She smiled at him. "Thank you, Jim."

Miller pulled his 4-Runner into Sharon's driveway and turned off the engine. "Are you okay?" he asked sympathetically.

She turned and faced him. "Come in for a drink, Jim," she said, barely audible.

Miller studied her face a few moments. "Are you sure you're not too tired?"

"I'm sure. I don't want to be alone right now."

"Alright, let's go inside," Miller said. She was surprised at how happy she was that he was coming in. Even if he left after the first drink, at least she wasn't walking to the empty house alone.

Miller had been there a few times over the years, just as she had been to his house. Their relationship was strictly platonic, although they often flirted. He was sitting on her leather couch and she was in the kitchen making dinks. Sharon just about made the best 7&7 he ever tasted.

She came from the kitchen, handed him a drink and joined him on the couch. She held up her glass and he raised his to hers. "To our friendship," she said.

"To our friendship," he repeated. They clinked glasses and took a drink. Miller sucked in air and laughed. "That took me by surprise. I don't remember ordering a double."

"Well, I figure if you were going to have only one, it might as well be a strong one.

Miller laughed lightly, and said, "I don't know what's going on in this head of mine, but I don't think I want to go home." He and Sharon both had smiles at the corners of their mouths.

"I don't know what's going on in this head of mine, either," she was saying, "because I know I don't want you to leave."

They leaned toward each other and kissed gently. Both were overcome with an excitement for each other that was so powerful it took them by surprise.

"My God, Sharon," Miller whispered. He kissed her again, this time touching his tongue to hers. It felt as if electricity was flowing between them. His eyes rolled back in his head, his fingers went numb, and as he felt the glass slipping out of his hand, he thought, *I'm lost in her kiss.*

The glass fell to the ground and bounced off the carpet, spilling everywhere.

When he regained himself, he focused his eyes on her and saw that her eyes were still closed. He touched his hand to her face and her eyes slowly opened, her head learning toward his touch. She set her drink down and pulled him on top of her. They kissed passionately and his hand went to her breasts. Sharon moaned with passion and rubbed her hand on his stiffening crotch.

"Oh, Jim," Sharon whispered. "Take me upstairs."

Miller picked her up and carried her to her bedroom, gazing into her eyes the whole way. He laid her on the bed and started unbuttoning his shirt. Sharon already had her shirt off and was working on her bra when Miller said, "Stop."

Sharon looked into his eyes and could read his mind. She closed her eyes, turned her head from him and said, "Shit."

"I'm sorry, Sharon. I can't. Not tonight anyway. Not with everything that's been going on." He sat on the bed and ran his fingers through her hair. She opened her eyes and looked at him. "I don't want us to do anything we might regret because we are vulnerable. Your friendship means too much to me."

Sharon's eyes filled with tears and she smiled. "Why do you have to always make sense?"

He leaned forward and gave her a soft kiss on the mouth.

"I suppose you're going to leave?" She asked.

Miller started unbuttoning his shirt again, "I would actually love to fall asleep holding you."

A tear fell from her eye, and her smile widened. "Can we be naked?"

"What other way is there?" he asked. Miller threw their clothes on the ground and lay beside her with her head on his chest. He gently stroked her hair and she ran her fingers lightly over his stomach. Sharon was asleep within two minutes.

Miller saw the remote control on the desk next to her. He wondered if the news was reporting about Allison Hayword. He leaned over, grabbed it and clicked it on. He saw Allison's home on the TV screen. The volume was turned down, but a reporter was talking, and the word "Live" was in the top right hand corner. He flipped the channel and saw his face. It was from earlier today. Miller clicked the TV off, shook his head, bent over and kissed Sharon's head, and closed his eyes.

Miller woke up in the same position as when he fell asleep. Sharon had scooted down the bed and her head was on his stomach. Instantly he wished they would have had sex. He looked at the clock on her dresser. It was 5:30 a.m. Thursday morning. He clicked the TV on.

"Are you shitting me?" he whispered. The picture was of Allison's house with a "Live" signal in the right-hand corner. He clicked it off. He remembered what Turner had said to him: *The shit has hit the fan.* "Boy, you weren't kidding," Miller said out loud.

Miller felt Sharon shift. "What?" she asked groggily, then she laughed. "Well, will you look at what I woke up to!" She turned her head to face him, "Okay, Jim, we both got some sleep. We're not vulnerable anymore—can we have sex now?"

Miller laughed. "She's back! There's the Sharon I know and love."

"Well, you know me, but you sure haven't done any of that other thing," she said jokingly. She put her lips together and Miller leaned down and gave her a kiss.

"As soon as we catch this guy, if you still want this old man, I'll be showing you a lot of that 'other thing.' Right now, though, I need to get my ass to Chino." Miller crawled out of the bed.

"It's a date," Sharon said, "and I better get my ass in the lab and solve this case."

Chapter 32

Miller pushed the button for the intercom on the outside gate at Chino State Prison.

"May I help you?" a voice asked. It was the same rough voice as the last time he was here.

Oh great, Miller thought to himself. He spoke into the box. "Yes, my name is Detective Miller of the San Diego Police Department and I'm here to see Warden Simmons."

"Do you have an appointment?"

Miller grimaced, "No, I don't, but—" He was cut off by the man's voice.

"I'm sorry. No one gets through the gate without an appointment unless you want to commit a crime. Then we'll give you a personal escort."

Miller heard him and another man laugh. It took all his strength to control his anger. "If you would just let Warden Simmons know I'm here, I'm sure he'll see me," Miller said in as nice a voice as he could muster.

The voice came back in a cocky tone, "The only thing the warden is going to see is your car turning around and driving away." The laughter started again.

"I'll be back," Miller said.

"Okay, Arnold," the man said, followed by more laughter.

Miller drove to the gas station he had called Turner from two days earlier, only this time he made it in about half the time. As he was dialing the warden's direct line, he said to himself, *I wish I was Arnold. I would drive right through that gate and blow your fuc*—Miller was interrupted by Jerry Simmons' voice.

"This is Warden Simmons."

"Jerry, this is Detective Jim Miller."

"How are you, Jim? Did you call to get some more information about Mr. Taylor?" he asked.

"Actually, Jerry, I'm down the street at a pay phone. I was hoping you might have a few minutes to spare to talk with me in person."

"Of course. Just let Larry know you're coming to see me."

"Is Larry the voice on the intercom at the gate?" Miller asked.

"That's right."

"Could you do me a favor and let him know I'm coming to see you?" Miller thought about telling him what happened, but decided against it.

The warden chuckled. "I see you already know about Larry. He likes his job a little too much. I'll talk with him as soon as we hang up."

"Thank you," Miller said, relieved. "I'll be there in about ten minutes." He hung up the phone.

Miller was waiting for Simmons in the visitor's waiting room. He could only imagine what the warden had said to Larry because he got from the gate to where he is now without any hassles. After only five minutes of waiting, the warden walked in the room. "What can I do for you today, Jim?" the warden asked, smiling.

"The case I'm working on has intensified greatly, and we're broadening our investigation."

"I can imagine. I saw you on the news last night."

Wonderful, Miller thought. He was hoping that the news coverage would be limited to San Diego. A foolish notion, no doubt, but one he was hoping for. "Yeah, I instantly went from the frying pan to the fire. I was wondering if you might be able to give me some names of the inmates Danny hung around. I would also like to know if any of them have been released from custody."

Just then, Dr. Richards walked through the door of the visiting room with a number of files in his hands.

Miller looked at Simmons. "I have helped many investigations over the years, Jim. I assumed you might want to take a look at Taylor's friends, for whatever reason it is that you might have," the warden said. He gave Miller a satisfied smile.

Dr. Richards handed the files to Miller with a disgusted look on his face. It was obvious he wanted nothing to do with any of this. He then left the room.

"Thank you, Dr. Richards," Simmons called to him. "You realize, of course, that I must remain present while you view those," he then said to Miller.

THE SUICIDE MURDERS

"Of course." Miller opened the first file. He read the name out loud, "Alan Thornson." He looked at Simmons.

"That inmate is more commonly known as Fruit Loop," the warden was saying, "but he is still in custody, with a couple more years to serve."

Miller set the file on a seat, then sat down next to it. Simmons sat across from him.

Miller opened the next file. "Jeremy Hart," he read. He scanned the file and looked up.

"Jeremy is due to get out next week. He is a quiet one. Mr. Hart is in for sleeping with a girl who was only sixteen. He claimed she had a driver's license that said she was eighteen. The girl's parents got involved and he was convicted of statutory rape." Miller put the file aside.

He looked in the next one. "Tom Prescott."

The warden crossed his legs. "Oh, yes. The inmates called him Frito. Such a peculiar one, he was. That little guy didn't go anywhere without a bag of Fritos. Danny took him under his wing and protected him. He was in here for stalking a woman and setting her house on fire, burning her to death. The thing is, he was innocent. He had seen the guy who actually did it and had his license number memorized. He didn't say anything to the

police though, and he was convicted. Mr. Taylor was actually the one to convince Tom to have his lawyer file an appeal so he could testify against the guy in court. Mr. Prescott won his appeal and was released about a month after Mr. Taylor was."

"Interesting," Miller said, and copied down Tom Prescott's information. He opened the next file. "Grant Boyd."

"Oh, yeah," Simmons said as if reflecting. "I haven't heard that name in a while. He was here for ordering his gang, the Grant Boys, to throw cherry bombs into a crowd at a gay and lesbian rally. He was released from custody a year before Danny. You might want to check him closely. He kept talking about getting revenge against, how did he put it—oh, yeah, he kept talking about getting revenge against the guys that drove their vehicles down the 'Hershey Highway!'"

Miller gave a chuckle, and as he put the file aside and opened the last file he asked, "Did any of these guys have anything against Danny?"

Simmons answered instantaneously, "No, Mr. Taylor got along with everyone very well." He then thought for a moment, then added, "I don't nearly hear everything that goes on in here, however."

"I understand," Miller said, then quickly scanned the file and read the last name, "Bucky Webber."

"Bucky Webber," the warden repeated. "More commonly known as Mad Dog. He was in here this last time on a violation. He was caught with and under the influence of speed. Mr. Webber was originally arrested about fifteen years ago for brutally murdering his girlfriend because she was talking with some guy at a party. He's actually a nice enough guy when he's on his medication, but he doesn't like to take it. He says the government's trying to control him with it. He just got out three weeks ago, but he's gonna be back. He's one of the people that keep the prison return ratio high."

Miller copied down Bucky's information, then opened Mr. Boyd's file and copied his information. He then handed the files back to Simmons. "Thank you, Jerry," Miller said. "I'll run a check on their social security numbers and see what I can come up with." He stood and shook the warden's hand. "If there's anything else you can think of, please feel free to give me a call. You still have my card, right?"

"Yes. Good luck with the investigation. I'll be watching the news to see how you're doing."

"Thank you for your help." Miller left the prison.

Chapter 33

It was 10:00 a.m. and Ron Turner was on his way to Danny Taylor's mother's house. He had struck out with Trey Reynolds, Danny's boss. It seems Danny goes to the office for about half an hour and is gone the rest of the day. He doesn't associate with anybody from work after hours as far as he knows.

Turner called Taylor's mother from Old Town and she agreed to meet with him so he could ask some questions. Danny had called her a couple of times during work and informed her of what had been going on.

Turner pulled up to the curb in front of Ms. Taylor's Poway home. He walked to the door and rang the bell. The door opened almost immediately.

"I saw you pull up to the curb," a gray-haired woman about seventy years old said. "I presume you're Officer Turner?"

"Well, Homicide Detective Ron Turner," he said, trying not to sound pretentious.

"Come in, Detective." Turner glanced around the house as she showed him to the kitchen. It was a modest one-story house that was well kept.

"You have a lovely home," Turner stated as he sat down at the kitchen table. She had a pitcher of lemonade and a plate of cookies set out.

"Thank you, Detective." She smiled at him.

"Please, call me Ron."

"Alright, and you call me Doris." She picked up the pitcher and asked, "May I pour you a glass of lemonade?"

Turner picked up the glass that was in front of him and held it out for her to pour. "Thank you, Doris."

"Help yourself to the cookies too." She set the pitcher down and said, "You know, Detective—I mean, Ron. I'm probably not going to be of much help to you. I don't want you to take this the wrong way, but you're the enemy."

Turner couldn't help but laugh. "I understand your viewpoint, Doris. I'm merely here to inquire about anybody your son might keep company with. Is there anybody Danny keeps in touch with from prison?"

"I don't ask my son about prison, or anybody from prison. Danny got a bum rap. He didn't kill that girl in Riverside." Doris was talking sternly. "He may have a few problems, I'll admit that, but Danny is no murderer."

"So, Danny doesn't associate with anybody you know of?" Turner questioned.

"My son is a loner. He doesn't hate people, but I can't say he really likes them—at least, not to the extent of being friends with them."

"I understand, Doris," Turner said. He took a sip of his lemonade and thought for a moment. "Does Danny have any belongings here I might be able to look at. Any pictures of him with anybody, maybe?"

"The only thing that Danny has here is some stuff from when he was a kid."

"Would you mind if I took a look at it?" Turner asked.

Doris thought about it for a moment and figured it wouldn't hurt anything. "I don't think it's going to do you much good, but here are a couple of boxes of stuff in the closet from the room he used to sleep in." She got up and said, "Follow me."

"I appreciate this," Turner was saying as he followed her down the hall.

She turned into the last room on the left and Turner was right behind her. She pointed to the shelf and the three boxes that lay upon it. "There they are. Knock yourself out."

Turner grabbed them one by one and set them on the bed. He opened the heaviest one. It was full of trophies. He opened the next box and saw that it had a bunch of pictures in frames. They were mostly of him growing up. There was none of him as an adult. Turner then opened the last box, having already given up hope of finding anything. There were a couple of books, a small stuffed animal, an old Pong game, some hand-held football and baseball electric games, some baseball cards, an old California Angels hat, and an old hand-held kid's labeler.

Chapter 34

"I want you to run the socials on those guys and find out where their addresses are. I also want you to download their criminal histories. "Miller was at the station downtown and he was talking to Duncan, the uniformed cop he had sent out to the first victim's home.

"Yes, sir," Duncan said.

Miller left him at the main computer and went to his office to call Turner. On his way he thought about sticking his head into the lab to say hello to Sharon, but decided against it. As he was sitting down, he looked at his watch. It was 12:00 p.m. He picked up the phone and dialed Turner's cell phone. It was out of range or no longer in service at this time. *People wonder why I don't have one anymore,* he said to himself.

Miller put his head back to think, and Duncan entered his office through the open door. "Sir, here is the information you wanted," he said.

Miller stood and took the papers from him. "Thank you, Duncan."

"You're welcome, sir. Is there anything else?" he asked.

"No," Miller answered. Duncan turned and was walking out when Miller said, "Shut the door, please."

He sat alone and looked at the papers in front of him. He read the information on Bucky Webber, aka Mad Dog, Snake, Grim Reaper. He was six-foot-three, two-hundred fifty pounds. In and out of institutions since he was fourteen. No known current address. Warrant for his arrest was issued two weeks ago for failing to report to his PO.

"Interesting," Miller said, and looked at the next piece of paper. He read about Grant Boyd, a.k.a. General Grant, founder of "the Grant Boys"—a group of thugs that had never quite made it as a gang. In and out of institutions since he was seventeen, five-foot-seven, one-hundred ninety pounds. Current address 323 Warner Avenue, Chula Vista, California.

Chula Vista, huh? Miller thought to himself and picked up the last print-out. He read: Tom Prescott, no known a.k.a.'s, five-foot-three, one-hundred twenty-five pounds. Arrested for murder—charges dropped. No other arrests. Current address 4474 Parker Street, National City.

Miller went to the Xerox machine and made copies. He went back to his desk and put three of the print-outs in one folder and three in another. He called Turner again, but got the same message. He left the station to see if either Tom Prescott or Grant Boyd was home.

Miller pulled up to 4474 Parker Street where Tom Prescott's current address was listed. It was an apartment, but he had no apartment number. He looked for a directory, but couldn't find one. He went to the manager's office and got the number from a grumpy fat man who threatened to "Kick that little fucker out on his ass," if he was giving problems with the law. Miller assured him he was merely asking questions regarding another person.

As he was walking to Mr. Prescott's apartment, Miller looked around and saw poverty. This apartment complex was a dump. He arrived at Apartment number 12 and knocked on the warped door. About fifteen seconds went by and he knocked again, louder this time. He made no effort to call out that it was the police, like they do in the movies. If he did that, and Mr. Prescott was home, there is no way he would answer the door—guilty of anything or not. People who have been arrested before seldom have high regard for cops.

After waiting another fifteen seconds, he left. Tom was most likely at work. It was only 1:00 p.m. Miller got in his car and drove to 323 Warner Avenue, home of Grant Boyd.

Grant lived in a small, one bedroom home. Miller knocked on the door and a voice from inside shouted, "Who is it?" Again, he wasn't going to announce he was a police officer—not until the door was opened. "It's Jim!" he shouted back.

The voice said, "Jim? I don't know any Jim. Do I, Ricky?" He obviously was talking to another person who was in the house also. The door opened and the man said, "Fuck, it's a cop."

"Do I look like a cop that much?" Miller asked.

"In this neighborhood you do," the man said.

THE SUICIDE MURDERS

Miller knew that if he asked this man if he was Mr. Boyd, he would say no. He figured it would be best to act like he knew it was him. "Mr. Boyd, I'm here to ask you a few questions about a person you knew in prison, Danny Taylor."

The man let out a little laugh. "I wish I could help you, but I'm not Boyd."

Just as I expected, Miller thought to himself. He then chose the rougher approach. "Look, Grant, do you want to answer my questions, or do you want me to take you downtown and run your prints? When they come back as Grant Boyd, I'm gonna bust your ass for lying to an officer of the law and interfering with an official investigation."

A laugh came from inside the house. "I think he's got a boner for you Double G."

Double G, Miller thought. *Of course, General Grant.*

The man at the door said, "What did Danny do?"

"That's not important. When was the last time you saw Danny Taylor?" Miller studied the body and face of Grant. He wanted to pick up on any signs that might indicate he was lying.

Boyd looked Miller straight in the eye and said, "The last time I saw him was in prison." He thought for a second, and continued, "That must have been one and a half, maybe two years ago."

Miller saw no sign of lying. "That's funny, I just happened to have talked with someone who said Danny looked you up when he got out," Miller lied.

"Hey, he couldn't look me up or down or sideways for all I know, but I haven't seen him since prison," Boyd said angrily.

Miller's bluff didn't work. "Do you know who Tom Prescott is?" Miller asked.

"Nope."

"How about Frito?"

Boyd laughed a hearty laugh. "Yeah, I know that fucking bundle of nerves." He looked off in the distance, appearing to think. "Fucking Frito. Is that his name, Tom Prescott?" Boyd asked.

"Yes," Miller answered. "Have you talked to him recently?"

"No, as far as I know, he's still in prison."

"Do you know a Bucky Webber? They called him Mad Dog."

"No," Boyd said.

"Are you sure?" Miller asked. "He hung around Danny in the Annex."

"Yeah, I'm sure. He must have got there after I was gone."

Miller thought for a second, then asked, "Do you remember when Dr. Richards put Danny on suicide watch?"

Boyd nodded his head as if disgusted. "Yeah, he was fucked up for a while on the psych drugs. Some people shouldn't take them."

"What do you mean?" Miller asked.

"The thing is, if you aren't crazy and you take those psych drugs it will fuck you up. The pills Danny was taking made him want to commit suicide. Everything became a fucking chore for him. He didn't even want to get up to eat."

"Danny's medication was changed though," Miller noted. "I talked with Dr. Richards and he said they found the right medication for him. That's why he was taken off suicide watch."

Boyd laughed an even heartier laugh than before. "Danny stopped taking his medication. That's why he went back to normal. That's why he was taken off suicide watch."

Miller couldn't believe what he was hearing. "Are you telling me Danny pretended to take his medication and lied to Dr. Richards?"

Boyd laughed again. "Danny's a smart motherfucker. He knew how to work the system. He took the pills that he palmed at pill call and sold them to other inmates for food or Pruno."

Miller thought about what Boyd just said. *Danny's a smart motherfucker. He knew how to work the system. He sure did. He knew how to manipulate a trained psychiatrist into letting him out of prison early. He lied straight to him and had him believe the medication he actually wasn't taking was helping him.* Miller was snapped away from his thoughts by Boyd's question.

"Is that all? I've got shit to do, you know."

"Yes, that's it. Thank you for your time." Miller walked back to his car as his mind whirled with questions. The one that kept coming back to him was, *How smart and manipulative are you, Danny; enough to think you can get away with murder?*

Chapter 35

Turner had gone to see Miller at 11:30 a.m., but Miller's car wasn't in his parking stall. He pulled into an empty spot to wait. He called his department to see if his team had come up with anything from the list of names Miller had given him last night. His assistant, Joe Riley, answered, "Hello. This is Joe."

"Hey, Joe. How did the search come out?"

"I was just about to call you. I have a name and address I think you should check out."

Turner grabbed his notebook from his back pocket. "I'm ready."

"Okay, the guy is named Tony Phelps. He calls himself Preacher. The alias you gave me this morning for him was the Reverend."

"I remember him. He was that pastor who was accused of telling members of his church that God wanted him to have sex with them."

"Right," Riley was saying, "and he was asked to leave the church. He was arrested for pulling down his pants during his last sermon."

Turner gave a slight laugh. "And he had 'Burn in Hell' written on his ass."

"Exactly. Do you have his address with you?" Riley asked.

"No, I left the list in the office this morning. Go ahead and give it to me. I'm ready."

"One twenty Burntwood Avenue, San Ysidro. Watch your ass too. This guy is over six feet and about two hundred forty pounds."

"What were you suspicious about with this guy?" Turner asked.

"Everyone on the list answered all my questions and cooperated, showing no nervousness at all. Everyone except Preacher. He just kept quoting the Bible and saying the end of the world was at hand. He gave me weird vibes."

"Alright, Joe. Thanks for checking them out." Turner hung up the phone and headed for San Ysidro. He decided he would talk with Miller afterward.

Turner pulled up to the Preacher's house at 12:30 p.m. It was an old, rotting eyesore. The kids in the neighborhood most likely thought it was haunted. Turner walked across the dead lawn and got a surprise scare from Preacher screaming at him.

"Good God, Lord Almighty!" He was standing behind his screen door and just about taking up all the space. "That's twice today! How is my grass ever going to grow back with the whole world trampling on it?"

Turner had frozen when the boisterous voice took him by surprise. He now hopped quickly to the walkway. "I'm sorry about that Mr. Phelps," Turner said.

"The name's Preacher!" his voice boomed. "That's what I told your snot-nosed partner earlier."

"What makes you think I have anything to do with anybody who may have come around earlier?" Turner asked.

"Because I'm not an idiot," he said, stepping onto the front porch. "You must be though, coming onto my property uninvited. I don't even know who you are." He slowly walked toward Turner. "You could be Satan himself!" he shouted.

Before Preacher could get his hands on him, he said, "My name is Detective Turner, homicide division."

Preacher stopped before him and stood face-to-face. Turner took two steps back. "Would it make you more comfortable to talk to me down at the station, Preacher? That's exactly where we're going to go if you get that close to me again. Understood?" Turner was stern, but calm.

"The Lord has my eyes wide open, Detective." He walked back to his front porch and turned around. "What is it that you want?" he said, agitated.

"I would like to ask you a couple of questions."

"I already answered the questions of your partner. I believe I have been more than cooperative for one day. Retribution is something you can't hide from. If you've sinned, then prepare yourself for what is to come. If you say you haven't sinned, you are a liar. If you are a liar, you will meet the fire." Preacher turned and walked in the house.

Turner when to his car and called Riley. He waited in the front of Preacher's house until the surveillance team arrived. He drove down the street and quickly briefed them. As he was driving away he said, "What a fucking head-case. This man just may be the killer."

Chapter 36

Miller and Turner had finally met up and briefed each other about the information they obtained. They were in Miller's office and the time was 3:30 p.m. Miller took four aspirin from the bottle he had sitting on his desk and washed them down with a drink of coffee. He offered some aspirin to Turner, but Turner declined.

"So, you think this Preacher character might be our killer?" Miller asked.

"Enough to put a tail on him," Turner answered. "He actually makes as much sense being the killer as Danny and our accomplice theory does. He's over six feet tall, just like the dope dealers said their new customer was. He also definitely matches the religious profile of the letters."

"I agree. You're sure he doesn't know he's being watched?" Miller asked.

Turner took a sip of his coffee and shook his head. "I put my best men on surveillance. Dell and Smith have been with me for eight years. I've got them watching him through tomorrow. If Preacher is our boy, there's no way there's going to be a victim number four."

"What about the kid's labeler you found at Danny's mother's house?" Miller asked.

Turner nodded his head. "I know. I never said Preacher was our killer, I only said he fit the profile. When I asked Doris if Danny had been to her house since he got out of prison, she said no. She did, however, take the boxes to his apartment when he was moving in. She said he rummaged through them, but said he didn't want any of the stuff. She took the boxes with her when she left."

Miller thought for a moment, then asked, "Does Danny have a key to her house?"

"She said he does," Turner answered.

"So," Miller said, "he could have taken the labeler out of the box when she wasn't looking, made all the notes, then returned the labeler when she wasn't home."

"Exactly," Turner agreed. "He might have then given the letters to his accomplice, knowing after he contacted you that you might put a tail on him."

"Or that we might search his apartment," Miller added.

They both sat in silence for a moment while they gathered their thoughts. "Is Danny as smart as we're giving him credit for? That's the question."

"From what you told me Grant Boyd said, he is," Turner pointed out. He then added, "Do you think Boyd might be Danny's accomplice?"

"No," Miller said, "but I'm going to put a tail on him anyway. I'll put a tail on Prescott too. If they come up clean tomorrow, I'll take it off."

"I'll do the same with Preacher, providing we have another victim claimed tomorrow. If no body is found, we're going to arrest every single one of these guys and sort it out later. All we need is for the killer to notice he's being tailed and hold back, then we pull our teams and he starts killing again."

"Exactly," Miller said. They both sat in silence again. Miller leaned back in his chair and rubbed his head. He took a deep breath and let air out noisily. "The thing that's bothering me, Ron, is the fact that Danny has been targeted as the sixth victim. What do you make of that?"

Turner crossed his legs and rubbed his hand on his face. He was looking off into an imaginary distance, then slowly said, "We originally thought it was to take heat off of himself. Maybe the killings will stop after the fifth victim."

"Interesting point," Miller noted "Or maybe, just maybe…" Miller's voice trailed off.

"Maybe what?" Turner questioned.

"It's a far-out thought, but I don't know how far-out Danny's thinking actually is. I don't think anybody does but Danny himself." Miller leaned forward and put his arms out on his desk with his fingers intertwined. "What if Danny is still suicidal? What if he never took his medication in prison at all?" Miller paused for a second, then continued. "What if he stopped telling Dr. Richards he was suicidal so he could be put back with his friends and be taken out of solitary confinement?" Miller stopped and shook his head.

Turner was listening intently to what he was saying. "Keep going," he urged.

Miller sat straight in his seat. "What if Danny is really schizophrenic, and is tired with his struggles of keeping himself together? Maybe he's just tired of being an alcoholic." Miller's face it up, as if being sparked by a revelation. "What if Danny wanted to commit the perfect crime? How much more perfect could a crime be than to have the killer claim himself as the last victim? The case would never be solved."

Turner smiled, showing how happy he was to have joined this new level of thinking. He was now on the edge of his seat. "Right! Maybe he even killed Allison Hayword because the murders weren't getting any publicity!"

"Exactly," Miller agreed. "Even though they were bizarre killings, we kept it out of the news for fear of a copycat."

The two men sat back in their chairs looking satisfied.

"I like working with you, Jim," Turner said, smiling.

"Fucking 'A' Right!" Miller said happily.

Chapter 37

Miller and Turner had just placed calls to their surveillance teams. Everybody was at home and everything was under control. Miller looked at his watch. It was 7:40 p.m., and in five minutes he and Turner were making a statement to the press in front of the downtown station. They didn't have anything to report, but they wanted to make the media happy, the public feel safe, and if the killer was watching—to make him think they were on to him.

Miller spoke into the microphones of about twenty different stations. He even noticed a microphone from the Mexican TV station, Telemundo. *This news story has definitely stretched farther than I thought it would*, he thought to himself. Cameras were flashing wildly, and he had a hard time finding a spot to look at without going blind.

"Thank you all for coming," Miller started. "Both homicide Detective Ron Turner and I will make a brief statement, but for security reasons we cannot answer any of your questions at this time. I'm sorry, but that is the way it has to be."

The killer watched the detective delivering his speech. He reached forward to his TV and turned the horizontal knob until Detective Jim Miller was shooting on and off the screen with a bunch of squiggly lines chasing him. The killer laughed.

"We have reason to believe the death of Allison Hayword was the third in a series of murders. We feel this way because we have found evidence at each crime scene that we have linked together." Miller had prepared what he would say beforehand. He didn't want to mention the letters, videos or audio tape. The threat of a copycat killer was very real. He also had to be careful to not let any of the suspects know they were being followed. He wanted his words to be bold though, challenging the killer so he would strike again, even if he thought he might be caught. As soon as he did strike, the surveillance team would take him down.

"There is no cause for public alarm, however," Miller continued. "We are very confident we will apprehend the perpetrator before he strikes again. We do ask that everyone please take extra caution and lock their doors, and be wary of strangers; not just now, but always. If everyone practices safety and good judgment against people they don't know, and even people they do know, the sick people of this world who prey on the innocent and trusting will no longer have any victims to attack." Miller felt as if he'd just given a sermon. He stepped aside and Turner went to the podium.

"I just want to reassure everyone that this violator of public safety and personal freedom is as good as caught. No one, and I repeat, no one comes into my city, our city, and gets away with something like this." Turner looked straight into the camera that was closest to him. "If the killer is out there watching—I'm coming to get you!"

Turner and Miller turned and walked back into the station amidst a barrage of photo flashes and questions being yelled.

Once inside, Turner turned to Miller and asked, "Well, was that good?"

"Absolutely. If I was the killer, I would be pissed off by the challenge." He patted Turner on the back.

The killer turned off his TV while laughing heartily.

Chapter 38

Preacher was in the shower singing...

"Jesus loves me, yes he do.
He would even love me if I were you.
Washes away my sins, through and through.
Forgives me no matter what I do."

Preacher turned off the water and dried off. While he was getting dressed, he looked at the clock, "...12:05 in the a.m.," Preacher said aloud. "It's almost time, Lisa, it's almost time. Lord Almighty! I've been looking forward to this since I saw you last week. Ask and ye shall receive. Isn't that right, Jesus? Ask and ye shall receive."

Preacher went back in the bathroom and looked in the mirror, admiring himself. "The Lord blessed you, Preacher. When He gave out good looks, I do believe you got in line twice." He opened the medicine cabinet and grabbed his lotion and rubbed it onto his bald head. He then winked at himself with one of his blue eyes. "That Lisa is a lucky girl." He turned off his bathroom light, went to his bedroom dresser and grabbed his keys and headed for the front door.

Dell and Smith were in their police-issued Ford Taurus down the street from Preacher's house. They were far enough away so Preacher couldn't see then in the car from his house, but they could see his front door and car, which was in the driveway.

THE SUICIDE MURDERS

Smith had just fallen asleep while Dell kept watch. Dell was the older of the two, at thirty-five. Smith was twenty-one. They both looked like cops. Dell had poured himself a fresh cup of coffee and was taking a drink when he saw the large figure of Preacher coming out of his house. When he got in his car, Dell nudged his partner, "Wake up, we've got movement."

Preacher started his car and sat a moment, letting it warm up. He leaned over and moved the stuff from the passenger seat to the back seat. It consisted of two Bibles, some religious tracts and a pair of women's underwear. He picked up the underwear, sniffed the crotch and threw them back in the back seat. *You're next, Lisa, he said to himself.* He kept talking as he pulled out of his driveway and away from the police. "The Lord is my shepherd, I shall not want." He laughed loudly. "At least not when I'm finished with her." The laughing continued.

Dell had no problem keeping up with Preacher. There weren't many cars on the road at this hour, and he had to stay a good distance behind to be sure Preacher didn't know he was being followed, but the man was driving nice and slow, obeying every law.

"Almost there, Preacher, you handsome man," Preacher continued talking to himself. As he pulled into a parking lot, he looked in the mirror and made sure nothing was on his nose. "All set," he said. He pulled back on the street and made a left on San Ysidro Boulevard. He gazed at the hookers scattered along the street. "Beware of the wolf in sheep's clothing, ladies." He slowly drove along the road, looking for his lucky lady. "There you are, you harlot," he said. He pulled up to her and rolled down the passenger side window. She walked over and leaned down to see in. She exposed Preacher to dangling breasts in a loose fitting top. He stared at them, smiling. She was studying his face.

"Don't I know you?" she asked.

Preacher ignored her and kept his eyes on the full view of her breasts, "Lord, Almighty!" he said. "The Lord is blessing his servant tonight."

The girl's face lit up. "That's how I know you. You're the guy who preaches to us girls that we're going to Hell." She smiled. "I've seen you drive by a couple of times. What's the matter?" She jiggled her breasts. "Did you change your mind about us?"

Preacher finally looked her in the eyes. "I only changed my mind about you. Are you going to stand there all night teasing me with those," Preacher pointed to her chest, "or are you going to get in, Lisa?"

She opened the door and got in. "Hey, how did you know my name?" she asked.

He laughed. "The Lord works in mysterious ways."

She laughed with him. "I like you. You talk funny, mister."

"The name's Preacher."

She laughed again. "That's a perfect name for you."

He drove a little ways and said, "Lord, Almighty! The Lord surely is blessing his servant tonight."

She laughed again. Lisa was a stunning girl who looked to be about seventeen years old. She was a true blond, with sparkling blue eyes. She had a beautiful petite figure and large breasts for her size. "So, where do you want to do it?" she asked.

"The Lord told me to take you to my house. He told me you were the chosen one."

She laughed and put her hand on Preacher's leg, just above his kneecap. "Did He tell you how much I cost?"

"I have been blessed enough to give you fifty dollars," he said, putting his hand on hers and pulling it further up his leg.

She continued her hand to his crotch and gave a gentle squeeze. Her head tilted back and she moaned. She put her right hand under her mini-skirt and rotated it in circles between her legs, lifting herself up. She opened her eyes and looked at Preacher, who was starting to sweat. His eyes were darting back and forth between the road and her right hand. She stopped rubbing herself and lowered her pelvis back to the seat. Her left hand continued squeezing his crotch and she said, "It feels like you got something in there dying to get out. For fifty, I'll take care of him right here, but for a hundred, I'll take care of him at your house."

Preacher's forehead was beaded with sweat and his throat had gone dry. He licked his lips, and when he spoke he had a hard time finding his voice. "The end is nigh, so I might as well indulge in the sins of the flesh." Preacher then spoke so loud, it made Lisa jump, "Sweet Mary, Mother of Jesus! Please forgive me, Lord, for I have sinned!" He wiped the seat off his forehead and laughed. "Beautiful temptress of the night, lead me down the wide path of sin."

She smiled. "Does that mean we have a deal?"

"That is exactly what that means," Preacher said, and smiled back.

She pulled her hand off his crotch and placed it with her other one, held together in front of her face as if praying, "Lord almighty! The Lord is blessing me tonight!" she shouted, and the two of them laughed as Preacher pulled into his driveway.

Dell and Smith had been contemplating what to do since Preacher picked up the hooker. They had called Turner at home, and he had told them to hold their ground until they could catch him in the act, but to not wait too long for fear of not saving the girl in time. When Smith hung up the cell phone he said, "No shit! Great advice."

Down the street they pulled to the curb and turned off their lights until Preacher and the girl went into the house. Dell sped down the street, with his headlights on now, and slowed to regular speed about one hundred feet from Preacher's house. As they drove by, they saw a light go on in a window covered by drapes. The drapes had a two-inch gap in the middle.

"What are the chances of that being the bedroom?" Smith asked his partner.

"Get out and find out while I park the car down the street. I'll be back to help you in a second," Dell said.

Smith jumped out and Dell was gone. Smith ran to the shadow of the overhang of Preacher's house. He could be seen from the street, but there was a rickety, old fence that kept him from view of the neighbor. It appeared that there had been a gate protecting Preacher's backyard at one time, but it looked like it had fallen off long ago. Smith moved flat against the fence and was edging closer to the window. He wanted to be as far away from it as possible when he looked in. He reached the spot where the gap in the curtain was and peered in. Dell came around the corner and scared the shit out of him. Smith waved him over and a chill went through their spines at what they saw.

Preacher was standing at the top of his bed, putting a pair of handcuffs through an opening in the headboard, then slipping the cuffs on her free wrist. He stood looking at her handcuffed, blindfolded and gagged. They heard him say, "Lord, Almighty! What a sight!"

Preacher then straddled her on the bed, clad only in what appeared to be the girls' underpants. They were stretched to the limits on him. He then lay flat on her, completely covering her naked body. The girl's legs wrapped around him and she thrashed wildly as if she were struggling. Preacher put his hand to the girl's throat and Smith grabbed his gun and smashed the butt against the window, shattering glass onto the bedroom floor. The girl screamed as best she could through the handkerchief and Preacher jumped to his feet, facing the window in the pair of pink panties that were bulging from his excitement. He had a look of surprised horror on his face as he saw the two men pointing guns at him from the window, and he shouted, "Sweet Mary, Mother of Jesus!"

Chapter 39

When Dell and Smith had Preacher dressed, handcuffed and in the back of the Taurus, they called Turner to find out what to do. Turner listened to what happened and informed them to take the prostitute into custody too, and to meet him at the downtown police station. He didn't want anybody booked. He told Dell to keep them in single-man cells and to not interrogate them. He then called Miller and asked him to get down to the station as quick as he could.

"So, you're telling us that Preacher wasn't attacking you?" Miller asked Lisa. He and Turner were in Interrogation Room I. Preacher was waiting in Interrogation Room II.

"Right. We were about to have sex." Lisa was trying to be tough, but it was obvious she was scared.

"He didn't threaten you or say anything strange?" Turner asked.

She rolled her eyes and let out air between her teeth. "No, he didn't threaten me. He said a lot of weird stuff, but these perverts almost always say crazy shit to get themselves off." Lisa looked at Miller as if she had seen his face before. She pointed at him. "Don't I know you?"

Miller looked at Turner and Ron gave him a shit eating grin and raised his eyebrows as if to ask, "Well, do you?"

"No, you don't know me," Miller said firmly. Lisa kept looking at him, trying to figure it out. "Did he say anything to you about suicide?" Miller asked.

Lisa looked back and forth between the two with a puzzled look on her face. She had never been busted for prostitution before. In fact, she was only seventeen, but these seemed like strange questions they were asking. Then she remembered where she had seen Miller. She pointed at him again. "I knew I knew you," she said. "I saw you on the news yesterday." A sudden look of terror ran across her face. "Hey! That guy I was with tonight, he isn't the guy who killed that Hayword news lady, is he?"

Turner looked at her sternly, "It very well could be."

Lisa sat there stunned, tears forming in her eyes.

Miller put his hand on her shoulder and said, "I know this is difficult, but please think hard. Did Preacher say anything to you about suicide, or anything like that?"

Lisa was doing her best to keep control of herself. She sat thinking, then shook her head no. "He just kept saying the Lord had blessed him tonight." She looked back and forth between them. "I'm sorry, but—" Her face lit up. "Wait, he said I was the chosen one. He asked me to lead him to the road of sin, or something like that."

Turner looked amazed. "And that didn't scare you? You didn't think that was strange?"

Lisa shook her head no. "Not at the time. I've heard a lot of unbelievable stuff come out of guys' mouths. It's tough to say no to somebody when you need the money."

"How old are you, Lisa?" Miller asked.

She looked at the ground. "Eighteen."

"All we need to do is run your prints to find out for sure," Turner said.

She looked up at him with scared eyes. "I'm seventeen."

Turner shook his head with pity. "Unless you want to end up dead by a horny lunatic, AIDS or a drug OD, I suggest you get off the streets." Turner left it at that. Lecturing her wasn't going to help, so he spared her the drama. He looked at Miller and made a head motion toward the door.

"That's all the questions we have for you right now, Lisa. We'll be back in a little while. Sit tight while we figure out what we're going to do."

Lisa nodded her head, then looked at the ground. "For what it's worth," she said, "I'm sorry."

They left the room with no response.

Miller and Turner walked into Interrogation Room II. When Preacher saw Turner, he said, "The Lord told me you were the one behind this."

"Did he also tell you that you're going to jail for a long time?" Turner asked. Preacher was sitting down on a chair at one side of a small wooden table. Miller sat in one of the two chairs on the other side. Turner stood against the wall, behind Preacher.

Preacher laughed. "For what? For two cops peeping through my bedroom window, then breaking the damn thing?"

"The immediate charge we have is soliciting a prostitute," Miller said.

Preacher laughed. "I didn't solicit anybody. That young woman came home with me on her own free will."

Turner and Miller both laughed, and Miller said, "Young is right. That girl is seventeen."

Preacher sat in silence and shifted in his seat.

Turner crept forward and stood behind Preacher, "Give it up, Preacher!" he shouted, and Preacher jumped. "The girl told us all the religious jargon you were babbling. She told us you said she was the chosen one and you wanted her to show you how to sin."

Deep down Turner didn't think this was the killer, and he was pretty sure Miller didn't either. This guy was definitely someone who deviated from normal sexual behavior, but Lisa didn't say he did anything to lead them to believe he was going to kill her. He also didn't say anything about her killing herself. There also was nothing found in his house that matched anything at the other crime scenes. He had no labeler, no duct tape, no video camera, no audio tape recording, and he wasn't forcing her to do anything. Turner was going to do the best he could to call Preacher's bluff just in case he was the killer.

"Why was she the chosen one!" he screamed.

Preacher jumped again.

Miller then spoke calmly. "Why her, Preacher? Why would you want to kill such a beautiful, young girl?"

Preacher wiped his now sweating forehead and spoke in a voice barely louder than a whisper, "Good God, Lord, Almighty." He then raised his voice so he could be heard better. "That's what this is about? You think I was going to kill that girl?" He looked into Miller's eyes and Miller saw sadness. "I wasn't going to hurt that girl. Lord, help me, but my problem is the sin of the flesh. I have a weakness for women that are forbidden. The women of the night stir something in me and I can't control my loins. Lord, forgive me, but that is why I got kicked out of my church a few years back. I was a reverend, but I couldn't control my lust for other men's wives because they were off limits to me. I had to have what I couldn't have." He lowered his head, ashamed.

Turner looked at Miller and made another head motion toward the door. He then spoke to Preacher. "I don't want to give you false hope because we are arresting you for soliciting an underage prostitute, but I am going to discuss with my partner about how cooperative you've been and that may be the only charge we file."

As they walked out of the room, Preacher called to them, "God bless you both."

Miller closed the door of his office behind him and Turner. Neither made a move to sit down.

"Well, what do you think?" Turner asked.

"I don't think he's our killer, but you never know. I'll keep him in holding cells and drag the booking process so there's no way he can make bail before the day is through. If another body shows up today while he's in here, he's in the clear. He'll only have the underage solicitation and near copulating charge."

"Okay. What about the girl?" Turner asked. "Do we bust her or do we cut her a break?"

Miler gave Turner a sullen look. "We have to bust her or we can't bust Preacher. If she doesn't have an arrest shown for this, the charges on him will never stick."

Turner nodded his head. "I guess this means our killer is still at large, huh?"

"I guess so," Miller answered, "but we've got our other suspected perps under surveillance."

Turner looked at his watch. "I guess that means we can go home and get some rest. It's only 3:00 a.m. What do you say you give me a call at 9:00 a.m.?"

"Will do," Miller said.

Chapter 40

Miller had just sat down at his desk when the phone rang. Instantly he got a bad feeling that this call was going to be about the fourth victim. He looked at his watch and saw that it was 8:30 a.m. Friday morning. He picked the receiver up and said, "Miller here."

"Detective Miller, this is Peterson."

"Is something going down with Taylor?" Miller asked.

"Not exactly, sir. The thing is, he's still in his apartment."

Miller looked at his watch again, then Peterson continued talking. "Murray came from the van and told us that Taylor called in sick."

"What time was that?" Miller asked.

"At 7:00 a.m. I've been trying you at the station ever since. I would have called you at home," he looked over at Duncan and smiled, "but Duncan told me not to wake you."

Duncan punched his partner in the arm and whispered, "You fucking liar." Peterson laughed to himself. After a week of boring surveillance duty, they were doing anything they could to amuse themselves.

"No," Miller said, "you did the right thing."

Duncan was mumbling obscenities when Peterson put his hand over the phone and said, "He's pissed off." Duncan's face got bright red and Peterson whispered, "Calm down. I'm just kidding. He said that was the smart thing to do." The dark color instantly vanished from his face and Duncan smiled. Peterson couldn't help but laugh at him.

Miller had continued talking, but Peterson hadn't heard him because his attention was drawn to his partner. He thought he made out the final words, "I'll be there in half an hour," but he wasn't sure, and Miller had hung up.

Peterson clicked the phone off and looked at his partner with a look that was filled with amazement, anger and humor. "Good going, spastic. I didn't hear what he said. I think he's coming to talk with Taylor."

"So, we just sit tight and wait for him."

Peterson laughed. "Do you even know how to sit tight?"

Miller pulled up at 9:20 a.m. and went straight to Danny's apartment without saying anything to either his team or Peterson and Duncan.

Miller knocked on Danny's door and was surprised with how quickly he answered. Danny's expression was that of total surprise when he saw Miller.

"Detective Miller? What are you doing here?" he asked.

"I just wanted to discuss a couple of things with you. Is it alright if I come in?"

"Of course." Danny took a side step and motioned with his hand to come in. He shut the door and offered Miller a seat on the couch.

"That's okay, thank you. I'll only take a moment of your time," Miller said. The two men remained standing.

Danny cleared his throat and asked, "What can I do for you, Detective?"

"I see you're home for the day. Are you feeling alright?"

"Yeah, I'm just tired. What with everything that's been going on, and all I decided to take a three-day weekend. By the way, I saw you on the news. You and that other detective sure did put the killer in his place."

Miller stared hard into Danny's eyes. "We wanted to let that lowlife know we're going to nail his ass."

Danny smiled. "You sure made me believe it."

What was that smile for? Miller thought. "Anyway," he said, "we got your drug test back and it came up clean."

Danny smiled even bigger. "Of course it did."

Miller's team was listening intently in the van. They didn't now why he was here, and the men had bets going with each other on whether or not Miller was going to bring Danny in for questioning. They also had bets going at 5-1 odds that he would arrest him.

Miller leaned against the wall. "The thing is, it shouldn't have."

Danny looked puzzled. "What?"

"We tested for the psychological drugs that were prescribed to you by the prison psychiatrist, Danny."

Danny nodded his head and gave a nervous laugh. "You've been checking up on me. Why? Do you think I have something to do with the killings?" Danny's voice was rising. "Do you think I'm schizophrenic? Do you think because I'm not taking those fucked-up psych drugs that I might be crazy?"

"That's a lot of assumptions, Mr. Taylor. I didn't imply any of that," Miller said, trying to sound innocent.

Danny was mad now. "You didn't have to! It was implied when you tested me! I have no court order to take that medication, Detective, and unless I'm under arrest, I'm under no obligation to talk to you. I have been cooperative and have answered all your questions and pretty much bent over backward to help you, but no more!" Danny put his hands out to be handcuffed.

"I'm not arresting you, Danny. I jus—" Miller was cut off.

"Then get out of my home! Please!"

Miller turned and left the apartment without saying a word.

Miller's team exchanged money between the winners and the losers.

Miller called Turner and met him for breakfast at Denny's.

"So Taylor kicked you out of his apartment," Turner said.

"Yes, he did. I don't know if I can really blame him." Miller took a drink of coffee. "He made some good points. He has been cooperative to the point of annoyance."

"He's a murder suspect. What does he expect?" Turner asked.

"Well, that's the thing. Danny doesn't know he is. At least he didn't before today."

"Of course, he did. He's an ex-con on probation for murder. This guy knows we're snooping around on him. Hell, he probably even suspects, or knows, that we still got a tail on him. Danny's obviously very smart and he's probably even a little paranoid about how cops work. I wouldn't doubt that he knows his place is bugged. His mother told me that he's been keeping her up-to-date on what's been going on by calling her during his workday from payphones."

Miller leaned back in the booth. "Interesting. You should have seen how quickly his mood changed when I mentioned that he wasn't taking his medication. I could tell he was holding back, too. If I wasn't a cop, who knows what might have happened?"

They both took a drink of coffee and thought for a moment.

"Have you heard anything from your surveillance team?" Miller asked.

Turner looked at him with a quizzical smile. "Jim, Preacher's in custody."

Miller closed his eyes and shook his head as if clearing the cobwebs. He then gave a chuckle and said, "Oh, yeah."

"You didn't go back to sleep this morning, did you?"

Miller took another drink of his coffee. "I tried, but I couldn't stop thinking that the killer is going to strike again today."

"Maybe we got lucky and we have the killer in custody."

Miller finished his coffee and reached for his wallet. He threw a ten and a five dollar bill on the table. The men got up and walked to the door, and Miller said, "I hope you're right, Ron, but I just don't think so."

Chapter 41

"Come on, Travis! You're going to be late for school if you don't hurry up!" Roland Perry shouted to his son. He was standing at the bottom of the stairs in his Rancho Penasquitos home.

"I'm coming, Dad!" his son shouted from upstairs.

"I'll be in the car!" Roland yelled back and headed for the garage. He opened the driver side door and got in his 1984 Mustang 5.0. He started the car and smiled, listening to the engine purr. He had always liked the '80s style Mustang, and had just bought this car two months ago from a kid down the street who needed money.

Roland honked his horn and his son appeared through the door that led from the house to the garage. Travis pressed the button on the wall and the garage door opened. As he got in the car he asked, "When are you going to get new batteries for the remote control?"

"I'll get some today before I pick you up." He backed out of the driveway and drove away. "I have to get home right after I drop you off. I'm expecting a conference call at 8:00 a.m."

Travis looked worried. "I hate leaving my bike in the garage when nobody's home and the garage door's up."

"It will be fine," Roland assured his son. "Besides, the Cadillac completely blocks it from view."

Roland pulled to the curb in front of Travis' elementary school, gave him five dollars for lunch and kissed his goodbye for the last time of his life.

At 7:58 a.m. Roland pulled into his garage, walked to the door leading to the house, pressed the button on the wall, watched the door fully close and entered his house. He was met by a large man with a gun. Roland Perry froze with terror. He then asked a question that made the man with the gun laugh. He asked, "Who are you?"

"Out of all the people I've killed," the man with the gun was saying, "over half of them have asked that stupid question."

Roland's face turned white.

"If it really makes any fucking difference, you can call me Mad Dog."

Roland put his hands chest high with his palms toward Mad Dog, showing he wasn't going to attack. Mad Dog laughed at the man. Roland was only five-foot-eight and one-hundred seventy pounds. Mad Dog was gigantic compared to him.

"How old are you?" Mad Dog asked.

"I'm forty-five," Roland answered.

"Good, then you're not young and foolish."

The phone range and Mad Dog turned away from Roland, momentarily startled. Roland started to lunge forward but Mad Dog was already turning around. Roland stopped, and Mad Dog laughed. "I take it back," he said. "You are foolish." He motioned for Roland to follow him to the living room while he held the gun steady on him.

"You can have anything you want," Roland said with a shaky voice.

Mad Dog laughed again. "That's good, because I want you to kill yourself."

"You're crazy," Rolland managed to say through quivering lips.

Mad Dog laughed so loud and crazily that Roland flinched. "That's usually a prerequisite to being a cold-blooded murderer." They were in the living room now, and Mad Dog motioned toward the floor. On the coffee table was a role of duct tape.

Roland said, "If I lay on that floor, I'm a dead man."

"You're a dead man anyway, but if you lie on the floor and do as you're told, your son won't have to die also."

Roland's face got angry. "I swear to God, if you touch my son, I'll kill you!"

Mad Dog motioned him into the kitchen. He grabbed a knife out of a wooden knife holder that was on the counter. He held the gun in his left hand and a good sized butcher knife in his right hand. "Take off your shirt," Mad Dog said calmly.

Roland looked into the eyes of his assailant and shuddered. They were wild, yet lifeless. There were dark circles around them and they were sunken. He looked like he had been awake for a week. Roland tried to rationalize with the man. "Please, if we can just talk about this, I know we…"

Mad Dog cut him off with his scream, "Take off your fucking shirt!" His face had turned beet red.

Roland cringed and pulled his shirt up over his head, and when it was in front of him, his arms still in the sleeves, Mad Dog sprang forward and jabbed the knife deep into his right shoulder. Roland jerked backward and fell to the floor screaming with pain.

"Now," Mad Dog said, "like I said, lay on the floor and do what I say and I won't have to kill your son."

Roland got up and staggered to the living room, dripping blood down his side. He lay down on his back.

"Turn over!" Mad Dog screamed with frustration. "Put your hands behind your back, with the fingers together." Roland did as he was told and Mad Dog straddled him, grabbed the roll of duct tape and rolled it around Roland's wrists until he was positive Roland was secure. He pushed Roland with his foot and told him to get up. Mad Dog laughed as Roland struggled to his feet.

"You promise my son is going to be safe, right?" Roland pleaded.

Mad Dog picked up the knife and watched Roland's eyes as they opened very wide. He quickly thrust the knife into Roland's left shoulder, then threw his head back in wild, sick laughter as Roland screamed in agony.

"Will you shut up and take the pain like a man? That fucking Hayward bitch had bigger balls than you."

Roland started crying because all his hopes of living just went out the window.

Mad Dog spoke in a cocky voice, and said, "If you think this is bad, just wait until you find out what we're going to do." He picked up the duct tape, put the gun in his belt, grabbed Roland's hands and led him to the garage with the knife pressed against the back of his neck. "Oh, by the way," he said in his most sincere voice, "I promise I won't hurt your kid—if you do what I ask, understood?"

Roland let out an inner sigh of relief and nodded his head.

"Alright then, it's time to pay the fiddler." Mad Dog reached around Roland and opened the door to the garage. He led Roland to the driver's side of his Mustang and helped him in the car. Mad Dog then went to the Cadillac and pulled out a large duffel bag from underneath it. He pulled out a flashlight, turned it on, then turned it off. He went to the wall and turned the light on. Roland was watching him with terrified curiosity. Mad Dog then grabbed the duct tape and walked to the garage door. He unrolled the tape around the outer edge of the door to block the air from coming in or out. He used a whole roll, taping the holes securely. He then pulled another roll from the bag and taped the door frame that led to the backyard.

Mad Dog then reached into the bag and pulled out a garden hose. He opened the passenger door and rolled down the window an inch. He stuck one end of the hose through it and led the nozzle to the back seat, then duct-taped the opening in the window.

Roland's eyes were wide with panic and he bent his head forward onto the horn. Mad Dog jumped from surprise, but quickly threw his body into the car, pulled Roland's head back and whispered in his ear, "Check it out, dipshit. This is really happening and you're really going to die." Roland had his eyes closed and he was breathing so hard he felt as if he was going to pass out.

"You can make it easy on yourself, or you can make it hard. You can be the only one who dies, or we can make it a family event. The choice is yours. You got it?"

Roland started crying and nodded his head.

Mad Dog reached into Roland's pocket and grabbed the keys to the car. "Don't be getting a boner on me now," Mad Dog said when he had his hand in Roland's pants pocket, "I'm only getting your car keys." He put the key in the ignition, then went to the bag that was between the two cars. He pulled out a tape recorder and a pad of paper. He put the tape recorder on the dashboard and took a seat on the passenger side. "Alright. This is the big moment. Open your eyes and look at me."

Roland slowly opened his eyes, tried his best to stop crying and turned his head toward Mad Dog. He was looking at the ground.

"Close enough," Mad Dog said. "I'm going to turn this recorder on and you're going to read from this paper. Now, just so you're not surprised, it says you're killing yourself, and so on. Please, spare me the theatrics. Just be a man and read it, and I promise you I won't touch your kid. If, however, you disobey me, or God forbid, say my name, I will do to our kid twenty times worse than I'm doing to you. Understood?"

Roland started crying again, but he nodded his head yes.

Mad Dog patted him on the head. "Now, before I start the tape, I have to ask you a question. Do you want me to start the car?" Roland was whimpering and he looked at Mad Dog like he had just been asked a trick question. "Do you want me to start the car, Roland?" Mad Dog asked in an agitated voice.

Roland's eyes were scared but now he held a minute amount of hope. He shook his head no.

Mad Dog laughed. "Wrong answer, Roland." He grabbed the duct tape, tore a piece off and put it over Roland's mouth. He turned the keys back in the ignition and the radio came on. It was "Happy Together" by the Turtles. Mad Dog laughed and blew Roland a kiss. He turned up the volume on the radio, grabbed the knife and plunged in into Roland's right thigh. Roland jerked wildly and tried to scream while Mad Dog danced between the cars.

When Roland settled down, Mad Dog turned the radio down and asked, "Do you want me to start the car, Roland?" He nodded his head yes. Mad Dog tore the tape from his mouth.

"Now remember, read exactly from the paper. Understood?"

Roland squeaked out, "Yes."

Mad Dog pressed record on the tape recorder and the reels started spinning. He waited five seconds, then started the car. He then grabbed the other end of the hose and walked around to the back of the car and stuck it a couple feet into the tailpipe. He then went to his duffel bag and pulled out an oxygen tank with an airtight mask. He put the mask on his face and pulled the rubber strap over his head. It was a tight fit, but he got the mask secure without tearing the hood off his head. He turned the tank on and got in the passenger seat with the tank sitting on his lap. He looked over at Roland who was watching him. Roland was horrified.

Mad Dog smiled at him and shut the door. He held up the pad of paper for Roland to read. Roland looked at it for a few seconds, his eyes quickly scanning it, then he looked at Mad Dog with pleading eyes. Mad Dog grabbed the gun out of his belt and Roland quickly started reading. He was dripping blood from both shoulders and also his right thigh. His head, as well as his wounds were throbbing and he felt like he was going to pass out; with determination he wouldn't let himself. The only chance his son had to live was if he read the letter. He opened his mouth and spoke as best he could. His defeated voice said, "Goodbye, cruel world."

He could already feel the effect of the car fumes in his spinning head. He breathed in deeply. "My pain is so deep," he continued, "that I have decided to take my own life." His eyes started tearing both from the fumes and from the thought of never seeing his son again. Mad Dog sat in the passenger seat holding the pad of paper, looking at Roland through the mask. His eyes were alive with a maniac's pleasure and he was smiling.

"I know this cowardly act will deliver me to the lair of Satan, but I feel confident he will embrace me and comfort me." Roland's voice was shaky, and it was going in and out, but Mad Dog felt he was doing well. He was almost finished with the letter, and that was good because he wasn't going to last much longer. He felt as if he was floating, and his voice was echoing in his ears.

THE SUICIDE MURDERS

"I long for his flaming hand of fire to stroke my head and sooth me. I say goodbye to the madness of this world and hello to the mysterious unknown."

Mad Dog turned the tape off and sat with Roland while he breathed in the deadly fumes. He watched as Roland breathed in deeply and chuckled when his eyes closed and his head leaned against the window. Mad Dog turned up the radio and listened to the music for another fifteen minutes. Roland didn't move a muscle the whole time.

Chapter 42

Miller pulled to the curb across the street from the downtown station. He didn't pull into the underground parking because he was only going in for a second. He talked to Sharon and she informed him she had made no progress. He told her that he was going home to take a quick nap. He looked at his watch. "It's 12:05 p.m. now—I'll be back at 3:00 p.m. Call me at home if anything happens."

She gave him a crooked grin. "Do you want me to come with you?" she asked.

He leaned toward her and kissed her cheek. "Yes, but no. I need to get some rest before I fall down."

He left the lab and headed for his car. When he got in, he noticed something underneath his wiper. He sat for a good ten seconds staring at it. "No fucking way that's on my truck." He got out and looked at it. It was envelope with his name on it. He leaned in the car, opened the glove box and took out a pair of latex gloves. He put them on, grabbed the envelope, and went back into the station to the lab.

When Sharon saw Miller she said, "That was the fastest three hours of my life."

"Tell me about it." He held up the envelope.

"Was the convict contacted again?" she asked.

"No, I was. The cocky bastard put this on my truck."

Sharon looked surprised. "I thought you had surveillance on all suspected perps."

THE SUICIDE MURDERS

"So did I," Miller responded. "Well, let's see what we've got." He opened the envelope and it was the same style, done with the kid's labeler. Miller read:

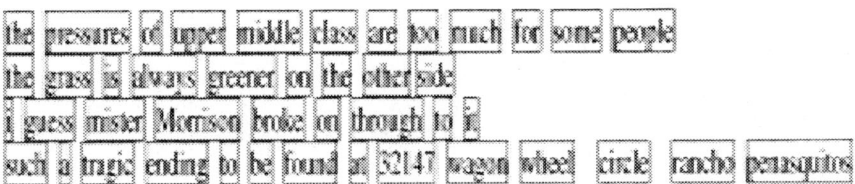

the pressures of upper middle class are too much for some people
the grass is always greener on the other side
i guess mister Morrison broke on through to it
such a tragic ending to be found at 13147 wagon wheel circle rancho penasquitos

"He's probably in love with himself," Miller said. "I got to get over to P.Q. See if you can get anything from this. He copied the address down and went to his office to call his surveillance teams. None of the teams reported anything suspicious, and nobody had gone anywhere near the station. He then called Turner and told him to meet him at the Penasquitos address.

Miller went to the house alone. He had told Turner to do the same. He wanted some time to check out the crime scene before the media got wind of it. He went to the front door and knocked. No one answered it. He knocked again, louder this time. Since he was going to most likely have to break in, he called out that he was a police officer. Still no one answered the door. He tried the doorknob, but it was locked. He walked around to the gate that separated the back yard from the front of the house. He reached over and unlatched the bolt.

Miller pushed the gate open a couple inches and called out, "Here, boy! Here, doggy!" but the backyard was empty. He left the gate open as he walked around to the back of the two-story house. On his way, he tried to open the door to the garage, but it was locked. He could smell exhaust fumes, but no car was running. At the back of the house he yelled, "Detective Miller, San Diego Police Department. Is anybody home?" There was still no answer as he tried the sliding glass window, which was locked. Miller then noticed the kitchen window above the sink was open, but blocked by a screen. He announced who he was again through the open window, then knocked the screen into the house with his fist. Miller hopped up and pulled himself halfway through the window when a pair of hands grabbed his legs. Miller instantly reached for his gun.

Turner said laughingly, "Hey, it's just me."

Miller let out a sigh of relief and pulled himself all the way through. When he got the sliding glass door opened, he gave Turner a look of amusement. He smiled and said, "Are you trying to give me a fucking heart attack?"

Turner chuckled. "Sorry, I just couldn't resist." He changed the subject. "Did you smell the fumes coming from the garage?"

Miller nodded his head yes. He made a head motion toward the garage. "I think I know where the fourth victim is."

As they walked closer to the garage, the smell of fumes became greater. Miller opened the door to the garage and the exhaust smoke billowed into the house. They both jumped back and the door shut.

"Holy shit!" Miller exclaimed.

"Well, there's no doubt about it. Whoever is in there is dead," Turner added.

Miller covered his mouth with his shirt and took a deep breath. He closed his eyes, opened the door, and ran his hand around the wall until he found the button to the garage door opener. He pressed it and heard the unit overhead struggle. The gears momentarily sounded like they weren't turning, then a peeling sound came from the garage door and it began to open. Miller closed the door and they went back through the house and out the front door, letting the garage air out.

When they approached the garage, fumes still permeated the air.

Turner pointed to the figure sitting in the Mustang. "There he is."

Miller shook is head. "Fucking suicide murders. When I catch this motherfucker, I'll show him what a suicide murder is. I'm going to hang him by his fucking nuts!"

"Should I call this in?" Turner asked.

"Yea, we might as well get this over with." He shook his head again and looked at Turner. "You realize, of course, the media is going to be all over our asses after what we said yesterday. We pretty much challenged the bastard to kill again."

Turner held up a finger to Miller, instructing him to wait a moment. He gave his assistant the information and address and told him to contact the Penasquitos Police Department. He hung up, then said to Miller, "Why do we have to let the media know this is part of the killings? No one but us knows this was a murder. It looks like a suicide to me."

"How are we going to explain us being the first ones on the crime scene?"

"We can say we got an anonymous tip that this might be another victim of the person who killed Hayword. Until we catch the killer, we can rule this a suicide."

Miller thought for a second as he saw the last of the smoky fumes float out. "That would certainly take the pressure off us." He walked to the passenger side of the Mustang and looked in the open door. He saw the victim, then looked at Turner. "I don't think our plan is going to work." Miller waved him over.

"Will you look at that shit," Turner said, disgusted. He saw the knife wounds and the blood. "He must not have gone quietly."

They walked out to the street and heard the approaching sirens.

Chapter 43

Mad Dog was in his dingy motel room watching TV. He was sitting on the bed with his back toward the headboard with two the thin pillows the motel had provided between his back and the headboard. He grabbed the telephone book that was on the lamp stand by the bed. It had a pile of speed on it with a playing card and a drinking straw that was cut in half. He pulled himself a line out of the pile and hastily snorted it up the straw and into his nose. There was no burning sensation that followed. He was way past that stage. Mad Dog was on his eighth day of being awake and he was doing a line every half hour.

On his way from Rancho Penasquitos to his National City motel room, he dumped the air tank and mask in a dumpster behind a grocery store. As long as it wasn't in his possession, it couldn't be tracked to him. He had pulled off a clean "breaking and entering" two days ago at a diving shop. He was very pleased with himself about the idea of asphyxia. The look on that guy's face when he got into the car with the oxygen tank was fucking priceless. It was well worth the price of admission.

He pulled himself another line and, like a magician, made the line disappear into his nose. He put the telephone book back on the night stand and lay down so the drug wouldn't drip out. He said, "I'm going to have to score some more shit tonight. No sleep until this is over." He laughed to himself. "Only one more person, Danny. One more person, then I'm coming for you."

Mad Dog got up, went to the TV and turned the volume up. He got in the shower and washed the drugs off his body. He could smell the chemicals coming out in his sweat. He turned the water off and heard from the TV what he'd been waiting for. He quickly wrapped the towel around him and sat on the bed in front of the set. There was a live broadcast from the house of the guy he had killed. He inwardly wondered if they had figured out how he got in and out of the house. There were no forced signs of entry, and everything was locked up when he left. He dumped the house key he had taken from the key ring in the same dumpster he had put the air tank in. He figured if they were lucky enough to find it—which was nearly impossible—then he would give them a lucky clue as to how he could monitor the death without suffocating himself. He didn't have a very high opinion of the police, and he knew they would never track this to him.

The TV was blaring and he turned it down a little as he watched the pretty reporter deliver the breaking story.

"I am at the scene of what is believed to be the fourth death in a series of grisly murders. The police have yet to make a statement, but we have been notified by an anonymous source that these killings are being called the "Suicide Murders.""

Mad Dog laughed while bouncing on the edge of the bed. He patted himself on the back. "I like that name, Mr. Anonymous. Yeah, it has a nice ring to it."

He then stopped talking so he could hear the news woman who was so beautifully delivering anonymous fame to him.

"We have been told his name was derived from a note by the killer which was given to an unnamed person who, in turn, gave it to Detective Jim Miller of the San Diego Police Department. This took place last Sunday, six days ago. According to our source, one person every two days will die, having committed suicide." The reporter half turned to show the house and the car in the garage. "This is the home of the latest victim, Mr. Roland Perry. He was found by the aforementioned, Detective Miller. With him during the discovery was Homicide Detective Ron Turner. As you remember, yesterday these two men publicly warned of a possible connection between the late Mrs. Allison Hayword and two other victims. They also publicly challenged the killer, which resulted in dire consequences. In the garage behind me is the scene of the murder/suicide. Mr. Perry was found dead in his car, a black Ford Mustang. There was a hose that ran from the exhaust pipe into the car. Mr. Perry died of asphyxiation, running out of oxygen and choking to death on the deadly exhaust fumes of his car. It appears, however, that he was forced to get into and stay in his car while he slowly suffocated to death. Mr. Perry was found with his hands duct-taped behind his back, and he had been severely stabbed in both his left and right shoulders, as well as in his right thigh. It appears as if this was done with his own kitchen knife."

Mad Dog was on his back laughing hysterically. "This is fucking beautiful.

There is going to be so much panic and commotion, that when Danny's dead, the cops are going to say he was the one doing this. There's going to be so much pressure to pin this on somebody they'll wrap it up and pin it on sucker schizo Danny—a con on probation for murder, and they have proof he wanted to do himself in." He stood up and looked in the mirror over the TV. "Mad Dog, you are a fucking genius." He leaned forward and kissed his reflection in the mirror.

The reporter continued. "Even though we don't have a formal statement at this time, the police urge everybody to stay on guard."

Chapter 44

Miller and Turner had successfully gotten away from the crime scene without answering any questions. They stormed through the center of screaming reporters and flashing cameras without saying a word. The anonymous tip had certainly screwed their game plan.

After listening to the tape in Sharon's lab, Turner went back to wrap up the crime scene. He and Miller had decided they would hold a press conference on Saturday to answer all the questions. There was no hiding anything anymore, not with the media being tipped off. At least their theory about Allison Hayword appeared correct. It most definitely looked as if she was killed for publicity.

Miller had called the surveillance teams and pulled them. He could better utilize the manpower elsewhere. He did keep watch on Danny though—mostly because he had no other options. Danny tied into all this somehow, Miller knew, but he had no idea to what extent. It was still very possible Danny was teaming up with someone. He was not ruling out the possibility of Taylor committing suicide to pull off the perfect crime, either. In fact, he wasn't ruling out anything.

There was still one accomplice Danny could be working with that made perfect sense, and that was Bucky Webber. Miller had the teams that were on surveillance now looking for Webber. He had them checking shelters, housing projects, cheap apartments, hotels and motels. They were running his name through the computers and his picture by the management and staff. If Bucky Weber was staying in San Diego, Miller was determined to find him.

Mad Dog had his belongings packed and had just snorted the last of the speed. He wiped the telephone book down with a wet towel to get the residue off. Even though he checked the motel room out under a false name, with a fake ID, the less attention drawn to him, the better.

Now that he had gotten the media going, and the city most likely in an uproar, it was time to get out of town. He figured since it was Friday night and he was out of dope, he would go to Tijuana for the weekend. He already knew the next person he was going to kill. He would party tonight and tomorrow and come back Sunday morning for victim number five. He had a pocketful of money from the Hayword woman. The guy today also had over two hundred dollars that he contributed to the drugs, alcohol and hooker fund. Mad Dog left the key in the room and headed for the border.

Miller finished a cup of coffee and let out a big yawn. He looked at his watch and saw it was 7:00 p.m. He decided to go home for the night. He was exhausted, and if he wanted to be worth a damn at all tomorrow, he needed some sleep. He and Turner were going to talk to the press at 9:00 a.m. He had teams working all night scouting the city with the name and picture of Bucky Webber. He also had his team listening in on Danny. Miller turned off the light in his office and headed for home.

Chapter 45

At 8:00 p.m. Mad Dog was walking on the bridge over the Tijuana River. He looked over the bridge and laughed. The water was about a foot wide and two inches deep. There were shopping carts, diapers, torn clothing and such at the bottom. It smelled like raw sewage, but then again, so did most of Tijuana. He took a deep breath and continued walking.

There was a mixture of people going toward Revolucion Avenue, but not many people coming back to the U.S. The traffic usually didn't start heading home until at least midnight. Mad Dog walked among college students, high school kids, off-duty military personnel, and tourists. He ignored the vendors selling their useless items and the mothers and children begging for change or selling Chiclets. As soon as you gave one of them a quarter or dime, you were an unwelcome target for the rest.

He was still flying high from the line of speed he had done at the motel, so he decided to get a couple of beers before he scored some dope. He was jittery and his hands were shaking. He snorted over a half gram, but he wanted to be sure he was good and high for the drive and walk in Tijuana.

He thought about taking a taxi from the border, but those pieces of shit reeked like exhaust, and it had taken him three showers to get the smell from earlier today off him.

Mad Dog made a left at the Arch, which looked like a miniature version of the St. Louis arch. He walked a little further and reached the street he was looking for. He made a right and was walking down Revolucion Avenue, the most popular street in Tijuana. He actually had been up too long to be partying in this area. He should actually be on Cohuela Avenue, but he wanted to try his hand with the schoolgirls first before he lowered his standards and went to the even dingier part of town.

He hadn't walked very far when he came to a club called Rio Rita. It was one of his favorites that he patronized when he was in town, and he wanted a young white girl. There were three levels and they were all underground. The funny thing was, most people only knew about the first level. People would walk in and see the bar crowded, then they would leave without walking to the back wall where a single staircase led to the second level. The same was with the second level to the third.

The thing was, the longer the people drank on the first level, the more chance they had of finding the second level. The longer they drank on the second, the better chance they had of finding the third. Mad Dog always went right to the third level because that is where all the really drunk people were. It just so happened to be where the dance floor was, and even though he didn't dance, he liked watching the eighteen-year-old sweethearts grinding with the drunken boys who were doing everything but fucking them, which, surprising to some people, happens in a lot of the clubs in T.J.; not in this one though. This club actually had ground rules, which was why the cleaner women come here.

Mad Dog grabbed an open four-man table, three stories under Mexican soil. He ordered a bucket of beer, which consisted of ten Coronitas. A Coronita is a miniature Corona and has six ounces of beer instead of twelve. If you looked like you would pay whatever it cost, they would charge you ten dollars. If you looked like you knew how the game worked, like Mad Dog did, they charged five dollars. He drank two of the beers down like they were water. He started on the third and finally felt the jitters going away.

The dance floor was empty, as was pretty much the whole bottom floor. He forgot that the bottom floor didn't really get going until after midnight. He finished his beer and carried the bucket to the second floor. Having been up for so long was making him paranoid. He felt like everyone was looking at him. He finished three more beers and felt much better. He was loosening up and felt like he was fitting in. By the time he finished the last beer out of the ten, he was feeling good. He ordered another bucket.

Mad Dog was sitting at the bar and was putting the miniature beers away with three swallows each. Besides the fact that his eyes were glossy and sunken, and he was sweating profusely, he fit in well. He had on a pair of Levis with a Harley Davidson tee shirt. His black tennis shoes were well-worn, but so were most of the other people's.

THE SUICIDE MURDERS

By the time Mad Dog finished the last beer of the second bucket, it was 11:00 p.m. He was buzzed, and all of a sudden very tired. He needed to score.

He walked down Revolucion Avenue for about a quarter of a mile and made a left on Cohuela Avenue. He was now in the part of Tijuana where he had to be careful. Unlike Revolucion Avenue, not many white people came to Cohuela Avenue. The ratio of Hispanics to whites was at least a hundred to one. Mad Dog actually fit in and felt better over here. Prostitutes lined the streets, and drugs were easily found.

A couple years back, Mad Dog had hooked up with a guy that always did square deals. He never got ripped off or got bunk dope, which is rare in Tijuana, since you pretty much play by their rules since you are on their turf. Mad Dog was a good customer. He always bought an ounce or more, and he came back frequently—when he wasn't in prison.

He went to a motel called La Tropical and got a room for two nights for fifty dollars. It was a six story building that had an attached strip club. If you liked the dancer, you gave her forty bucks and took her up to your room for sex. The dancers were a lot cleaner than the hookers who walked the streets.

Mad Dog went to his room and called room number 24. His drug dealer had stayed in that room for the last three years.

The man picked up the phone and said, "Bueno."

"Enrique, it's Mad Dog."

Enrique's voice was excited. "Mad Dog, my friend. You are calling from one of the rooms here?"

"I'm on the fifth floor in room 51."

"What do you want tonight, my friend?"

"I'll take an ounce of rocket fuel."

"Okay, very good. I got some very good shit. Meet me in the bar in an hour."

"Alright. I'll be in a booth near the dance floor."

Enrique laughed. "Pick out a pretty one, my friend."

"I'll see you in an hour." Mad Dog hung up the phone and headed for the strip club.

Mad Dog got a four-man booth right at the edge of the dance floor and no sooner did he sit down than a waiter came over and took his order. All the workers in these clubs were young, bilingual Mexicans. They ranged anywhere from twenty to thirty. The dancers mostly knew a minimal amount of English and were usually eighteen to twenty-five years old. Some clubs had girls that were as young as fourteen. The streets had girls as young as twelve and as old as fifty.

Mad Dog ordered a Dos Equis. The waiter came back with two. It's common knowledge that the strip clubs in Mexico bring you two drinks for every one you order. Why? No one actually knows, but that's the way it is. Most likely it's to get you drunk so you buy a lap dance, or take a girl up to a room for sex. He gave the waiter six dollars, five for the beer and one for him. As long as he kept tipping him that dollar, the beers would never have a chance to get empty. They will continue serving you until you pass out—then they take your money and carry you out to the sidewalk.

Mad Dog took a long drink and sat back to watch the dancer. She was an attractive Hispanic girl that looked to be about twenty.

The dance floor was about fifteen by fifteen feet with a pole in the middle. There was some old disco song playing that Mad Dog didn't recognize. The lights were out except for a strobe-light that was flashing. There was also a fog machine blowing onto the dance floor. Mad Dog laughed at the girl spinning on the pole. He had been up too long for his mind to accept the girl being in one spot when the light went out, then being in another spot when the light came back on. He felt like he was in some erotic nightmare. He reached for his beer and watched in amazement as his arm appeared to grow, getting closer and closer to the beer until his fingers wrapped around it. He closed his eyes and drank the entire beer down. He kept his eyes closed until the song was over. When he opened them, the lights were on and the girl was bending down on the stage looking at him. Mad Dog jumped, then laughed. The girl smiled. He reached in his pocket and gave her two dollars.

She gave his a kiss on the cheek and said, "I come back. You buy me a drink?"

He nodded his head and said, "Why the fuck not?" She smiled and walked to the back room to get dressed. Mad Dog knew better than to buy these girls a drink. It was the number one racket the club had. It cost ten dollars for them to drink a 7-Up with you while they rubbed their tits against you and grabbed your cock, the whole time trying to get you to take them upstairs. If you were not careful, while they're touching you and kissing you, they try to slip your watch off, or reach in your pockets for money. Mad Dog was hip to those tricks, but he liked this girl, and as soon as he met up with Enrique he was going to show this girl what a real bone-job felt like.

He took a drink of his other beer and closed his eyes, thinking about how the girl was crouched in a position that reminded him of a catcher in a baseball game. Her arms were resting over her knees, which were spread apart, and he could see right into the pink inside of her pussy. He was getting hard thinking about it. He opened his eyes and saw her walking toward him. She had on a skimpy red dress that barely covered her tits and ass. He picked up his beer and drank it down as she sat down next to him. The bartender was behind her.

"Another beer for you?" he asked.

Mad Dog nodded his head and said, "And whatever she wants." The waiter smiled and left without the girl saying a word. *Here comes the ten dollar 7-Up*, Mad Dog thought to himself.

The girl didn't waste any time. She put her hand right on his crotch and smiled when she saw he was already hard.

"Did you like my dancing?" she asked as she rubbed her hand up and down the length of his penis. Mad Dog didn't have underwear on, so he had grown to full length down the side of his left leg.

He laughed as she was stroking him through his jeans. "Yes, and I like you."

The waiter came back and she pulled her hand away. *What a stupid thing to say*, he thought.

The waiter set down two more beers and a shot glass with a liquid in it that was carbonated. "Fifteen dollars," he said.

Mad Dog did a dangerous thing by pulling out his wad of cash in front of them, but he wanted to have a little fun. If they thought he was able to be scammed by the oldest trick in the book, he wanted to see just how far they would go. He flipped through the money and gave him eighteen dollars. He had a hard time holding back his laughter when they saw all the cash he had. The waiter's eyes almost fell out, and the girl got a huge smile and her hand went right back to rubbing his penis.

"If you need anything," the waiter said excitedly, "let me know; pot, speed, cocaine—I can get anything you want."

"Maybe later," Mad Dog said. The waiter nodded his head happily and went to another customer.

Mad Dog put the money deep into his pocket and away from the girl's roaming hands.

"You take me upstairs?" she asked.

He moved her hand off him and onto her lap. He had her hooked now. "Let's finish our drinks first." Mad Dog picked up one of the two bottles and drank the whole thing down. He was getting way too tired and starting to feel drunk. The girl sipped her 7-Up and made a face like it was strong. Mad Dog laughed. He then turned the tables on her and put his hand between her legs. She smiled and lifted the dress that was barely covering her. She had no panties on.

Just then the lights went out, the music started, the fog floated across the cane floor, and the strobe light came on. Mad Dog looked at the girl and a smile was slowly pulsing wider and wider on her face. She looked down between her legs, and he followed with his eyes. She pulled his hand up to her pussy and he felt how warm it was. She took his middle finger and rubbed it slowly and softly, up and down her lips until he felt her getting wet. His finger slid into her as she continued moved it up and down. Gradually she was slipping his finger deeper inside of her. Mad Dog was rock hard as he watched her guiding his finger deeper and deeper. The strobe light was flashing and he looked up at her face. She had her head back against the booth and her eyes were closed. Her mouth was slightly open and he saw her tongue running along the edges of her lips.

Mad Dog started feeling lightheaded. He closed his eyes for a second to regain composure. When he opened them, he looked at the dancer. She had her legs on either side of the pole and was pulling herself along the ground toward it, then away from it. She kept doing this over and over while her back was arched and her head was tilted back. The fog was swirling, the lights were flashing and the music was blaring. The song was by the Red Hot Chili Peppers. It was called, "Breaking the Girl." The dancer now got on her knees.

Mad Dog looked down at his hand between the girl's legs and saw that she had his index finger in her also. He looked up at her through the flashing light and saw her head rocking back and forth. She was biting her lower lip. He turned his head back toward the dancer on the stage. Everything seemed to be moving in slow motion. He heard the words from the song as the dancer crawled over to him and shook her breasts in front of his face...

> "Twisting and turning, you're feeling the burning,
> you're breaking the girl. She meant you no harm.
> Think you're so clever, but now you must sever,
> you're breaking the girl. She meant you no harm."

He looked down between the girl's legs and she was squeezing her legs open and closed, while rubbing the tips of his fingers vigorously over her clitoris. His forehead was covered in sweat and he was about to stand up when a pair of hands grabbed his shoulders from behind.

"I see the ladies like you, my friend!" Enrique shouted.

Mad Dog looked over his shoulder as the girl jumped and let go of his hand while pulling her skirt down.

"We need to take care of this now," Enrique said. He then spoke to the girl next to Mad Dog. "He'll be right back. I just need to borrow him for half an hour."

THE SUICIDE MURDERS

The girl looked at Mad Dog and he motioned for her to get out of the way.
"You coming back?" she asked as she got up.
Mad Dog looked at Enrique, then at her. "Oh yeah, I'll be back for you!"
The girl smiled and watched them walk away.

When the deal was done, Enrique left Mad Dog's room and told him he looked forward to seeing him next time. Mad Dog started to draw himself a line from the pile he had dumped from the ounce, but changed his mind and decided to lie down for a few minutes. He locked the deadbolt on the door, an old habit he had whenever he had a bunch of dope and not going to be in a defensive position. His head was still spinning from that fucking strobe light. He started laughing as he lay down and closed his eyes.

"What a fucking scene," he said. "That girl is definitely fucking hot." Two seconds later Mad Dog was asleep.

Chapter 46

"I still got teams continuing the search for Webber," Miller was saying. He and Turner were in his office going over the game plan before they talked to the press. "There is a motel in National City," Miller continued, "that has the manager swearing he had a customer matching the picture of Webber. The name in the computer for that room, however, was Donald Ryan. When the officers knocked on the door at 3:00 a.m., nobody answered. The manager let them in and the room was empty. The key had been left in the room."

"Did they pull prints?" Turner asked.

"Yeah, they're running them now to try to find a match, but you know how many prints are in a motel room," Miller said.

"I know." The men sat silent for a moment. It was 8:50 a.m. Saturday morning. "If the prints do come back as a match for Webber, what are you going to do?" Turner asked.

Miller scratched his head, "Not much, but at least we'll know an alias he's running under."

"Why did your guys knock on the motel door anyway?" Turner asked as an afterthought. "Webber can be arrested only for his outstanding warrant. Shouldn't they have staked the motel room out and followed him to see if they could catch him in the act? We don't have any DNA to link him to the murders, and unless he confessed to them, there's no way he can be charged for them."

Miller was nodding his head. "I had a long talk with those officers, believe me. I contacted all remaining teams and told them that we wanted Webber under surveillance only. The only way he is to be arrested is if he is perpetrating a crime."

Turner looked at his watch and saw it was 8:55 a.m. "Did you get to talk with the warden about Webber?"

"Yeah, and he talked to the psychiatrist for me. Bucky was never on suicide watch, but he takes medication to keep himself under control. Without it, he is violent beyond comprehension."

"Does he have a court order to take it?" Turner asked.

"Yep. That may be the reason he didn't report to his PO." Miller looked at his watch. "Shit, it's time to throw ourselves to the wolves."

Miller and Turner walked out the front door of the downtown station and Miller got a feeling of déjà vu. The crowd was strangely quiet, which was good and bad. It was good because the press was going to let them talk without interruption. It was bad because they wanted assurance. They wanted answers about what was going on to stop this maniac.

Miller stepped up to the podium and once again saw the red lights in the front of the cameras, which were most likely doing live feeds. For better or worse, they were now going to know the details of this case.

"Good morning everyone. There have been a lot of rumors and speculation circulating since I spoke to you on Thursday, and they have compounded greatly since the tragic death yesterday of Rancho Penasquitos resident, Robert Perry. Let me start by saying that both myself and Detective Turner, as well as every officer on the San Diego police force, are doing everything in our power to track down and catch the perpetrator of these horrifying crimes.

"What we are dealing with is a man who has no respect for human life. He has no respect for the law. When you add these two together, it makes for a very dangerous situation. Please realize I'm not speaking to you today to scare you, even though what I'm about to tell you is indeed scary. Without going into extreme detail, I'm going to inform you as to what is really happening in our city. Everyone has a right to know. Everyone has a right to be informed." Miller was standing straight and speaking with confidence. He was standing before the crowd, the TV cameras, and the flashing bulbs. He was standing before the countless microphones and he was speaking from the heart.

"There is a heartless, merciless, cold-blooded killer on the loose in San Diego who is making innocent men and women commit suicide. It is, in fact, true I have received a letter from the killer. He has self-titled the killings…he has a strange fascination with suicide. Of the four victims, it is confirmed that three of them resisted him in one way or the other and they were, in turn, tortured. They were tortured and their loved ones were threatened until the victims took their own lives.

"I want everyone to be on guard and to keep watch in your neighborhood. People with children and grandchildren should be especially careful, since this seems to be a form of leverage he likes to use in order to make people do what he wants. If you see anything or anyone suspicious, please do not try to apprehend them yourselves. Call the police and we will follow up on all calls. Remember everyone, I am not up here to scare you, but merely to inform you. Please know we are working twenty-four hours a day to bring this man to justice.

"At this time I would like for you to direct any questions you may have toward homicide Detective Ron Turner."

Miller stepped aside while Turner stood before the podium. Questions were being shouted from every spot in the crowd. Turner was the one to answer the questions because this was his investigation. He had full jurisdiction in San Diego when someone was murdered. Miller had often worked with him over the years, and they made a good team.

Turner pointed to a reporter for the first question.

Chapter 47

When Detective Turner walked away from the podium and he and Detective Miller disappeared into the police station, Danny turned off his TV. Turner had been evasive in his answers, which was expected. They couldn't give too much information away. Danny was actually surprised at how much they did say though. *They must not be close to catching him at all*, he said to himself. *Tomorrow is another murder and the last one is Tuesday. These suicide murders are going to go unsolved.* He thought about the letters the killer sent him and spoke aloud, "Chase your tails, Keystone Cops, the suicide murders are unsolvable."

Miller and Turner were discussing their plan of action. They were in Miller's office. Sharon just left, having informed them she had struck out with the latest note and audio tape.

"I've been thinking, Jim," Turner said.

"Shit! Do you think the crews are still outside because this is headline news?" Miller laughed.

Turner smiled and said, "That's funny. I'm surprised you can think of something funny right now." Turner's smile turned into a wicked grin. "I thought all your attention was still on Sharon's ass."

Miller's mouth fell open, and he stared at Turner, dumbfounded.

Turner nodded his head. "I knew it! Did you guys finally get together?"

"What do you mean?" Miller asked, trying to sound innocent.

"Come on Jim, there's chemistry between you two. I'm just surprised this hasn't happened sooner."

"Really?" Miller was truly surprised. Until the other day, he never thought he and Sharon would be an item. "Well, first of all, we didn't get together. We have had something spark between us lately though."

"What are you waiting for?"

"You don't think I'm too old for her?"

"Shit, she'll probably teach you a thing or two," Turner said, smiling.

"Right now I've got to concentrate on this case."

Turner threw his hands up in mock surrender. "Okay, whatever you say. Now, getting back to my thought. I was thinking we should let Taylor know he's been targeted as the sixth victim. If this kid is innocent, he needs to know."

Miller thought for a quick moment. "You're right. I'll let him know we got a tail on him again, too. Whether he does or doesn't have anything to do with what's going on, Tuesday will be a very interesting day. For right now, I'll keep my team listening in on him and keep the two-man surveillance. Monday I'll have him crawling with undercover cops. Tuesday I'll have him safer than the president."

The phone on his desk rang, and he answered it on the first ring. "Miller, here." He listened for a moment, and said, "Interesting. I'm actually going over there right now. I'll check in with you when I get there." He hung up and looked at Taylor. "That was my team. I guess Danny watched us on a live broadcast. When it was over, they heard him talking to himself. He said the suicide murders were going to go unsolved. He also said, "Chase your tails, Keystone Cops, the suicide murders are unsolvable."

Turner's eyebrows went up, and his eyes widened with surprise. "That's just what one of the first notes said, isn't it?" Turner asked.

"Exactly," Miller replied.

Chapter 48

Miller and Turner pulled up to Danny's apartment in Miller's 4-Runner. They had discussed different ideas of what to do on the drive over. They were going to question Danny about Bucky Webber, but decided against it. If he was teaming up with him, that would screw everything up. They also contemplated not telling Danny about being the sixth victim. If he was partnering with Webber, and he was going to commit suicide as the sixth victim to pull off the perfect crime, letting him know he was under surveillance again might cause him to change his game plan. In the end, they decided to tell Danny he was the sixth victim. If he was innocent, he needed to know. Starting today, they were not only going to tail him, they were going to put two undercover cops with him. If he was planning on committing suicide, he was in for a surprise. They were also going to call Danny's boss and tell him Danny needed Monday and Tuesday off. After that, they didn't know what they were going to do. But for now, this was the plan.

They checked in with the team in the van and found out nothing new, then went to Danny's apartment and knocked on the door.

Danny opened the door and let out an exaggerated sigh when he saw the detectives. "Are you here for another drug test?" he asked sarcastically.

The two detectives looked at each other.

Danny spoke again. "I saw you guys on TV. You don't have any leads, do you? That's why you're harassing me, isn't it?" Danny asked.

"Danny, we have been contacted by the killer and you have been targeted as the sixth victim," Miller said.

Both he and Turner studied Danny's face closely. They wanted to pick up any and everything in his reaction. What they saw was sheer surprise.

"You're kidding, right?" Danny asked through a forced smile.

"No, we're not," Turner answered. "Can we come in, please?"

Danny was staring off into space, but he stepped aside so they could enter. He shut the door and locked it. He pointed to the couch. "Please, sit down."

They sat down, and Danny remained standing.

"We know this must be a shock to you," Miller said. "We want you to know we've started the surveillance on you again. There is a team outside right now, but we don't want you to know they're there. Also, we've got two officers on the way over here right now who are going to be with you twenty-four hours a day until this is over. Do you understand?"

Danny nodded his head yes. He was still absorbing what was happening.

Miller continued. "Officers Williams and Frost will watch over you in the apartment. When you leave, Frost will accompany you. She will pretend to be your girlfriend."

"She?" Danny asked.

"Yes, Officer Frost is a woman. We are going to notify your boss that you will miss work on Monday and Tuesday. After that, we don't know. Most likely we will have the killer in custody by then. We are putting you with a female officer so we don't scare him away. We want you out and about, and it will look more natural with a woman."

Danny finally put two and two together. "You're going to use me as bait!"

"Frost will be armed," Turner said, "as well as Williams and the surveillance team in the car. You will be perfectly safe."

There was a knock at the door. "That's going to be them now," Miller whispered, "but we'll hide in the bathroom just in case."

Danny unlocked the door and opened it slowly. It was a man and a woman.

"Danny Taylor?" the man asked. Danny nodded his head. The man looked over Danny's shoulder and whispered, "Detective Miller sent us over. Is it alright to come in?"

"Yes, come on in," he said. They walked inside with a duffel bag each. "It's alright!" Danny yelled toward the bathroom. Miller and Turner came out.

"Danny," Miller said, "this is Officer Darren Williams and Officer Karen Frost."

Williams was six feet tall and weighed one hundred ninety pounds. He had brown hair and blue eyes. Frost was an attractive woman and was five foot seven inches tall and weighed one hundred forty pounds. She had long, black hair, which she wore in a ponytail and green eyes. Williams was about thirty-four while Frost was thirty.

The two officers shook hands with Danny. Danny couldn't help but think how much he lucked out with Frost. She was definitely pretty, and someone he would consider dating if he were only viewed better by the eyes of society. Danny all of a sudden felt uncomfortable with how small his apartment was. "I don't know how we're all going to live in this tiny place for the next couple days."

"This will be fine," Karen said.

"Yeah," Williams agreed, "as long as we have TV, we're all set."

"Okay, Danny," Miller said, "whenever you leave this apartment, you will go with Frost. From right now until I say otherwise, you and her are a couple. You will act like a couple, not only when you leave the apartment, but also while you're in the apartment. We do this because we want you to look natural when you're with each other in public, which you are going to be. Karen has been given an allowance for the two of you. From now on you are to look like love in bloom. Officer Williams will stay out of your way. You are not to talk to him or acknowledge him in any way. At first you may feel uncomfortable pretending you two are a couple, but it will pass. Officer Frost was a method actor in college, so she'll make you feel at ease." Miller smiled at her. "Won't you, Karen?"

She walked over and gave him a kiss on the mouth.

"This isn't going to be so bad, is it, Taylor?" Miller asked.

Danny was blushing. "It's going to take some getting used to. Is all this necessary though?" Danny asked.

"Absolutely," Turner answered. "We need you to feel comfortable with each other, especially in public. If the killer suspects she's a cop, the whole operation is shot. Also, there's no talking about any of what's going on, even in the apartment."

"Alright then. That's about it," Miller said. "You two go out for dinner tonight. Go somewhere you'll have a lot of leftovers. Don't order Williams anything. Just bring him your scraps." Miller laughed and patted him on the back.

"I get no respect," Williams said in an imitation of Rodney Dangerfield.

"Call the surveillance team, Ron, and see if it's clear to go," Miller said. "Alright. First, Williams, good luck. Keep alert and be careful. We will have no more contact until it goes down. Understood?" They both nodded their heads yes.

Turner hung up the phone, gave a thumbs up, and they were gone.

Chapter 49

Danny and Karen were eating dinner at Round Table Pizza. Pizza, coincidentally, was Karen's favorite food, just as it was Danny's. He was having a great time with her. She was dressed in faded blue jeans, a casual blouse, and a Chargers hat with her hair pulled out the hole in the back. Danny was growing to think she was not only attractive, but beautiful. He had only been with her a few hours and he was falling for her. It has been over three years since he had been with a woman, and her touch was driving him crazy. Her kisses felt so real and he was kissing her in return as if they were. Even though this was going to end in a couple of days with his heart broken, he didn't care. He talked sweet to her, kissed her soft lips, held her hand and did everything else she would allow. He smelt her hair, rubbed her shoulders, told her jokes, nibbled on her ear, and so on. He was having such a good time, and it felt so real that he didn't want to go back to the apartment. He knew that as soon as they were alone she was going to slap the shit out of him for going too far.

Karen had to keep reminding herself she was on an assignment. Every now and then Danny was taking things a little too far, but she really didn't mind. He was smart, funny, good looking, tall and he had the prettiest blue eyes she had ever seen. She was a very good judge of character, and that was one of the reasons Miller had put her on this duty. Not only was she supposed to protect Danny, she was supposed to get a feel for his character, and unless he was the smoothest manipulator she's ever encountered, she couldn't see how he could be the killer. In fact, she knew he wasn't the killer. She also knew he had nothing to do with the killings. Karen felt bad for Danny. He was a man who had been wrongfully accused of many things, past and present. He was just a man who had a knack for being in the wrong place at the wrong time.

A couple times she had to excuse herself to the bathroom to regain her thoughts. It was so unlike her to feel this way about a man, let alone so quickly, let alone an assignment. She actually thought about taking herself off this assignment because she was second guessing her logic. She felt her judgment was being swayed by her emotions. Her instincts had always proven correct in the past though, so she decided to trust them now. If something ended up happening romantically between her and Danny, she didn't know how she was going to explain it to Miller. That was at least three days away though—a lifetime away. For now she was just going to let nature take its course while she protected Danny with her life.

While they were driving back to the apartment, Danny took a deep breath, reached over and held her hand. She held it back. "I had a great time with you tonight, Karen. I'm glad to have you as my bodyguard."

She laughed and playfully twisted his hand. "I'll guard your body any day, Danny."

He smiled at her. His head was whirling. This was all fake, right? He felt like a pathetic pervert, but he couldn't hold back. He asked her a question as a joke, even thought he was serious. "So, if I had a bedroom, would you be sleeping with me?"

Karen's heart was pounding. Her thoughts were racing. She decided to open her mouth and see what would come out. "I don't know." She looked at him and realized that was a lie. She squeezed his hand, looked out the window, and said, "Maybe."

Danny squeezed her hand back and left it at that.

Chapter 50

It was Sunday morning and Officer Williams was lying on Danny's couch resting. Danny and Karen were out having breakfast. He had been kept awake till the early hours of the morning while his partner and Danny watched movies. They had stopped by the video store on their way back from the pizza parlor. Williams had gotten a feeling about them last night; either they were acting really well, or there was something happening between the two of them. She clung to Danny during the scary parts of *Halloween*, a movie that Williams thinks Danny is obsessed with. He seemed to know every line. She also snuggled with him during the romantic comedy, *Cousins*. It wasn't his place to judge though. All he cared about right now was that they brought him some food. Danny didn't have any food in the place.

"What do you think he'll want?" Danny asked Karen. They were in Vons Food Store doing some shopping for Williams. They had just eaten breakfast at the IHOP.

"I don't know. What do guys eat?"

"Well, I know what I like, but I doubt many people have a disregard for eating healthy as I do."

"I don't know. I love junk food," she said.

"Really? Do you like pizza for breakfast?" he asked.

"It's the best!" Karen answered enthusiastically.

They walked down the frozen food aisle holding hands. Karen was finding him sensitive and caring. He was also polite and sweet.

"I agree," Danny said. "Let's just hope Williams feels the same way." He opened up one of the freezer doors and grabbed some frozen pizzas. He put them into the hand-held basket. He held her hand again and they walked to the chip aisle. Karen was turning out to be better by the minute. They had so much in common, and he truly felt she liked him.

She stopped in the middle of the aisle, looked Danny right in the eye and asked, "Is it just me, or do you also have an incredible desire to put our lips together?" It was a line from *Cousins*. He set the basket down, put his hands on her cheeks, pulled her gently to him and softly kissed her mouth. The whole world disappeared. He wanted so badly to tell her how he felt about her, but he couldn't do it here. He would take her to a nice quiet restaurant tonight and tell her then. He was positive he felt something in her kisses. If he was wrong, then tonight he would look like an idiot.

If he was right, then tonight would bring reason—a reason to stay sober. Ever since last Saturday, when this nightmare began, he wanted a drink more than anything. Not now, however. Now he wanted only to be with Karen. He wanted to see her smile, to hear her laughter, to watch the way her hips swayed when she walked, to listen to what she had to say. He wanted to make love to her. He wanted to make her happy. Tonight could be a new start for him. Tonight was his destiny.

Chapter 51

Mad Dog was walking naked on the beach in Playas with the stripper from La Tropical. She was naked also, but she was wearing a scarf over her nose and mouth.

She grabbed his arm and stopped him. She held her index finger out with her thumb up like it was a gun, and she pointed it at him. "I'm sorry I have to do this," she said, "but you never came back for me the other night."

Mad Dog laughed and asked, "What the fuck are you talking about?"

She looked at him with a sad expression. "If I don't make any money for the club, do you know where I'll have to work?"

Mad Dog realized she was talking in perfect English. He looked at her with a puzzled stare. "No, I don't. Where will you have to work?"

"Housekeeping," she said, now with a Spanish accent. "Housekeeping. Housekeeping."

Mad Dog was looking at her scarf. Every time she said that word, it billowed away from her face, but her voice was muffled. She then bent her thumb forward toward her index finger. She did this over and over like she was firing a gun, and every time she did, it sounded like someone knocking on wood. Mad Dog closed his eyes and she started shouting. "Housekeeping! Housekeeping!" An anger was building in him that he couldn't control. He opened his eyes, ready to strangle her, when he realized he was in his motel room. He heard a knock on the door and a Hispanic woman's voice say, "Housekeeping!"

"Alright!" Mad Dog screamed. He got up and walked to the door while trying to gather his thoughts. Did he fall asleep last night and not go back to the strip club? He looked at his watch and saw that it was 11:00 a.m. He opened the door just far enough to tell the annoying bitch he didn't need any fucking maid service, but not enough for her to see the dope on the table. "No housekeeping for me," he said, then shut the door. She knocked again and he kept the door closed but said, "I don't need housekeeping. Come back tomorrow."

The maid said, "You need to check out or pay more money."

He opened the door and gave her an evil look. "I paid money for two nights, Okay? I paid for Friday and Saturday."

He was about to shut the door when she said, "Si. Today is Sunday."

A million thoughts went through his head at once. "Today is Sunday?" he asked.

"Si. Do you want to pay more money?"

"No, I'll be out in twenty minutes." He shut the door. *How could this happen?* he said to himself as he sat down to the table to do a line. *Fuck, I crashed for a day and a half. I was supposed to be at the bookstore when it opened at 10:00 a.m.* He pulled a gigantic line from the pile, rolled up a dollar bill, and snorted it down in two tries. His nose instantly started running and he laid on the bed for a minute to keep the drugs up his nose. He then took what seemed like a three minute piss, followed by a two minute shower. He did another line, dumped the rest of the pile into the bag and tied it. He put the bag into his underwear, which were an extra tight pair of briefs he wore specifically to carry the drugs in.

He left the motel, grabbed a taxi and headed for the border.

The taxi dropped him off about a hundred yards from the border. He gave the driver six dollars and got out. He reached in his underwear and situated the drugs between his legs so there would be no extreme bulge in the front of his pants and started walking toward the customs building. When he walked through the open double doors, he let out a sigh of relief because the dogs weren't out. He was home free without the drug sniffing dogs patrolling the two lines. He got in the left line, the shorter of the two.

It was always hot in this building, but today had to be about ninety degrees. With the combination of the heat and the speed, Mad Dog was sweating uncontrollably. He reached the metal dividers that split the two lines into smaller lines leading to the border agents. He looked ahead and saw which agent wasn't paying much attention to the visas of the Mexicans and chose that line. If he wasn't vigorously studying the documents, then he wasn't going to pay the slightest bit of notice to a citizen of the United States.

Mad Dog reached the agent and said, "U.S.," without the agent asking him his citizenship. He was waved through, just like every other time he has ever walked across. The only real risk of bringing drugs into the U.S. was if you drove across. The agents in the booths were paranoid and would pull you over to "Secondary" for not making eye contact with them. Once you were in "Secondary," you were fucked.

Mad Dog crossed the bridge over the 5 Freeway and found his car in the parking lot. It cost eight dollars a day to park there, but your car was safe. He pulled up to the attendant and paid him sixteen dollars. He drove over the bridge and got on the 5 Freeway going north. He got the bag of speed out from between his legs and set it on the passenger seat while he accelerated to seventy. He wanted to drive faster, but he didn't want to get pulled over.

Mad Dog reached in his pocket and pulled out the little bit of money he had left. He chose the newest, most crisp bill and rolled it up. He tore a small hole in the bottom corner of the bag of dope where all the powder was and stuck the bill in it. Mad Dog looked around to make sure no cars were next to him. Nowadays it wasn't only the cops you had to worry about. Nowadays everybody had a cell phone and was more than happy to call 911 if they saw someone breaking the law—let alone snorting drugs while driving. He saw that the coast was clear and took a big sniff. His right eye instantly started watering. He set the bill and bag on the passenger seat and tilted his head back the best he could while he repeatedly sniffed to keep the escaping drugs in his head.

Mad Dog pulled off the next exit ramp and drove into the parking lot of a liquor store. He laid on his passenger seat until the speed had dropped down his throat. He went in the liquor store and bought a six-pack of Miller Genuine Draft, then went to the pay phone and made a call.

Chapter 52

Mad Dog was driving down Mira Mesa Boulevard at 1:00 p.m. and cursing at himself for wasting time and going the long way. He was driving toward the 15 Freeway, the one he should have connected with almost half an hour ago. He finished the last bit of his third beer and saw the Mira Mesa Mall on the left.

It was a dying little strip mall, and the fifth victim was an owner of a bookstore there. Mad Dog pulled into the parking lot and drove around back to the bowling alley. He found a spot by the front door. He opened the glove box and pushed the button to open the trunk. Then he grabbed the bag of speed and held it in the palm of his hand while he went to the trunk. He unzipped his backpack he had stocked with a roll of duct tape, gloves, socks, a roll of twine, a tape recorder, a cassette tape, a towel, and an envelope with the note. He tore off a piece of duct tape and put it over the hole in the bag. Mad Dog left the dope in the trunk and slung the backpack over his right shoulder. He shut the trunk and headed for the mall, only about forty feet away.

He walked through a break in the shops that served as a side entrance and exit to and from the strip mall. He made a right and headed down to the second to last store on the right. There were only four people walking around. He was beyond angry with himself for not getting there right at 10:00 a.m. when the owner opened for business. Now he ran the risk of potential witnesses. Mad Dog took a chance that no one would be in the store and walked right in. He had to hurry because he still had a very busy day ahead of him. He still had to abduct Danny before the police had him swarming with protection.

The store was empty, and as the bells that were attached to the door rang, Mad Dog heard an elderly man's voice call out, "I'll be right there."

Mad Dog turned the sign in the door from *Open* to *Closed*. He walked to the back and shut the door that separated the store from the office.

A gray-haired man of about seventy-five turned around from a stack of books and looked at Mad Dog, startled. "Young man, I said I would be right out."

"Shut the fuck up, old timer!" Mad Dog exclaimed. "You're staring into the face of the Grim Reaper."

The man looked at Mad Dog with a look that was both confused and frightened. "Are you planning on robbing me?" he asked. "I only have twenty dollars in the register."

Mad Dog whispered to him, "Didn't I tell you to shut the fuck up, old man?" He then stepped forward and punched him in the gut. The man collapsed onto the floor while Mad Dog laughed. He knelt down beside the old man and opened the backpack. He pulled out one of the socks and waited for the man to catch his breath, then he shoved it in his mouth and put a piece of duct tape over it. The old man's eyes were wide with fright and he was gagging.

"You better not throw up, Gramps," Mad Dog said. "If you do, you're going to drown in your own vomit." He then slapped him across his face and laughed. "I bet when you woke up this morning you were glad to be alive, to be able to live another day. Well, now look at you. Now I bet you wish you would have died in your sleep last night." Mad Dog grabbed him by his armpits and set him on his chair at his desk.

Mad Dog sat down Indian style in front of him and mocked the old man. When the man showed pleading eyes, Mad Dog gave pleading eyes in return. When he cried, Mad Dog pretended to cry. This went on for about five minutes until the man finally closed his eyes. Mad Dog stood and flicked his middle finger against the man's forehead. His eyes shot open in surprise. Mad Dog laughed. He then stroked the man's head with a sympathetic touch. "I know this is hard for you," Mad Dog said, "but now that it's started, the only way for it to finish is for you to die."

The man's eyes were wide with shock and he shook his head no. Mad Dog's eyes imitated his and he nodded his head yes.

"Here's what's going to happen," Mad Dog said. "We're going to climb the ladder to the roof, and if you give me any trouble, I'm going to kill everybody that's in those pictures." He made a motion of his head to the man's desk. The man looked at the pictures of his kids and grandkids and immediately got up and walked to the ladder. Mad Dog laughed and patted him on the head.

Mad Dog looked up and asked, "Can you open that hatch?" The man nodded his head yes. Mad Dog put the backpack on both shoulders and pointed toward the roof. The man started climbing and Mad Dog was behind him. The roof was only fifteen feet high, so the climb was short. The man unlatched the hatch, pushed it up and climbed through. Mad Dog held on to his ankle until he climbed through just in case the man had thoughts of doing something stupid.

Mad Dog looked at his watch. It was 1:30 p.m. He didn't have any time to fuck around with the tape recorder. He opened the backpack and grabbed the twine. He tied the man's hands behind his back. Mad Dog walked the man to the edge and peeked over.

There were too many people now to fuck around with trying to get him to jump. Also, if he didn't land just right, he might not die. Mad Dog led him along the strip mall's roof to where the side entrance was. He would just dump the old fucker on his head and run back to the bookstore and make a clean getaway. As they neared the edge, the man meekly struggled in protest. Mad Dog hit him in the stomach and, as the old man bent over in pain, Mad Dog launched him over the edge head first. He heard a loud thud, then sprinted toward the hatch of the bookstore. He closed it behind him and climbed down the ladder.

On his way out, he went to the register and opened it. "That lying fucker," Mad Dog said, "there's over a hundred dollars in here." He took the money, checked under the drawer, which was empty, and put the money in his pocket. He opened the door and walked casually out.

The side of the mall was empty. The middle of the mall where the old man had landed had the few people that were shopping gathering to see what the commotion was. Mad Dog went around the long way, around the department store that was at the end of the mall. He walked slowly and calmly until he reached his car. A small crowd was now gathered around the old man, but Mad Dog could see that he was dead. He backed out of the parking stall and looked to his right. He had a clear view of the man and saw that he was bent over backward. His back had broken during the fall. Mad Dog laughed to himself at how easy that was as he pulled out onto the street. He made a right at the light, then a right on Mira Mesa Boulevard. He reached down to the passenger side floorboard to grab one of the remaining beers when he was struck with the realization that in his haste to get the murder over with, he had forgotten to wear gloves.

He pulled into the mall parking lot again to figure out what to do. The sinking feeling in his stomach was overwhelming. All the careful planning and meticulous attention to detail had been for nothing. His anger rose to unmatched levels and he began to pound on his steering wheel. "Fuck! How could you be so fucking stupid?" he shouted. "Fuck! Fuck! Fu—" Mad Dog stopped suddenly. He looked in his backpack and started laughing. He reached in and pulled out the envelope with Detective Miller's name on it. He had forgotten to leave the note in the bookstore. "Fuck it!" he said. He got out of the car and walked to the far end of the mall where the bookstore was, carrying the envelope in his back pocket. He looked around the corner at the front of the store and saw no one was there. He quickly walked to the window, looked in and didn't see anyone. He placed the envelope on the floor, just inside the door, and ran to his car.

They were going to find his fingerprints on the door, envelope, cash register, ladder, hood, and office. There was nothing he could do about that now. Once he abducted Danny and took him to the safe house in Riverside, he would be safe until he killed him. He would have to go to Mexico after that. He would start moving drugs for Enrique and live there from then on.

Mad Dog drove to a liquor store, got some more beer, made a phone call, and headed to Danny's apartment.

Chapter 53

At 2:30 p.m., Detective Miller's phone rang. His gut clenched because he knew it was about the next victim. He had been waiting for the call ever since he arrived at the station at 7:00 a.m. He picked up the phone. "Miller here."

"Number five has turned up," Turner said.

Miller reached for his aspirin. "Where?"

"Do you know where the Mira Mesa Mall is?"

"Yeah, it's a little strip mall on Mira Mesa Boulevard, right?"

"Right. It's right next to Mira Mesa Lane. The owner of a bookstore over there took a nosedive off the roof of the building."

"Alright, I'm on my way. I'll meet you there," Miller said, and hung up the phone. He dumped four aspirin in his mouth and dry swallowed them.

When Miller pulled up to the mall, it was crawling with spectators and media. He parked his truck and walked toward the crowd. He flashed his ID to the officer at the police tape and the officer let him through. Turner spotted him and took him to the body.

"Nice," Miller said. "You don't see many people jump off a building with their hands tied and a gag in their mouth." He looked at Turner. "Where's the letter and audio or video tape?"

Turner pulled out the letter from his jacket pocket and said, "This is all that was found."

Miller looked surprised. "Really? Where was it found?"

"In the victim's bookstore down the way. Come on. I'll show you." Turner and Miller walked through the crowd and into the bookstore, which was also blocked off with crime scene tape. Turner pointed to the ground as they entered. "It was found right here by one of the Mira Mesa police. I guess another store owner recognized the victim as the owner of this bookstore and told the officer. He came to see if everything was alright and found the envelope. He put two and two together with what's been going on and notified his sergeant. His sergeant called me, then I called you."

Miller gave a chuckle. "Funny how that works, isn't it?" Miller looked around. The forensics crew was dusting everything for fingerprints. He nudged Turner and said, "I would hate to have their job on this one."

"No kidding," Turner said. "You know how many different fingerprints must be in a bookstore?"

"Have you read the letter yet?" Miller asked.

"I haven't had time," Turner replied.

They walked to the back room to find some privacy, but they were dusting for prints in there, too. They went back in the store and found a spot that was clear. Miller borrowed a pair of gloves from an officer and opened the envelope. He straightened the paper out and said, "Shit. Our fingerprints are going to be on the envelope."

Turner said, "I wouldn't worry too much about it. He hasn't left us any prints yet." He looked down at the letter, then jumped when Miller shouted, "Oh, shit! I can't believe I didn't tell you. We got a confirmation on Webber's prints from the motel room."

"When did you find out?" Turner asked.

Miller shook his head, disgusted with himself. "Yesterday."

Turner pretended like he was mad. "Wait a second, you found that out yesterday and you're just now telling me at a crime scene a whole day later?"

Miller felt bad. He didn't think Turner would react like this. "I'm sorry, Ron. It's just with everything that's been going on it slipped my mind."

Turner shook his head and said, "That's alright. My crew told me a match was made yesterday, also."

This time Miller shook his head, "And you didn't even call me?" The two men laughed and Miller raised the note. It was the same style, done with a kid's labeler. He read:

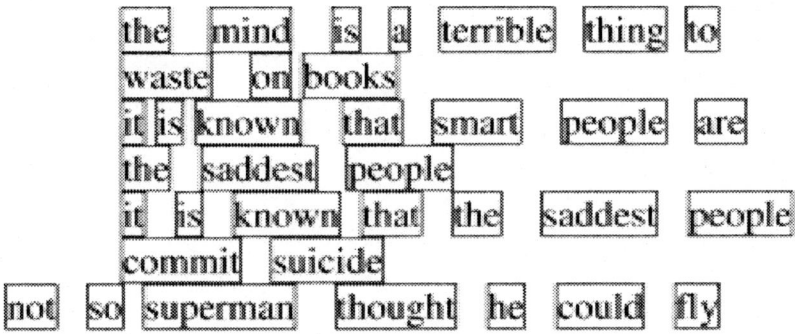

"I'm going to run this over to the lab and see if Sharon can get anything from it besides our prints," Miller said. "You don't need me here, do you?"

"No. Are you going to talk to the press?" Turner asked.

"No way," Miller said.

Chapter 54

Mad Dog parked around the corner from Danny's apartment. It was 2:30 p.m. He knew there was a surveillance crew watching Danny. There was also an Econoline van that had been parked in front of the apartment complex for a number of days. The cops most likely had Danny's place bugged. He had been right; they had him as a murder suspect. If he hadn't fucked up today, he would have been in the clear. Mad Dog shook that thought off and tried to figure out how he was going to get to Danny without getting busted.

"Are you ready, Karen?" Danny asked. He decided he couldn't wait until dinner to tell her how he felt. He was going to tell her during lunch that he was falling for her.

"Yeah. Where are we going?" she asked.

"I told you, it's a surprise." Danny opened the door and waited for her at the railing.

She laughed at him and grabbed her purse. "Alright, alright! I'm coming. What's gotten into you, Danny? You can't sit still."

Danny shut the door and held her hand as they walked to his truck. "I'm just hungry, that's all."

She shot him a furtive glance and smiled. Something was going on and she couldn't wait to find out what.

Danny pulled onto the street and the surveillance team followed. Mad Dog was right behind them.

"Who the hell is that fucking chick?" Mad Dog said out loud. He reached under his seat and pulled out his dagger and kissed it. "It's time to wake up, baby," he said to it. "We've got our work cut out for us today!"

Danny drove to a little romantic Italian restaurant located in Poway. He and Karen barely spoke to each other the entire drive there. Danny kept rehearsing what he was going to say to her in his mind.

Even though it was crazy, Karen kept hoping something special was going to happen between them.

When they pulled into the parking lot of the restaurant, the surveillance team parked in the far corner with a view of the door. Mad Dog pulled into the adjacent parking lot, which had a view of them and the door.

Danny and Karen were seated in a quiet corner. Karen looked around and thought it was quaint, and liked it very much. They placed their orders and sat in silence.

"Thank you for bringing me here, Danny," Karen finally said. "It's very nice."

He smiled nervously and said, "Thanks. I'm glad you like it. It's right around the corner from my mom's house. I thought we could go see her after we eat."

Karen gave him a big smile. "You want me to meet your mother? That's sweet."

Danny took a drink of water and cleared his throat. "Karen, this is hard for me to say, considering the circumstances." Danny's heart was pounding. "I've only known you a very short time, and I know I'm just an assignment for you, but I enjoy being with you."

Now Karen's heart was pounding.

He continued, "You make me happy and that's not easy to do, believe me. I'm trying to be logical about our relationship, but I can't. I know it's fake, but it feels too real." He looked down at the table, and said, "I just wanted you to know I think you're special, not to mention beautiful."

Karen reached out and touched Danny's hand, and he looked up into her eyes. To his surprise, they weren't cold and uncaring. They were filled with joy and compassion. "Do you know how happy I am that you told me that?"

Danny gave a nervous smile. "Really?" he asked in a whisper.

She nodded her head gracefully. "Yes. Danny, you are somebody special. You make me feel good about myself, and I love being with you." She let go of his hand and looked at him sternly. "But right now I have a job to do. Tuesday is only two days away and if I don't protect you, I can't be with you when this is over."

With a huge smile on his face, he reached over and grabbed her hand back.

"This is absolutely unbelievable. Do you know that? What a way to meet a woman; a lunatic gives me a note, people start dying, I'm then told I'm the sixth victim, they give me a fake girlfriend who's a beautiful cop, and we end up falling for each other. Absolutely amazing."

The waitress brought their meals and they were both all smiles. Karen looked down at the enormous plate of pasta in front of her and said, "Now that is amazing."

Mad Dog took a drink of his beer as Danny and the girl came out of the restaurant. He watched as they pulled onto the street, followed by their tail. Mad Dog waited for a few cars to get in front of him, then pulled out. Danny pulled into a residential area, then pulled into someone's driveway. The tail pulled to the curb two houses away. Mad Dog had no choice but to drive past. Danny was busy opening the truck door for the woman and didn't pay any attention to him.

This was his opportunity. If he waited, he would miss his chance. There was no way he was going to be able to abduct Danny from his apartment; not if it was bugged. He wouldn't be able to get him in public either with the fucking tail on him.

Mad Dog drove to the street behind the house Danny parked in front of. He reached under his seat and grabbed his sheath. He slid the dagger into it and got out of his car. He put the sheath in the back of his pants and pulled his shirt over it. He walked up to the house directly behind Danny's mother's house. He walked onto the porch and knocked on the door. He knew he would have to kill everybody inside, but it was the only way to get access to the other house without the cops seeing him. Nobody answered and Mad Dog knocked again. Still no answer, so he tried the door handle. It was locked.

Mad Dog walked to the gate at the side of the house and reached over. He felt a padlock, but it wasn't locked. He pulled it off and unlatched the gate. He chuckled as he pushed it open. He went around to the back sliding glass window and tried to pull it open, but it was locked. Mad Dog surveyed the inside of the house through the window and saw no one. He knocked on it, but no reply came. He went to the fence that separated the backyard of the house he was at from the backyard of the house Danny was in. He hopped up and looked over. The curtains were open and he could see Danny, the woman, and an old lady standing in the living room.

"Oh, don't be ridiculous," Doris was saying, "I'll be back in a jiffy."

"Mom, we just ate. We're full."

"I'll be right back," she said as she grabbed her purse and headed for the door. She was going to get some snacks and sodas from the supermarket. "I can't entertain without some goodies to display."

"At least let me go," Danny said. "My truck is blocking you in anyway."

She batted a hand in the air as if dismissing what he just said. "Nonsense. You two sit down and relax. Give me your keys, unless you think your mother is too old to drive a stick."

Karen laughed and Danny gave up. He gave her the keys, and she said, "I'll only be a minute."

Once she left, it was like two teenagers who had a lust for each other being alone for the first time. Danny pulled Karen to him and kissed her passionately. Before she let logic take over, she grabbed him by the butt and thrust her hips into him. Danny was already hard and she wiggled herself back and forth on him. He hurried to the door, locked it, picked her up and carried her to his old bedroom. He left the door open so he could hear when his mother returned.

Mad Dog ran back to his car and grabbed his backpack and his gun. He put the backpack over his shoulders and put the gun in his front waistband. He ran back to the divider fence and quietly climbed over.

Mad Dog crept across the backyard of Doris' house, keeping out of view of the bedroom Danny and the woman were in. He tried the sliding glass window and almost laughed aloud when it slid open. *Don't they know there's a killer on the loose?* He pulled the dagger out of the sheath and the gun from his waistband. He left the sliding door open and walked quickly to the bedroom with the gun in his right hand and the dagger in his left hand. He turned down the hallway with lightning speed. This would be no problem with the element of surprise in his corner. He could hear sex sounds as he made the turn into the bedroom. It couldn't have been any more perfect. Danny was on top of her, blocking him from her view. Her legs were up in the air on both sides of Danny. Mad Dog moved with speed and grace. Without breaking stride, he raised the gun and brought the butt of it down hard onto Danny's head. He then shoved Danny aside while bringing his left arm up, high above his head. As soon as Danny was off her, he plunged the dagger into her throat. He withdrew it instantly and drove it deep into her heart. He left it there as he turned and pointed the gun at Danny.

Danny was out cold. He turned and looked at the girl. She was dead. He pulled the dagger out of her chest and picked her clothes off the ground to clean the blade. He saw her gun and badge underneath them and started laughing. He took the backpack off and threw the dagger and his gun in it. He tore a piece of duct tape from the role and put in over Danny's mouth. He then clipped the badge onto his waistband and tucked in the front of his shirt. *That will come in handy if someone sees me taking Danny to my car*, he thought. He picked up the gun and turned toward the woman. He spoke aloud, "If you would have been doing your job and not trying to get yourself off, you would be alive." He bent down to her and sucked on her bloody nipple. "You stupid bitch," he said through bloody lips.

Mad Dog went to the kitchen and got a glass of water. He then went back to the bedroom and poured it on Danny's face. Danny slowly opened his eyes until his mind registered what it was seeing. His eyes then sprung open, filled with horror and disbelief. He realized Mad Dog was standing over him with a gun.

Chapter 55

Doris got back to her house about half an hour after Mad Dog took Danny away by gunpoint. She tried the front door, but it was locked. She set the bag of groceries on the ground and got her keys from her purse. She unlocked the door and opened it.

"Danny, I'm back. Why did you guys lock the door?" Her question went unanswered so she picked up the bag and took it into the kitchen. She then started to walk toward his old bedroom. "Danny, I'm back from the store. You're not in there showing her your old trophies, are you?"

She entered the bedroom, saw the bloody dead body of Karen, and just stood there. Her mind wasn't comprehending the scene her eyes were viewing. She stood there unblinking for thirty seconds. She then became overwhelmed and started shaking.

Crying hysterically, Doris ran as fast as her old legs could carry her, out of the house and down the street.

Peterson and Hudson were still sitting in their car two houses from the house Danny and Officer Frost had gone into. An old lady had taken Taylor's truck about half an hour ago.

"What do you think they're doing in there?" Hudson asked.

Peterson smiled. "Why? Are you jealous?"

"Of Taylor?" Hudson asked, astonished. "That'll be the day."

Peterson nudged his arm. "Here comes the lady in Taylor's truck." They watched her pull into the driveway and get out with a bag of groceries. "I guess they didn't get enough to eat at the restaurant."

When she reached the door and sat the bag down to get her keys because the door was locked, Peterson nudged his partner's arm again and started laughing.

"What the fuck did Taylor lock the door for?" Hudson asked angrily.

"Relax," Peterson said. "I'm sure they just locked it because of what's been going on. Either that, or she's inspecting his concealed weapon."

The woman entered the house and left the door open. About a minute and a half later they saw her running out the front door, crying. She continued down the street. They both looked at each other, and at the same time said, "Taylor."

Peterson was in the passenger seat and was out of the car first. Hudson was right behind him. They were running toward the house with their guns drawn. Neither of them slowed down at the door. They ran straight through it, yelling to the empty rooms and lifeless corpse that they were police officers.

Hudson was the one who found the body and went into a fit of range.

Peterson entered the bedroom and said, "I'll call Miller."

Chapter 56

Sharon entered Miller's office without knocking. She was smiling from ear to ear. "I hope you're ready to start our torrid affair, because this case is over!" she said excitedly.

Miller smiled and asked, "What are you talking about?"

"I got prints and a match in the computer from the envelope today!"

Miller laughed. "Let me guess, the killer is me and my accomplice is Turner."

"I got prints—nice clear prints—besides the two of yours. I got a positive ID for a Mr. Bucky Webber!"

Miller's mouth fell open, "You're fucking kidding."

"I fuck you not—well, at least not yet," Sharon said.

Miller jumped up from the desk and went to her and kissed her. He picked her up and twirled around. "I fucking love you!" he shouted.

Everyone at the station looked toward his office. Somebody from the back said, "It's about time."

"Come on," Miller said as he grabbed her hand and led her out of the office. "Show me the match in the computer." They were five feet from the office when his phone rang. Miller said, "Run a printout and bring it to me."

On the third ring he picked up the receiver. "Miller here."

"I got great news!" Turner said happily.

"So do I. Sharon got Bucky Webber's prints from the envelope today!" Miller said, equally as enthusiastic.

"That's amazing," Turner said. "I just got a call from forensics and Webber's prints are all over the bookstore."

"Interesting," Miller said. "I wonder why all of a sudden his prints are showing up."

"I don't know, and I don't really care. I have an APB out on Webber as we speak. Call the surveillance team that's watching Taylor and tell them to bring him to one of our protective custody condos until we catch Webber. There's no use keeping him as bait now that we know who the killer is."

"Absolutely. I'll also call the news channel that Hayword worked for and give them an exclusive breaking story. That should make them happy and also get Webber's face out to the public. We should have him apprehended in no time."

"Call me later," Turner said.

"Will do." Miller hung the phone up and Sharon walked in with the match of Webber's prints next to his mug shot.

"It's definitely a match," she said as she handed him the printout.

"I believe you. What I want you to do is fax that to Allison Hayword's network, KRRV, and send it to Tawna Sally. We're going to do them a favor and let them break the story. I'm going to call them right now."

Sharon left his office and he checked his list of numbers he had for the networks. He looked at his watch and saw it was 5:30 p.m. Perfect. She would be doing a live broadcast right now. Miller dialed the direct number to the news producer and informed him of the fax that was being sent specifically for Tawna Sally to report. After numerous thank-yous for the exclusive, Miller managed to hang up the phone. As soon as he did, it rang. He answered it right away.

"Detective Miller, this is Peterson." He sounded frantic.

"Peterson, I was just about to call you," Miller said, detecting the urgency in Peterson's voice. "What's wrong?"

Peterson didn't know how to say what he had to, so he just blurted it out, "Officer Frost is dead and Taylor is missing."

Miller fell to his seat as if someone pushed him down. "What?" he asked dumbfounded.

"Officer Frost is dead and Taylor is missing."

Miller could hear Hudson cursing in the background. "Where are you? Are you at Taylor's apartment?" His mind was racing and he was trying to collect his thoughts.

"No sir. We're at some old lady's house in Poway. It must be Taylor's mother."

"Is she there?"

Peterson explained to him what happened, and after a moment of silence he said, "I'm sorry, sir."

"There's nothing you could have done," Miller said. "The one at fault here is Officer Frost."

"Should I call this in over the radio, or will you call it in?" Peterson asked.

"No, you call it in." Miller took the address down and sat at his desk, thinking. Officer Frost had been naked and it appeared she was having sex voluntarily with Danny. She had no bruises or broken nails that might have occurred during a struggle. What the fuck was that all about? Did Danny manipulate her into having sex with him, then kill her? It would make sense. He could have sent his mother to the store so he could have sex with Frost, and once she was vulnerable, pull a knife from under the bed and kill her. Then he could escape through the backyard.

Miller was leaning back in his chair with his eyes closed when he suddenly opened them and sprung forward, rocketing himself to his feet. He slammed his fist on his desk and shouted, "Where Webber was waiting for him on the street behind his mother's house!"

Miller called Turner and said, "Put out an APB on Taylor also…"

Chapter 57

Mad Dog was standing on a ladder tying a noose to a ceiling beam. Danny was tied to a metal chair over in the corner, naked. The chair had slits in the back and his arms are through them, tied together with a long piece of sturdy twine. The chair was strapped to a two-by-four in the wall, which was part of the frame of the house. Mad Dog had knocked apart the drywall in that area and drilled a hole through the wood, which he ran the twine through. He then ran the twine through the slits in the back of the metal chair. He did this repeatedly, until he was sure the chair was secure. There was only a six-inch gap between Danny's tied hands and the wall.

Mad Dog had knocked Danny out with chloroform as soon as he got him out to his car. He had never seen anybody so confused and pissed off in all his life as when Danny awoke on the floor in his mother's house. He was confused because he couldn't figure out what Mad Dog was doing there, especially with a gun in his hand. He was pissed off when he saw the dead bitch on the bed.

Mad Dog had left Danny's hands untied so he could climb over the fence. That ended up being a very stupid move. He didn't anticipate Danny attacking him, especially when he was holding a gun on him, but he did. Mad Dog had to hit him on the head with the butt of the gun again, knocking him out once again. He duct-taped Danny's hands together and carried him to the backyard fence. It took all his strength to lift Danny up over the fence. Danny hit with a hard thud and woke up again.

When Mad Dog hopped up on the fence, Danny was already getting to his feet. As Mad Dog jumped down into the other backyard, Danny was running clumsily toward the open gate. Mad Dog caught him at the front of the house and forced Danny to his car. He then forced him into the passenger seat and locked the door. He ran to the driver's side and got in just as Danny was leaning over and banging his head on the horn.

Mad Dog shoved Danny's head back against the window with his right hand and opened the glove box with his left hand. He pulled out a small towel wrapped around a bottle of chloroform. He dumped the bottle onto his lap as he held Danny's head against the glass. He grabbed the bottle and put the cap between his teeth while he turned it. The cap loosened, but didn't come off. He turned it upside down toward the towel and it poured out the sides as he shook it up and down. Within five seconds the towel was well covered with the ether-like fluid.

Mad Dog continued holding Danny's head with his right hand as he leaned over and shoved the towel with his left hand into Danny's face, covering his nose and mouth. Mad Dog was impressed with the brief struggle Danny put up. The fumes were getting to him and he was feeling lightheaded. Thank God Danny passed out when he did or there would have been two dead people in the car.

When Danny stopped fighting him, he left the towel on his face another five seconds for good measure. He then rolled down the window and stuck his head out for a deep breath of fresh air. Mad Dog got out of the car and took the backpack off. He opened the trunk and threw it in. He had Danny's clothes in it, but he was going to leave the little fucker naked now. He was making this way too difficult.

Mad Dog shut the trunk and saw a couple of people looking out their windows. He pulled the badge from his waistband and held it in the air for them to see. He made a slow circle with it, in case there were people watching that he couldn't see. He got back in the car, tightened the cap on the bottle and put it back in the glove box with the towel. If Danny woke up again, he would just leave it on his face until he suffocated.

That didn't happen though. Danny was still knocked out and Mad Dog didn't doubt he was in a comma. He had knocked the fucker out twice with the gun and once with chloroform. He also knocked him against the window pretty hard, not to mention dropping him over the fence. Mad Dog laughed at the thought and stepped down from the ladder to admire his work. "Not bad," he said. "Not bad at all."

Mad Dog went to the kitchen that previously belonged to an old man named Rudy Trotter. Mad Dog knew old Rudy, and knew that no one would be making a fuss if they didn't see him around. Rudy was a hermit, which made him easily disposable. Mad Dog had killed him last Friday, the night before he had the guy blow his head off. He buried Rudy in the backyard late that night in the middle of his five-foot weeds.

As he grabbed a beer out of the refrigerator, he wondered why he was going through all this hassle. He really should just kill Danny quickly and get to Mexico, but he had put so much planning into this that, even though he had fucked up earlier today, he was still going to see it through. Man, what a brilliant and psychotic plan it was, and it all fell to shit because he fucking fell asleep in Mexico.

"That's not going to happen this time," Mad Dog said to himself as he sat down at the kitchen table to do a line.

Chapter 58

Turner was sitting in Miller's office and the two men were discussing the call that just came in.

"I can't believe the lady saw Webber force Taylor into a car, naked, gagged and wrists taped together at roughly 5:00 p.m. She waits two hours, then calls us with a suspicious activity phone call," Miller said, astounded.

"She thought he was a cop," Turner joked.

Miller gave a tired and frustrated chuckle, and said, "At least she got the license number of Webber's car." Turner nodded his head. Miller continued, "So, where do we stand right now?"

"Right now we have every cop from San Diego to Sacramento looking for Webber and his car. The media is helping us get exposure of his picture to the public, and they're showing Taylor's picture also. We've set up a special hotline number for anybody with information as to their whereabouts. There is also a small reward for anybody that gives information that leads to an arrest."

"Alright," Millers said. "Have you notified the authorities at the border?"

Turner was nodding his head. "Yes, and not only the San Ysidro border, but also the Otay Mesa and Mexicali borders."

Miller leaned back in his chair. "He could already be in Mexico right now. He had a couple hours head start."

"That's true," Turner agreed, "but he didn't know we were on to him before. In fact, he still may not know."

"Exactly. I think he's going through with his plan." Miller rubbed a hand over his two-day beard. "Can you believe it? Danny was innocent the whole fucking time, and we couldn't even protect him with a surveillance team and an armed bodyguard." He leaned forward and looked Turner straight in the eye. "If Taylor ends up dead, it will be my fault. I don't know if I'll be able to live with that."

Chapter 59

Danny slowly opened his eyes. It felt like a hammer had been taken to his head. He looked up and saw the noose hanging from the ceiling beam and instantly remembered what was happening. His head was pounding, and he felt as if he'd been drugged.

Danny tried to stand, but realized his hands were tied together behind the chair. He gave a slight struggle, trying to free himself, but the rope was too tight. His head was spinning, and he leaned forward and retched.

Mad Dog opened the refrigerator and got another beer. He had just done another line and was wired to the max.

Danny heard the noise in the kitchen and called out, "Hey, Mad Dog, you sick fuck! Do you get off on tying naked men to chairs?" His head was throbbing. "I hear you in there! Hey, fuckhead!" Danny closed his eyes and winced from the pain in his head.

When Danny had called out, it made Mad Dog jump. He smiled and slowly walked to the living room where Danny was tied up. When Mad Dog saw Danny, he started speaking the words to "Enter Sandman," a song by Metallica. His voice was low, angry, and evil—just like in the song itself. His eyes were huge and wild from the speed. He walked to Danny and said, "Hush, little baby, don't say a word. And never mind that noise you heard. It's just the beast under your bed. In your closet, in your head."

Then he started singing and shouting at the same time, "Exit light! Enter night! Take my hand, we're off to never-never land!"

Danny was wincing from the pain caused by the shouting. When Mad Dog was finished, he started bowing and waving as if a crowd was cheering for him.

Danny looked at him as if he had never known this man before in his life. "What the fuck is wrong with you?" Danny asked. "What the fuck are you doing this for?"

Mad Dog walked toward the kitchen, and said, "All in good time, Danny. All in good time."

Danny heard a cabinet bang, then Mad Dog returned with a bottle of Seagram's 7. "First, I'm going to get you drunk."

Danny spit in his direction and said, "Fuck you, I'm not drinking shit."

Mad Dog started laughing. "Oh, but I think you are. I would hate to have to go back to that old lady's house and kill her." He looked at Danny and gave him a knowing smile. "Who was that? Was that your mommy?"

Danny thrashed wildly in his chair and struggled with trying to free his hands, but to no avail. He looked at Mad Dog with a hatred and anger that Mad Dog had never seen before. "If you think about touching my mom, I swear to God, I'll kill you."

Mad Dog laughed. "It's up to you," he said. "Just drink this bottle and listen to my story and I promise you I won't touch her."

"Alright. Untie me so I can drink it," Danny said.

Mad Dog threw himself to the floor and rolled back and forth on his back while kicking his legs in the air. He was holding his belly and was laughing hysterically. "Oh, come on. After what I went through earlier today with you? Fuck no!" He walked toward Danny and unscrewed the cap. He held it under Danny's nose and asked, "Doesn't it smell like Heaven?"

Danny took a whiff and instantly his mouth started watering. He looked up at Mad Dog and asked, "If I drink this, you're going to leave my mother alone?"

"You have my word," he said.

Mad Dog's word didn't mean shit to Danny, but it was the best thing he could hope for right now. "You're also going to tell me what the fuck all this is about?"

Mad Dog laughed and said, "You couldn't stop me from telling you."

Danny leaned his head back and opened his mouth. Mad Dog poured the liquid into his mouth. Danny held it in his cheeks for a moment, getting his stomach ready for it. After a moment he gulped it down and was surprised at how smooth it actually was. He expected it to burn since he hadn't had a drink for over six months. He instantly felt warm inside. Danny opened his mouth for another drink.

Mad Dog chuckled and patted him on the head. He poured another mouthful and said, "That's the Danny I know and love. Once an alcoholic, always an alcoholic." He sat the bottle down, walked over to the noose and batted it with one hand. "I had the perfect fucking plan, Danny." He turned toward him and said, "I think it borders on genius."

Danny was amazed at how badly he wanted another drink. He figured he was fucked anyway, so he might as well get drunk. It was better than dying sober. He made a head motion toward the bottle and Mad Dog smiled. Mad Dog poured some into his mouth and waited. He held it up after Danny swallowed, and Danny nodded his head yes. He opened his mouth and Mad Dog filled it.

Danny could feel his headache disappearing. Too bad he was going to die, because he sure would like to start drinking again. Man, did he like to drink alcohol. In a way—a deep down, fucked-up way—Danny felt sorry for people who drink and aren't alcoholics. Those normal, social drinkers will never know the true pleasure that alcohol provides.

After a hard night of drinking, the next day is filled with horrible pain. Sometimes it's just a tremendous headache, and sometimes it's a headache with vomiting. Sometimes you can't even move your head without wanting to cry. Non-alcoholics tough it out and suffer. Some even swear off alcohol for a while, while others swear off it for good. Not alcoholics though. This is the time when alcoholics shine. There is nothing better than feeling good when you once were feeling bad. Everyone should know the ecstasy of having your pain slowly ebb away with each drink. Everyone should know the pleasure of having your sickness make you well.

Danny's sickness was making him well at this very moment. He was feeling more alive with each drink. If it wasn't for the fact that we was going to die, Danny was almost thankful for Mad Dog showing him his purpose in life. His purpose was to drink.

Mad Dog gave Danny another drink, then another. The bottle was half gone and Mad Dog sat it down. "Yep, I had the perfect fucking plan," Mad Dog said, "but I had to go and fuck up."

Danny was halfway to being drunk, but he was listening intently. Knowing why he was going to be killed by someone he thought was a friend was very important to him. Knowing why he was going to be killed was almost worth dying for. It's almost like the person willing to die if they are told the meaning of life.

"Danny, Danny, Danny!" Mad Dog was saying as he looked up at the noose. "Remember back in prison when you, me, Fruit Loop, and Frito were friends? Back when I was taking my medication," he looked at Danny and laughed, "and was relatively normal?" Danny nodded his head. "Remember how everybody told their stories of why we were in there? Well, everybody but you, right?"

Danny shook his head no. "That's not right," Danny said through slightly slurred words.

Mad Dog picked up the bottle and gave Danny another drink. "I told my story before you got there, but nobody believed that I was innocent, so I stopped telling it. The only person that believed me was Frito."

Mad Dog gave Danny a drink that overflowed his mouth. Danny choked and had a hard time catching his breath. Mad Dog patted him on the back and said, "There, there. Take it easy. We don't want you drowning, now do we?" He took a drink from the bottle and made a face of disgust. "You actually like this shit?" he asked.

Danny nodded his head, and Mad Dog poured more into this mouth. Danny's eyes were getting heavy and he was officially drunk. "What does my story about getting arrested make any difference in anything?" Danny asked.

Mad Dog tilted Danny's head back and Danny opened his mouth. Mad Dog turned the bottle upside down over Danny's mouth, pouring the rest of the liquor out. Danny did the best he could to keep swallowing, but there was too much liquid and it overflowed down his chin, onto his chest and down his body. Mad Dog flung the bottle across the room and it shattered against the wall. He looked at Danny with the eyes of a demon.

"I'll tell you why your story makes a difference, you stupid fuck!" Mad Dog shouted. "When you left prison I asked Frito to tell me why you were in. I was curious, you know. The little fucker wouldn't tell me. He said you said not to. That made me even more curious. I had to fucking know, so I got him drunk and the little guy told me the whole story."

Mad Dog was walking around the room in a circle, and every time he went by the noose he swung on it by his arms.

Danny was having a hard time following what he was saying because Mad Dog was talking so fast; either that or he was hearing slow because he was so drunk.

Mad Dog laughed an evil laugh and continued, "I almost shit a fucking brick when he told me."

Danny lifted his head as well as he could and managed to say, "Big deal. He told you my story. If it means that much to you, I'll tell it to you right now."

Mad Dog quickly crossed the room and slapped Danny across the face. "The fuck you will, cocksucker!" he screamed. His eyes were wild with hatred and he started laughing. "Have you ever heard the expression, 'It's a small world?' Well,

I'll be dammed if it isn't. The woman you were convicted of killing was my woman, you stupid fucker!" He pointed at Danny and laughed. "You were the guy in the shower when I did Margi in! You went to jail for me, 'cause I killed the bitch." Mad Dog started laughing.

Danny couldn't believe what he was hearing. Mad Dog's laughter was echoing in his head. His face became flush and the room started spinning. Danny felt as if the whole world had come crashing down. What were the chances of this happening? What were the odds?

Mad Dog continued. "And to think that I had you as a friend. In my book, friends don't sleep with other friend's women."

"I didn't know she was your girlfriend," Danny said innocently. "I didn't even know she had a boyfriend. I didn't even know you at the time!"

"That's a lot of things you didn't know, isn't it?" Mad Dog asked. "If you ask me, you're guilty by association." Mad Dog laughed, climbed up the ladder and stuck his head in the noose.

"Anyway, I thought long and hard about how I was going to get you back. I was just going to kill you outright, but what fun would that be? Not much, believe me. Killing just doesn't have the same zest as it used to."

He jumped off the ladder, but held onto the rope above his head. "I finally decided to frame you." He put his feet back on the ladder and took his head out of the noose. "Please tell me you weren't hoping that I was going to accidentally hang myself. How droll!"

Danny sat silent and stunned.

"It's amazing how clever I can be without my medication," Mad Dog said. "I planned this scheme from the time I found out about you. Hell, it would have worked too if I hadn't fucked up and left my prints at the crime scene today. I had the cops thinking you were the killer. Did you know they had your place bugged?"

Danny was sitting there looking dumbfounded.

Mad Dog laughed. "I keyed on the suicide thing because of your psychiatric profile. Pretty ingenuous, huh? I even had a suicide note from you that explained why you did it. I was even going to make it seem like you were working with an accomplice. Then you were going to hang yourself without the cops catching you, thus pulling off the perfect crime."

Mad Dog went into the kitchen and Danny heard him snorting something and heard the refrigerator open and shut. Mad Dog came back in the room with a beer. He turned the TV on and said, "Enjoy. I'll be back when I get back. I need to get some more beer." He started walking toward the door and turned around.

"Don't fool yourself into thinking you can get out of the chair, Danny. I chose twine on purpose because it's thinner and it holds just as good as thick rope. Do yourself a favor and pass out. When you wake up, you'll be dead." Mad Dog was laughing as he went out the door.

Chapter 60

Danny was so drunk he could barely keep his head up. Maybe if he could get a little bit of sleep he would be alright. Danny closed his eyes and was about to pass out when he heard a special report on the television.

"Good evening. This is Luke Bradford bringing to you the latest developments in the bizarre serial killings that are being labeled. Tawna Sally of KRRV, reported earlier tonight in an exclusive report that the killer, who is still at large, is ex-convict, Bucky Webber. Bucky Webber has abducted fellow ex-con, Danny Taylor, who the San Diego police department say was targeted as the sixth and final victim in his killing spree. During the abduction, Officer Karen Frost of the San Diego Police Department was killed in the line of duty by Webber. Officer Frost was working undercover on a special covert operation. We asked that anybody with any information that might be helpful in this case, please call the toll-free hotline number on the bottom of the screen. We will report more to you as the investigation progresses."

Danny let his mind absorb what he just heard. He might have a chance to live after all. They showed Mad Dog's picture, as well as his. They also displayed the make and color of Mad Dog's car and his license plate number. Somebody might remember the car and call in. Hell, Mad Dog was out getting beer right now, which meant there was a chance he would be recognized. "What an idiot he is," Danny said as his head remained sagging.

Danny wanted to sleep very badly. Maybe if he fell asleep, all this would be over when he woke. The cops were probably arresting Mad Dog right now.

"No!" Danny shouted as he lifted his head. He knew if he passed out he was dead. He tried to free himself, but Mad Dog had tied his hands too well. He pulled them and pushed them, pulled then and twisted them, but he couldn't get the twine past his thumb bones. His hands were bleeding, and he decided to try to break the chair. He stood and smashed it down one time before he cursed at himself for being so stupid. The chair was metal.

He sat, defeated. He had just about given up when he thought about Karen. He couldn't let her die because of him, then go out this way. If he was going to die, he was going to go out fighting.

Danny started to feel his senses returning as the anger built up in him. As the anger built up in him, he started remembering all the violent things he'd done while he was drunk, and realized why he was a person who wasn't able to drink. There was the time he beat the shit out of that guy and then pissed on him. Why? Because he was drunk and the guy bumped into him.

He remembered breaking his hand by punching a brick wall because his girlfriend was talking to another guy. The guy mouthed off to him and Danny broke the guy's jaw with his broken hand.

When he was drunk, Danny had a high tolerance for pain. That and his size caused him to win most all of his fights. Even though he may get beat up bad, he beat the other guy worse because he didn't know when to stop. If he could just get free, he would do whatever it took to avenge the years spent in prison, the loss of Karen, all the turmoil Mad Dog had thrust into his life. His anger was at a boiling point.

He pulled and pushed as hard as he could on the twine, but he couldn't get it over his thumbs. His heart was racing and he was sweating profusely. He let out a scream and started thrashing wildly in the chair. He suddenly stopped and looked behind him. He thought for a moment, then stood up. Danny took a deep breath, pointed his thumbs at the two by four and thrust all his weight into the chair and at the piece of wood. Mad Dog screwed up by tying his hands back-to-back, instead of palm-to-palm, so his thumbs were easy targets for the wood.

Danny missed on the first try. He took another breath and pushed with all his strength backward. His right thumb hit square and he heard a loud snap. He fought back the urge to throw up, and tried to pull his hands free. He was close, but he had to break the other thumb too. Danny pushed the chair backward and hit his right thumb again. This time the urge was too strong and he turned his head and threw up. Without wasting any time, he threw his weight backward again. This time he hit his left thumb square on and it snapped louder than his right thumb.

Sweat was dripping off him and he sat down. He twisted, pulled and pushed his hands. Blood was flowing from the rope burns, helping his hands slide through the twine. He was pulling his hands free just as Mad Dog came through the door.

Chapter 61

Mad Dog came through the door with a twelve-pack of beer in his hand. He looked over at Danny, saw him sweating and laughed as he shut the door. He walked over to Danny and saw the vomit on the floor and the blood behind the chair from Danny's hands. Mad Dog sat down on the floor about ten feet in front of Danny and opened the twelve-pack. He cracked one open, took a long drink and started laughing uncontrollably.

"What the fuck have you been up to?" he asked. "I told you there was no way out of that."

Danny fought back the pain of his broken thumbs and said, "You might as well give it up, Mad Dog. When you were gone there was a special report about you. The cops know your name and they're looking for us right now."

Mad Dog crawled over to the TV and turned it off. "I never should have turned that on for you. TV warps the mind."

"Someone probably recognized your license plate when you went to the store. The clerk probably recognized your face. Just give it up—it's not worth it."

"Shut the fuck up!" Mad Dog screamed. "Just so you know, lame-ass, I walked to the store and the car is on the side of the house with a cover on it. As for you hoping the liquor store guy will recognize me—he knows me. He's a friend of mine whom I've known for years. He's a real friend, Danny. He's a friend who wouldn't even think about sleeping with my woman."

"Wake up, Mad Dog!" Danny screamed. "I didn't know you when I slept with Margi, and I didn't know she had a boyfriend."

"Like I said, guilty by association." Mad Dog took another drink of beer and Danny was about to lunge at him, when he said, "Now that you know why I went through all the trouble to set you up. Aren't you curious as to how I did it?" Mad Dog finished the beer and opened another. "I didn't get out of prison much before I had that old man blow his brains out, but I had the people I was going to kill scouted long before. I had help in placing the notes. I had a lookout to make sure the coast was clear. Even when I was elsewhere, I knew where you were."

He drank his beer, then held out a finger. "That undercover cop you were fucking, that took me by surprise. My partner let me down on that one, but he'll get his—trust me." Mad Dog stood up and walked over to the door. "I can see you're getting bored, so I'll get to the really exciting part."

Mad Dog opened the door and gave a whistle and a head nod. He took another drink of beer, then turned toward Danny. He held out one arm wide toward the door. He held his other arm out wide toward Danny as if presenting something.

What Danny saw come through the door first was an arm holding a bag of Fritos. Danny's heart sank. The arm was followed by the body of his old friend Frito. Danny closed his eyes in disbelief.

Chapter 62

"What's the matter, Danny?" Mad Dog asked. "You didn't actually think this stress case had any loyalty in him, did you?" Danny opened his eyes and Frito turned his head away, as if ashamed. "After I got him drunk and he blabbed your story, he was so afraid of me that he would of blown me if I told him to." Mad Dog patted Frito on the back. "Lucky for him I had Fruit Loop for that."

Danny was shaking his head. "After everything I did for you, Frito. How could you do this?"

Frito was looking at the floor. "I'm sorry, Danny. I really am. You left me though, and I had to do what it took to survive. You don't know what it's like to be me. When you left, Mad Dog started running the place and if we didn't do what he said, he beat the shit out of us."

Mad Dog was strutting around the living room drinking his beer and laughing.

"He told me if I didn't help him frame you, he would kill me."

"What do you think he's going to do to you now?" Danny asked.

Frito looked at Mad Dog with a scared and confused face. "You and I are partners, right? You said it was you and me."

Mad Dog smiled, then spoke in a soothing voice, "That's right, Frito, that's what I told you." He went over to him and held out his arms. "Now, give me a hug, partner."

Danny was going to jump up from the chair, but he saw the knife in the back of Mad Dog's waistband. He opened his mouth and yelled at Frito to watch out just as Frito was hugging Mad Dog. Mad Dog pulled the dagger out of the sheath at the same time Frito heard Danny.

Frito pulled away from Mad Dog just as he thrust the blade up into his belly. Frito staggered back and fell to the ground on his butt. He looked at Danny with terrified eyes as his life was quickly draining away. He opened his mouth to say something, but no sound came out. He fell onto his side and died with his eyes open.

It took every ounce of willpower Danny had to not charge at Mad Dog. He had to be smart or he wouldn't be able to win a flight with two broken thumbs and Mad Dog's dagger.

Mad Dog turned to Danny and said, "You're right. I was planning on killing him all along. The suicide note I was going to leave from you admitted Frito was your accomplice. Pretty good, huh? I would've pulled off the perfect crime. Remember when you talked about the perfect crime in prison, Danny? Remember back when you had to kill Tiny Tim? Well, this was the perfect crime." Mad Dog finished the beer he was holding. "If only I had stayed awake in Mexico."

"So, what's going to happen now? The cops are looking for you everywhere. They know your car and your face has been plastered over the TV."

Mad Dog opened another beer. "What's going to happen now is, I'm going to kill you." He said with a sneer, "Old man Rudy met an untimely death and willed me his car with a full tank of gas. I'm going to take old Rudy's car and head to Mexico." Mad Dog walked toward Danny and said, "Now that you know everything, just like I promised, it's time to die. I'm going to kill you, then hang you."

Mad Dog came at Danny and stood in front of him. He raised the dagger above his head and Danny pulled his arms out from behind the chair. Mad Dog's expression transformed into one of complete surprise. He then showed his teeth and snarled, while bringing his right arm down with the dagger toward Danny's heart. Danny sprung to his feet and sent his left hand behind Mad Dog's head, pulling Mad Dog toward him. At the same time, he sent the four fingers of his right hand slamming into Mad Dog's Adams apple, crushing his windpipe and killing him instantly. The dagger went into Danny's chest just below his left collarbone.

Danny let Mad Dog fall to the floor as he pulled the dagger out with the palms of his hands. He sat down in the chair and heard sirens in the distance as his consciousness slipped away from him. "I hope they're coming for me," he managed to say as darkness overtook him.

Epilogue

Danny woke up in the hospital Monday afternoon. The room was full of flowers. He reached over to look at one of the cards and winced from the pain. He didn't know which pain was worse—the pain from the knife wound or the pain in his head.

The toilet in the bathroom flushed and Danny turned to see who would come out. It was his mother.

"Well, look at who finally woke up," she said.

Danny smiled and asked, "Who are all these flowers from?"

"The San Diego Police Department—mostly Detective Miller." She went to the bed and gave him a kiss. "I'll go get him. He's in the waiting room."

She left the room and Danny smiled again. The thought of Miller hanging around to see him made him happy for some reason. Hell, who was he kidding? Just being alive made him happy. He had won the battle over Mad Dog. He remembered how he had escaped and looked down at his hands. His thumbs were in splints. Funny, but his thumbs didn't hurt at all.

Miller came through the door, and for some reason Danny laughed. "Thank you for visiting me," Danny said. "Oh, and thank you for the flowers."

"How are you feeling?" Miller asked.

Danny shrugged his shoulders, then made a face from the pain. "How did I end up here?" Danny asked. "I thought I heard sirens right before I passed out."

"You probably did," Miller said. "The hotline number got a call from the neighbor of a Mr. Rudy Trotter. It appears the neighbor saw somebody that looked like Webber go into Trotter's house last night, so they called the Riverside police. The police found you passed out in a chair and Bucky Webber and Tom Prescott dead at the scene. What happened?"

Danny ran down the story to Miller and he listened with fascination. Miller went to Danny and patted his leg. "I'm glad you're alright, Danny." He walked to the door and said, "Try to keep out of trouble."

Danny smiled and Miller smiled back.

Miller walked to the waiting room and Doris went back to Danny's room. Sharon stood up and asked, "Are you ready to go?"

He walked over to her and gave her a tender kiss. "Are you sure you want to get involved with an old man like me?"

"Too late," she said. "I'm already involved." They held hands and walked out of the hospital.

Danny closed his eyes and thought about the nightmare of last night and about what the future would hold. He was amazed at how much his thinking process was messed up while he was under the influence of alcohol. Yesterday was an end to six months of sobriety, but today was the first day to an even longer period of being sober—a lifetime's worth.

To Mary Ann,

Thank you for being supportive and helping make this book be published. After all you are very #1 fan. You are the best!

Scott